MOMENTS OF MEANING

MOMENTS OF MEANING

Charlotte Vale Allen

NEW ENGLISH LIBRARY

First published in the USA in 1979 by The New American Library, Inc.

Copyright © 1979 by Charlotte Vale Allen

First NEL Paperback Edition May 1982

NEL Books are published by
New English Library,
Mill Road, Dunton Green, Sevenoaks, Kent,
a division of Hodder and Stoughton Ltd.

Printed and bound in Great Britain by
Cox & Wyman Ltd, Reading

British Library C.I.P.

Allen, Charlotte Vale

Moments of Meaning.
I. Title
813'.54[F]   PS3551.L392

ISBN 0-450-05454-3

For Lola

Part One

---••◆•••---

One

———◆◆◆———

The only time the shaking stopped was when she was in the pool. So she spent as many hours a day floating in the heated water as she could. Numb. Being turned a dark brown by the sun without any of her usual efforts. No suntan oil. No after-sun lotions. Nothing at all. Just out there, floating around the hotel pool from ten in the morning until after four in the afternoon. Turning brown.

Away from the water, in her room, or walking along the streets, the shaking would take her over. Internally. Aside from an almost unnoticeable tremor in her hands, nothing showed on the outside. A fact that seemed extraordinary to her. That she could be shaking herself to death on the inside and look unchanged on the outside. Amazing. Somehow, she thought, it would have been infinitely more appropriate if she'd looked altogether the way she felt.

Every so often, that last scene would replay in her mind and she'd stare at it, her breathing stopping almost altogether as she watched it run through. And at the end, she'd be gasping for air—as she had been in reality—and running backward; running wildly as a dreadful animal whine came pushing up out of her throat.

She tried not to think about it.

And kept remembering the story about the camel lady. Not all of it. Just the essence. Because, at first, she'd found it very difficult to tune in to what the woman was telling her. So she'd missed parts here and there.

A woman alone. With camels. Walking her way across the Nullarbor.

She'd taken off her dark glasses in order to see the land below more clearly. And, without thinking, had turned stiffly to ask the woman in the seat beside her, "What is that, do you know?"

The woman had stood halfway up out of her seat,

leaned past Lyle—her perfume enveloping Lyle very pleasantly for several seconds—then had sat down, smiling, saying, "We're passing over the Nullarbor."

She'd said it: Nulla-bore.

And then she'd started telling Lyle about the camel lady. Lyle had begun listening after a few moments, captivated by the story. And by the idea of being alone. With camels. Crossing the Nullarbor. She visualized the woman. Grey-haired, perhaps. And strong. With a very straight spine, fiercely erect posture. And eyes much-lined at the corners from squinting directly into the sun.

There'd been a part having to do with wild camels coming out to attack the tamed ones. And Lyle had once more had to break her silence to ask, "Wild camels?"

The woman, obviously gratified to have an interested audience, had explained, "Camels were brought here around the middle eighteen hundreds, or so. Somewhere along about then. Beasts of burden and so forth."

Lyle had said, "Oh," and nodded and returned her eyes to the sights below. Staring down through the cloudless sky at the convoluted land-swirls and strange, beautiful patterns of the earth below. Its odd colorless colors and mesmerizing rises and falls. What looked to be roads, every now and then, that came from the horizon and ended nowhere. Lines intersecting the vast emptiness. Seeing all this while the woman's voice had continued telling about the camel lady. Lyle had absorbed it, awed by the idea of all that strength and independence. Going alone across the Nullarbor, accompanied only by camels. Walking. She desperately envied the camel lady, wishing she had that sort of adventurous, determined spirit. Seeing a projected image of herself as someone strong, and erect, and clear-eyed, squinting defiantly into the sun.

She hadn't any idea at all what she'd been doing. Running. Waving down a taxi and gasping out, "The airport. Take me to the airport."

"Tullamarine?" the driver had asked.

"Yes. There. Take me there."

One first-class seat available on a flight departing for Perth. Already boarded, with eight minutes to takeoff. She'd paid in cash for a one-way ticket and run. Boarded the plane and sunk into her window seat. Aware then for the first time of the shaking. In her throat and stomach.

Feeling as if the skin had dissolved from her bones and she was a chattering, rattling skeleton with dark glasses. Seat-belted into place. Until the plane had been well and truly airborne. And was following the coastline on a perfect, cloudless afternoon. The view compelling and starkly beautiful.

She'd refused the offers of drinks and food, requesting only a glass of water so that she might belatedly take her dramamine tablet; perferring to sit, gazing down at the land below. As if some message might be written down there for her. Laid out with branches and rocks. Perhaps with a smoking fire to draw her attention. The shaking had diminished some after the first forty minutes. She'd closed her eyes, saw it all happening again, and the shaking overtook her full force. She'd opened her eyes, looked out. Then asked the woman next to her, "What is that?"

She tried very hard not to think about any of the things that had happened during her stay in Melbourne. Because as soon as she started remembering, her chest shrank, her lungs seemed to deflate. She'd made such an effort to adapt to Ian's ways, to understand him, the country, the people. Loving the country, the people—for the most part. Which was why she couldn't bring herself to leave now. And so was staying on, on the very edge—both of the country and of her decision to return home.

At moments, she felt oddly peaceful when she thought of where she was. Insulated somehow by the exceptional beauty of Perth, its orderly layout, its mix of architectural styles, the broad avenue of palms running along the riverfront. And the black swans on the river. They fascinated her.

She'd taken a walk in the late afternoon of her fourth day at the hotel. Turning left out of the Sheraton, toward the river. So pleased by the sight of the palms. And astonished by the swans. She'd stood at the water's edge and half a dozen of the larger birds had come waddling up out of the water anticipating being fed. And, aloud, she'd apologized, saying, "I'm sorry. I don't have anything to give you." She was disappointed when, as if understanding her words, the birds had clumsily turned away, making their way back to the water. She promised herself she'd come again the next morning with bread or rolls from her room service breakfast.

Then, rather like an echo, she'd heard herself talking aloud to the swans and had laughed. The laughter alien, odd; creating an instant feeling of guilt. She couldn't, shouldn't laugh. Should she? No, no. It's all right, she'd told herself. Good to laugh. All right to laugh. She'd remained at the water's edge for half an hour longer before making her way back to the hotel, shaping as she went her plan to return to feed the swans on the following morning. A small, but definite destination. One decision made.

And, thereafter, had begun each of her days in this city by making her way down to the river to feed the swans, quietly reassured to see others on a like pilgrimage. Tour buses, too, unloading people whose necks were heavily hung round with cameras and whose hands stretched eagerly toward the birds.

She felt mentally and emotionally paralyzed, unable to do more than pick at the room-service meals she routinely ordered; floating away her days in the hotel pool, making her early-morning trips to the river with her paper napkin filled with toast or rolls. Whatever identity she'd once had was gone. Destroyed along with everything else. Ian . . . She couldn't, wouldn't. Fought off the trembling, told herself to remain calm. Get up, go down, walk out, feed the swans.

Into her second week. She stood watching the swans retreat from her, asking herself, Why don't I go home? I ought to go home. There's no point to my staying here. Why don't I go?

Because Perth is beautiful, is clean, has me quietly caught. And I'm not yet ready to relinquish so much beauty. Summer here and I like the idea that I'm so close to the Indian Ocean, to the river, the palm trees, the swans. I'm not prepared to return home, face winter, the cold. Or all those too-long hours of flying needed to get me home. Not ready. I'm not.

She dusted the crumbs from her hands, lit a cigarette and stood trying to think, watching a group of people from one of the tour buses feeding the swans, taking photographs. Finding it almost impossible to think. Feeling ghostlike. As if Ian had succeeded in destroying her, too. No! She shook her head to clear it and drew hard on her cigarette. Thinking of the camel lady. Thinking, I have no capacity for heroics. Or for small assertive, independent **acts.** Or for making decisions. I don't know what to do.

*   *   *

His morning stop by the river marked the start of his workday. He'd drive into the city, park in the layby at the shore and watch the swans being fed. Enjoy a quiet cigarette, then start up the drive to the office. He'd started the routine without plan. It had simply evolved after that first morning when he'd been utterly unable to face going directly into his workday after the horrendous night with Mag. He'd needed something—anything—to remove him from reality for just a few minutes. And the river, the swans had offered that. Kept on offering that. So he stopped for ten or fifteen minutes each weekday morning.

He could get his thinking done, seemed able to see his life with more clarity at these times. Trying to be grateful—working hard at that—for all he did have. Trying not to bemoan the failures. Spilt milk. What was the point of going on and on about that? None. Just as there was no more point to asking why things had to be the way they were and wondering if they'd change. Nothing would change. Time had spelled that out to him all too clearly. So, get on with it, his common sense had told him some time back. Get on with it.

He was aware of her the first time. Just aware. His eyes passing over her. Another someone—no doubt a tourist—there to admire the swans. He gave her no thought, smoked out his cigarette and looked at her a second time as he drove past. Nothing very much registered.

The next morning, she was there again. Unusual. The tourists didn't too often come back a second time. So he took a closer look. She was wearing the same dress she'd worn the day before. Navy blue. A little shorter than the popular look just then. The girls wearing those long, flowered skirts and skimpy skivvies on top, with those godawful wedges. This woman was wearing shoes. Ordinary shoes with heels perhaps two inches high. The girls thinking those wedges, those thick soles, made them look good. They didn't. *Shoes* looked good. He looked again at her feet and ankles, mentally congratulating her on resisting fashion.

Midday, when he went over to Miss Maud's on Murray Street to get a sandwich from the takeaway, then walked back up Murray and he found himself thinking about that woman. It occurred to him he hadn't looked at her face. Which was too bad. He really should've taken note of her face. Now, he'd probably never be able to remember any-

thing more of her than her shoes. And he had to smile to
himself, thinking that. Unlikely he'd remember her in any
event.

But she was there again on the third morning. Standing
surrounded by the swans, tearing up pieces of bread and
dropping them to the ground. He watched, noting how
absorbed she seemed to be in this act. As if it was something very serious. Which struck him as a little odd. He
continued to watch, this time seeing her whole. Not just a
pair of shoes.

The same navy dress, same shoes. A tallish woman, very
tan. With long bare arms and legs. Slim, long-bodied. With
shoulder-length dark blonde hair. And an attitude of great
concentration. He couldn't quite make out her features.
and wished he was closer, just in order to satisfy his curiosity, to know what she looked like.

When she'd finished with the bread, she backed away
and went to sit down on a bench nearby, opening the
large, red canvas bag she carried. She lit a cigarette, set
the bag down on the bench beside her and crossed her
legs. Gazing straight ahead. She seemed unaware she was
being watched, so he continued to indulge himself, studying her; noticing she had quite graceful hands. They
moved smoothly. The cigarette going to and from her
mouth until it was smoked down. Then she dropped it,
stepped on it, retrieved the stub end and set it down on
the bench beside her. Crossed slender legs once more.

With a start, he looked at his watch, saw the time and
started up the car. He'd overstayed. And pulled out, taking
one last look to see she was lighting another cigarette.

During the course of the day he was surprised to find
himself thinking about her, wondering if she'd be there the
next morning. Wondering, too, if she'd be wearing that
same dress. Thinking about the aura of frailty about her,
despite her dark tan. Something vulnerable about those
bare arms, the graceful hand gestures, the seriousness with
which she fed her crusts of bread to the swans.

Years ago, Mag had had an aura about her, too. A
brightness, gaiety. I haven't changed all that much, he
thought. Leastwise not for the bad. To the good, I'd say.
But Mag. Is it chemical? he wondered, considering articles
he'd read, things he'd heard. Or is it something I could
never give you, Mag?

Well, never mind. At least the kids were to the good.

Thank God for the kids. And the life wasn't bad. Not really.

He couldn't have said what prompted him to do it. Curiosity. Or loneliness. He wasn't ashamed to admit to being lonely. It might have been that. In any case, the next morning he climbed out of the car and went to sit beside her on the bench. Sat down and lit a cigarette, then looked at his feet. Feeling foolish. What was he thinking of? Never mind, he told himself, looking over at those swans swimming nearer in to the shore. Anyone might sit on a bench, share a bench with a stranger. He glanced sidelong at her, then away. She was younger than he'd thought. Not young. Well, not old. Just not a kid. Thirty-five or so.

She wasn't aware of him for several moments. She was thinking about *it* again: that moment coming through the door. The shaking started up and she opened her bag for a cigarette. Got one out and groped inside the bag for her lighter. A hand appeared in the air in front of her. A hand with a cigarette lighter. She looked at the hand, held the cigarette to her mouth. A flame appeared. She drew in. The hand went away. She said, "Thank you," to the air where the hand had been. Felt herself going through that door again and her throat seized, closed; the shaking again in control of her.

"Good start to the day," he said, returning the lighter to his pocket, "coming down to see the swans."

She nodded, trying to get past the blockage in her throat.

"I've been coming every morning for years now."

She nodded again, venturing to turn her head somewhat in order to see him, attach the voice to a face. A middle-aged man with a pleasant face, fairish hair. A rather battered look to his face. But so pleasant. An overweight, middle-aged man with very blue eyes. He smiled at her.

"American?"

"Yes." Her voice was no good, hadn't been since it happened. The rattling inside, as if her chest was filled with empty tin cans and every breath she took sent them crashing against each other noisily.

"On holiday?" he asked lightly.

She shook her head. "No." Then thought about it, changed her mind and said, "Yes."

His eyes registered a degree of confusion. She saw it

and thought again how pleasant-looking he was. Comfortable-looking. He made her feel the way she had the first
time she'd seen her house. Knowing at once she'd buy it
because it offered the potential of comfort.

"Are you from here?" she asked, wondering what had
happened to his nose. It looked as if it had once upon a
time been broken.

"Lived here all my life." He smiled at her.

"It's beautiful," she said soberly, eyes on the river.
"Very beautiful. What I've seen of it." For no valid reason, she added, "I'm supposed to be in Melbourne."

"Well," he said companionably, "you're better off here.
It's better all round." And was rewarded with a slight
smile. Her head turned and the corners of her mouth
lifted.

"You're the first person I've spoken to here," she said.
"Except for the hotel people. And they don't count. I did
speak to a woman on the plane. As we were passing over
the Nullarbor." Saying it the way the woman on the plane
had. Feeling stupidly proud of her retentiveness. "She told
me about the camel lady."

He nodded, listening.

"You've heard of the camel lady?" she asked.

He nodded again.

"You're the only two people I've talked to," she said,
looking at the cigarette between her fingers. "That sounds
strange." Her voice lost most of its volume.

"Strange country for you," he said, understanding. She
was shy. Terribly shy. "It's not always that easy," he went
on, "talking to people."

She looked at him, visually agreeing.

"Not something I do myself all that often," he added,
"talking to people. New people."

"It's not the same as business," she said. "That isn't the
same. Talking to people all day long. But you're not really
talking. Oh, sometimes. But so rarely."

"What've you seen of the city?" he asked. "There's a lot
to see."

"I've walked some."

"You need someone to take you around," he said, deciding he'd show her. He enjoyed showing off the city.
"Would you like a bit of a tour?"

Perhaps, she thought, I should be afraid. But I'm not.
Not at all afraid. Had Ian killed that, too?

She answered, "Yes," and sat waiting to hear what he'd say next.

"Jimmy Ballard," he introduced himself, reaching for his wallet and a card, presenting her with the card.

She accepted it, staring down, seeing the print but not reading the words.

"Lyle," she said. "My name is Lyle Maxwell."

"I knew a girl once named Lyle," he said easily.

It aroused her interest.

"Did you?"

"Journo. C grade. When I was with the paper. Years ago. Nice girl she was, Lyle."

"A journalist?"

"That's right." He smiled. He did have a nice smile. Small white teeth. "Second Lyle I've met."

"I've never met another," she said, wanting to reciprocate, return the smile but unable to. So many things she couldn't force herself to do. Smiling being one. "I was furious with my mother for naming me that. When I was young. Now, it's just a name."

"That's how it happens," he said, dropping his cigarette to the ground, grinding it carefully under his heel as she watched. "It all changes, getting older, seeing things differently."

She thought then about the flights. The one from New York to Los Angeles. Changing terminals, airlines. Boarding the second plane. Stopping first in Honolulu. Seeing the tourists in the airport and the miles of too-brightly-lit shops. Macadamia nuts crated, ready to be sent anywhere. Then reboarding the plane. She'd taken another dramamine and dozed off. To land again at four a.m. in Pago Pago. Reeling off the plane, hearing the music. Seeing the troupe of natives singing and dancing. Beautiful smooth-looking faces, lovely music. The air soft. Palm fronds slapping together in the darkness. Moths death-dancing in the spotlights focused on the small stage area. She'd stood watching, listening; wanting to laugh and cry simultaneously. So touched. Wishing, as she did less and less each passing year, she'd never surrendered her doubtful talents. There were so many shifting images here she might, some other time, have captured. So she'd stayed there, smiling, dim-eyed with fatigue; fearful of arrivals, disillusionment, getting old, traveling alone, living. Hopeful of too many nebulous possibilities, and of miracles.

Jimmy watched her eyes go vague and used those few seconds to study her face. A face that wouldn't stand out in a crowd. Unless you were the sort to attempt to read beneath surfaces. Then, you might be arrested by this woman's face. Because there was a quality to it. A fine face, he thought. Straight nose, firm chin. Her mouth. He was stopped by her mouth. And by the fact that when he spoke she looked not only at his eyes but at his mouth as well. As if she'd never seen someone in the actual act of speaking, forming words. Her mouth looked soft, revealing. Whatever she felt might be reflected in the tensing or relaxing of her lips. Not the eyes as was usual, but the mouth.

"What is C grade?" she asked, abruptly back in the present.

He was late. What was down in his diary for the day? Nothing that couldn't wait until Monday.

"A grade or two down from the top," he said distractedly, deciding. Brightening. "Look, why don't I give you a tour? Would you like that?"

"I might be crazy," she cautioned quietly.

He caught her meaning and smiled. "You *might* be. I probably *am*. It's a fine day and I'm proud of the city." He looked past her at the nearby buildings. "Come on," he coaxed. "Do us both good." Returning his eyes to hers, he said, "You've nothing to fear."

"I know that," she said, all seriousness. "All right. Yes."

"Good! My car's just here."

She looked at the car. A dusty, dinged, comfortable-looking station wagon. "This is very kind of you, Mr. Ballard," she said, moistening her lips. Wondering what she was doing, not caring. Such a pleasant man. The worst he could do was kill her.

"Jimmy," he corrected, slipping his hand under her elbow to assist her up from the bench. "It's all anybody ever calls me."

As they walked toward the car, he could hear Mag's voice shrieking. *Bastard! Bloody bastard!* He held open the door as Lyle slid in, waited until she'd settled herself, then closed the door and went round to the driver's side. Feeling everything in him lifting. An adventure. A break in the routine.

Two

---◆→---

He drove slowly, with care, following the road along the river.

"What's the river called?" she asked, finding it odd sitting in what should have been the driver's seat, her eyes on the water.

"The Swan. Are you fond of boats?" he asked, glancing over at her. Deciding anew she was a fine-looking woman.

"To look at. I suffer terribly from motion sickness."

"That's a pity," he sympathized. "I'll show you the boats, though. They're mad for sailing here. Some beautiful boats."

Beautiful. She thought of how all the people she'd met in Melbourne had called everything "beaut." That's beaut. Or beauty. That night Ian had taken her to the theatre to see Reg Livermore. Wonder Woman. And that man in the bar at intermission who'd grinned at her, his eyes on her breasts. Someone had pushed into her from behind and she'd found herself shoved up against the grinning, bearded man. Fire burning her face and neck, her chest, she'd pulled away and the man had whispered, "Oh beauty! Beauty!" She'd turned away, panicked, searching the crowd for Ian, who'd finally returned with the drinks to rescue her. Beauty. No one but Ian had ever looked at her that way. She'd wanted both to fly away and also to go back close to that grinning man to find out what he'd really meant. Perhaps to have him say more, do more.

"My father had a boat," she said, eyes on the river. "He didn't use it for sailing, though. Of course, as a child, I didn't know that."

"What did he use it for?"

"Women," she said flatly.

"Oh."

"I found that out when I was eighteen." Going to the marina in Rowayton, thinking to surprise him. Always

13

hoping to find some new way to win his favor. She'd run away that time, too. What else could she have done? She'd run, despising him. So angry. She'd never spoken of it to anyone. Until now.

"He was quite famous, my father. Very famous, really."

She turned toward him. "He was a comedian," she said. "Very funny."

"But you didn't think so."

"When I was little I did. Before I knew what he really was." She stopped, wondering about the changes that kept happening to her. Earlier in the day she'd felt endangered. Now, she felt safe, sheltered inside the big, banged-up, smoky-smelling car with this easy, interested man. Removed, somehow, from all the old patterns of her life. "He wasn't funny," she continued, looking again out the window. "My God! He *wasn't* funny!"

"I'll show you a bit of the town," he said, swinging the car away from the river, into the stream of traffic heading toward the city center.

"All right," she said absently. Examining her anger. Shaking again. What is *happening* to me? This isn't me. "I'm sorry," she said. "That was vitriolic."

"No," he disagreed. "Probably something that's been needing to get said."

"You feel that way about things?" she asked, turning back to look at him.

"You get to a point."

"Yes, you do."

She wondered suddenly if it was his intention at the end of this "tour" to attempt to make love to her. The idea causing her shaking to accelerate. She opened her bag for a cigarette, thinking, Please don't do any of that to me. Please don't. I can't, couldn't.

He pulled open the ashtray and said, "London Court just there. It's an arcade. Some very nice shops." She'd grown very tense, he could see. And wondered why. "Have you had breakfast?"

"I keep ordering meals from room service and not eating them."

"Well, then, we'll have something to eat."

He found a slot and parked the car. "There's a place just along here," he said, removing the key from the ignition.

She blinked, wet her lips, tried to smile. Couldn't. Got

out of the car and walked along at his side and into a small café. They were the only customers.

Jimmy said, "Be right back," and went to the gents, trying to decide what was wrong with her. Something bothering her badly. Fair dinkum, he thought. Something bothering me badly, as well. Everyone's got his something. But this, with her, it's like shock. Like some of the lads in the war. After the ship was torpedoed and they were out there in the rafts floating around, waiting to be picked up. The lads with their eyes going in and out of focus. Disbelievingly. This couldn't be happening to them, not to them. He'd been just a lad himself. Only he'd never felt young. Not like the others.

She was staring at the small, spattered menu, reading the same line over and over, unable to force her eyes to move.

The waitress came over and stood waiting to take their orders.

Jimmy, sensing Lyle's difficulty, said, "Two coffees, white. Eggs and toast."

The waitress removed the menus and went away.

"What do you do?" Lyle asked him, lighting a fresh cigarette.

"I have a small business. Printing. Worked on the newspaper for years until I couldn't take any more of the journos. Knowing everything. Knowing nothing. Kids with opinions on everything and no flexibility, no giving. And you?"

"I thought I'd be an artist." She waved away the cigarette smoke from between them. "I do needlepoint designs. Paint canvases. I have a shop in Connecticut. That's where I live."

"And you still paint?"

"I wasn't good enough. No. Not anymore. Every so often I think I might. I buy supplies, set them up, then stare at them for days. Finally put it all away. Until the next time." Hearing that old instructor at Pratt. Practically shouting at her. Free up! *Free up!* It's all there but you're not letting one damned bit of it come out! "You're married?" she asked.

He nodded.

"You have children?"

"Two. They both work with me."

"That's very nice," she said softly, liking the idea of that.

"Both married," he went on. "Good kids, nice kids. You're married?"

"No. I was supposed to be. It's why I came to Australia." She swallowed, looked over at the door, then down at the table. Australia. It's where I am God how did I get here how do I leave? "It's the biggest thing I've ever done," she said, "coming here." She looked up at him. "Before this trip, I'd never been farther from home than Vermont. No, that's not true. I went to Chicago once. But nothing like this. It all . . . I should go home. I've been trying to make up my mind to go. But I didn't think . . . I made arrangements to be away longer. I've . . ."

"Would you like to tell me what happened?" he asked. "It's sometimes a help to talk it out."

"I don't think I can," she said, looking stricken so that he felt all at once protective of her and very sorry for whatever it was that had happened. She appeared to be far out of her depth and drowning with it. "I can't believe any of . . . these things. I should go home. It's just that I can't. I can't seem to make myself go."

"I've a mare due to foal soon," he said. "She's had two fillies. I'm hoping this time for a colt."

"You have a farm?"

"Just the horses. You like horses?"

"I don't know. I don't know anything about horses."

"Susie's a beautiful mare," he said. "I'll take you out to see them."

"What do you do with them? Do you race?"

"Susie's a trotter. A good breeder. It's just for pleasure, really. I'm up at four-thirty every morning to tend the girls before I come into the city. Ben went this morning for me. My son," he explained. "We're keeping a close eye on Susie now."

The waitress set down the plates of food, the coffee, and went away. To stand behind the counter looking bored and angry, picking at her nails.

Jimmy started on his eggs and after a moment Lyle picked up her knife and fork and followed suit.

"Where are you staying?" he asked, glad to see she was eating with some degree of appetite.

"The Sheraton. It seems ridiculous to come all the way to Australia to stay in an American hotel. The food's aw-

ful. I stayed at the Hilton in Melbourne. The view was
wonderful. It doesn't seem right, though. Ian booked me
into the Hilton. And here, when I got off the plane . . . it
sounded familiar and I needed something familiar. But it's
familiar in all the wrong ways. The pool's good, though.
It's all I've really done. Float in the pool. Like some kind
of therapy. You know?"

"Maybe that's just what it is."

"I haven't felt able to do anything else. I suppose a psy-
chiatrist would say it's something fetal. I don't know. It's
a heated pool. And sunny out there. There hasn't been
anything else I've wanted to do."

"Do you know," he said, unintentionally switching subjects, "that Western Australia has some of the most beautiful wildflowers in the world? Probably the largest variety,
as well."

"No, I didn't know that."

"You like flowers?"

"Yes." She had that desire to laugh and cry again. He
was such a kind man, trying so earnestly to learn her likes
and dislikes.

"We'll go to the park," he stated.

"Mr. Ballard," she began. "Jimmy. I don't know what
you think I am or if you think I'm something. What I
mean . . ."

"It's all right," he cut in. "I know what you're trying to
say and it's all right. We'll just have a drive, I'll show you
the city. That's all."

"I'm sorry," she said quietly. "It's just everything that's
happened." She swallowed hard. "It's been . . . bad. And
I don't understand why. I mean, I do. But I don't."

"We'll talk about all that," he said, making it sound like
a promise. "Now just you relax and finish here before
your food gets cold. I know you're upset."

"How do you know that?" she asked stupidly.

"It shows," he said. And then smiled to make her see
that it really was all right.

"I have a younger brother," she was saying. "He's a
stockbroker. Bachelor. He has an apartment on Fifth Avenue in New York. We're exact opposites, Richard and I.
He's outgoing, extroverted, aggressive. Like our father.
No, not really like him. But I'm not like either of our
parents. My mother. She's young. It feels strange to think

sometimes . . . how young my mother is. Fifty-five. I get older and older and she gets younger. I'm thirty-five." She stopped talking and looked over at Jimmy.

"I'm coming up to fifty," he said. "That feels pretty damned strange, I can tell you. Thinking of myself getting on for fifty. All those years used up. I know what you're saying. Your parents are still living?"

"My mother is. My father died twelve years ago. They did a television retrospective. I watched and couldn't believe how funny/sad the man was. No one I'd ever known. Someone else who never came into our house."

"Tell me, how did you meet your chap from Melbourne?"

"He came into my shop. To buy something. But it isn't the kind of shop he thought it was. He wanted to buy a finished piece of work. And I don't sell work that's already been done. We talked. And"—she paused, then hurried on to the end—"that's how we met."

We met and he did with his eyes some of what the grinning man in the theatre did with his eyes, looking at me, at my body and it was exciting, dangerous. Something different. Attention. I was a fool for attention. Willing. Years and years of telling lies. To myself and everyone else. Saying I was perfectly content with my life, saying I wanted nothing more when I wanted everything more and still secretly believed I could have anything, everything. But he seemed so sincere, so urbane and charming and generous. Where is the best place in town to eat? he asked and I told him and he said, Good! We'll have dinner there tonight. Tell me where you live and I'll come collect you at seven-thirty. Is that a good time? Seven-thirty. I said, Collect me here.

He came in his rented car. Admired her with words and his eyes. Gave her wine and rich food and kissed her on the mouth before saying, Good night, I'll see you tomorrow same time.

Tomorrow same time different restaurant. More wine and rich food, more kisses on the mouth on the throat. He was on loan to I.B.M. Something to do with computers. He was always vague—intentionally?—about his work. Telephoning her at the shop to say, Do you know I'm in love with you? And she had to laugh with the shock because she hadn't any words in her vocabulary to deal with such a declaration.

Every night for a week, then two. Kisses on the mouth, the throat, the neck, the ears. Persuasive hands stealthily curving round her waist up over her breasts. Her treacherous body illicitly blossoming beneath these wrong-feeling caresses. Something was happening and it felt like love. He called it love and she allowed herself to be persuaded. She'd wondered all of her life what it was, how it was. At thirty-five finally finding sufficient boldness within herself to accompany him to his Howard Johnson motel room. Where with not a little difficulty and a great deal of further persuasion—in varying forms—he succeeded in placing his body within hers. Creating pain and confusion and a disappointment she refused to accept. Because he hastened to assure her the first time was always bad and next time—he insisted on a next time and she felt so relieved, so grateful—would be better. Which it was. But only somewhat.

He'd seemed content, though. And she went with him again and again and again. Making plans. He said, Come to Australia. Marry me. And she said, Yes. But caution or reserve—something quietly negative—told her not to leap in all the way. A three-month visitor's visa. And only two good-sized suitcases. Because there was always the possibility she mightn't like Australia. Never any doubt in her mind she wouldn't like Ian in Australia. Because it never occurred to her that he'd show himself to be anything other than what he'd been all along.

"It never occurred to me," she said, her mouth dry, "that someone could change so. . . so drastically. I don't know."

"Oh, people do, though," Jimmy said philosophically.

"But not that way. Not such a complete about-face. I . . ." They were passing a grassy area with benches overlooking the water. "Could we stop, do you think? Would you mind?"

"Not at all." He pulled the car over and they got out, walked across the grass to sit on one of the benches.

"Tell me about your children," she said. "They sound so nice."

"Ben's a good lad. Twenty-six. Married close on to four years now. Donna's my baby. Twenty-two. Married last year. Nice chap. Dutch."

"And your wife?"

Three years ago, when he'd first talked about Mag to

someone outside the family, the feeling of disloyalty he'd
had then had nearly crippled him. Wrong, he'd thought, to
do this to Mag, to us. Even with words. But what's she doing to me, to us? he'd countered. And where's the help?

"Mag's an alcoholic," he said bluntly. "We've lived
apart more than two years now."

"That's a shame," she said, at once captured by his
problems; wanting not to have to think about her own.
"It's very difficult, I know. Several family friends were al-
coholics."

"Tried A.A.," he said. "Nothing. The thing is, she won't
admit to having a problem. She stayed off five months last
year. I was all set to move back. Then she started in on
the beer, rang me up one night raving and that was it for
my moving back. It's a bloody pity. A beautiful, intelligent
woman. Young still, too. I just can't understand why. How
did it happen?"

"Did she always drink a lot?"

"Not always," he answered consideringly. "Once the
kids were grown it seemed to take hold of her. She'd ring
the office when I'd have people there. One afternoon she
rang thirty-one times. I finally had to have it out with her,
to get her to stop." He was feeling it again. That sick
sense of disloyalty. I shouldn't talk about Mag to a
stranger. Yet this woman doesn't feel strange to me. Not
in the least. Nowhere near as strange as Mag feels to me
now. "Why do you say you weren't good enough at your
painting?"

"Because I wasn't."

"Somebody told you that?"

"Nobody had to tell me. I simply knew."

"Maybe you were wrong."

"No, I wasn't wrong."

"Sometimes it's not up to us to judge. Other people have
to decide."

"I'd have been embarrassed having anyone else see my
work."

"Maybe," he repeated, "you were wrong."

"Why do you say that?"

"Because it's always a possibility. Would you mind if I
ask rather a personal question?"

"I don't mind."

"It's about your dress."

She looked down at her lap. "I haven't any clothes," she

said, smoothing her skirt over her knees; feeling the flush overtaking her face. "This was what I was wearing . . . I bought the bathing suit but I couldn't stay in the shop long enough to buy anything else. I've been having the dress cleaned every other day. If you put your clothes in with the valet by nine in the morning, they're delivered back by four-thirty or five in the afternoon. I put the dress in in the morning and spend the day in the pool."

"I see. You must be getting tired of it by now. How long's it been?"

"Two weeks."

"Why don't we finish up this drive for now, go back to the city and buy you a dress?"

"You don't mean to buy me a dress?" She looked alarmed at the prospect.

"No," he smiled. "I'll let you buy yourself whatever you fancy."

"I saw a very good movie on television last night," she said, apropos of nothing. " 'Sunday Too Far away.' "

"Right. It's a good one," he agreed.

"Have you ever been out to a station?"

"Years ago."

"Shearers. It seemed to me, watching, such a—removed life. All the petty trivialities blown to such importance simply because people are living so far from everything. I keep wondering if everything that's happened isn't simply trivial and just a case of my having blown it all out of proportion because I've lived for so long so far removed from reality."

"You don't seem unreal to me."

"I feel . . ."

"How?"

"Scared. Like a fool. Scared."

"What happened, Lyle?"

"I saw two other Australian films," she said. "*The Getting of Wisdom*. That was wonderful, really wonderful. The other one I hated. *Picnic at Hanging Rock*?" She lifted her eyebrows. "Apparently, it's won all sorts of awards. I hated it. I hate things that don't . . . that aren't resolved. I can't talk about . . . I *want* to talk about it. It's just that I can't." I sound demented, she thought. Running back and forth between subjects like a white mouse in a maze.

"Would you like some fresh clothes?"

"Yes."

"Shall we get you some then?"

"I should, shouldn't I?"

"You probably should." He smiled and patted her head. She suffered his touch, then got up to walk back to the car. Halfway there, she stopped and turned to face him. "You're a nice man," she said, "being very kind to me. Putting up with the way I'm behaving, because I know I'm behaving very strangely. It's just that it was all so— ugly. *Awful*." She shuddered, seeing the door open; seeing herself standing there, moving forward, slowly realizing what Ian had done. Feeling the horror.

"Not so strange," he said. "And in any case you remind me a bit of someone."

"Who?"

"Myself."

Her eyes widened slightly. "In what way?" she asked, again walking at his side.

"Oh, different ways. Knowing you've got things to do, things needing to be done, but unable to get yourself to do them. Different things."

"Do I look like a rich American tourist?"

"A little," he admitted with a smile.

"I was," she said. "For about a week. I felt horribly ostentatious going into the banks, changing my money. But people are so friendly, so interested, wanting to know do I find many differences here, what's it like in America." She smiled for the first time with her eyes as well as her mouth. "I couldn't answer about the differences."

"Foolish question for starters," he said.

"I needed more time. Some things you can see right away. The obvious things. Driving on the wrong side of the road. Palm trees. The accents. But others, other things need time to see. Like people. How can you know if the way they show themselves to you is actually the way they are? You can't tell, can't be sure. You can't!"

"He wasn't what you thought he was," Jimmy guessed, opening the car door for her.

"No," she said breathlessly. "Not what he pretended to be. Not." Why did Ian have to do that? she wondered. God! *Why?* All the rest of it and then that. Such a sick, cruel thing to do. And all along encouraging her to enter into performance with him. The shame of it. Throwing everything away. Giving every last particle of herself to someone who valued none of it. She saw herself in the act of making love with Ian and squeezed her eyes shut, hating seeing it.

"Are you all right?" he asked, sliding behind the wheel, noticing her hands had begun to tremble.

"I shouldn't have believed . . . any of it . . . nothing . . ." It was going to happen and she couldn't stop it. Sobs rising from her chest, refusing to be held down or suppressed; erupting from her mouth. She covered her face with her hands and bent until her head was resting on her knees. Feeling she'd go mad, crying so hard, making so much noise. "I'm sorry!" she cried, her voice totally out of control, her words punctuated by sobs. "He burned . . . destroyed . . . I went back thinking we'd . . . talk. Talk. And he was out . . . not there. Then I thought it was a good thing . . . he wasn't there . . . I'd take my things quickly and go but everything . . . *everything*. I'm sorry, sorry."

"No, no, no," he said softly, stroking her hair. "It's all right now, all right. Don't you be sorry. No need for that."

Once before she'd cried this way. Years and years ago. Closed herself into the hall closet. She couldn't, for the moment, seem to remember why she'd been crying. Only that she'd done it. Remembering the feeling, the terrible hurt and the fear. Because of something that had happened that she couldn't remember. Simply couldn't.

Three

———◆———

I want to die just let me right now right this minute die. It hurts and there's nowhere to go with the pain I've acted the fool made a fool of myself how can I go back? It was all just a game, some sort of conquest to him. But how could it have been? He said, Marry me, come to Australia. He said it almost from the beginning. But he changed day and night unrecognizably. Trying to make me uncomfortable about my money. Then doing that, what he did. Die just let me. Now.

Jimmy was, in an unexpected way, impressed by her tears, the grating sobs. To be able to let go, just open up and let all the misery come flooding out. He wished he could. It had to be a good thing, a healthy thing. Not holding it all inside, containing it year after year the way he had for so long. Mag screaming at him, You've got no bloody balls! You don't care! You don't! It's all your fault! Yours!

What, though? What did I ever do that was so wrong or so bad? I did all the things I was supposed to do. And a lot I thought was right. Providing for her, for the children. Holidays and gifts on birthdays, Christmas. Education for the kids. A nice home. I cared about her, cared about making her feel good. In bed, too. I loved you, Mag, and look what you did to it! It wasn't me drinking, unable to stop; drinking myself right out of control. No, you. I tried to help. Stopped drinking altogether around the house and tried not to come in smelling of the small scotch I took after leaving the office. You didn't get it from me. I wasn't ever the sort to start in on the beer of a Friday evening and not leave go of it until Sunday when my words were running down my chin and my eyes were bleary. I never was. I cared. About you, about the kids. I wish I could cover my face with my hands and cry that hard, that loud, get it all out from inside me.

"I'm sorry," she said again.

"Never mind that," he said, relishing the babylike softness of her hair under his hand. "You just go on and cry it all out. Get it out of your system. It's good to let it go. Don't be sorry. Here." He pushed his handkerchief into her hands. "There's all kinds of time," he said, watching the breeze blow up whitecaps on the water; liking the way the grass bent under the wind.

She thought of how she'd come out of the customs hall at Tullamarine and Ian had been so busy talking to some man that he hadn't even seen her, so she'd had to stand there with her luggage on the trolley. Waiting like a schoolchild for him to notice her. The pills and thirty-three hours of transit time turning her vision wavery. Her stomach churning, upset. She'd felt grimy, gritty-eyed; the airport sounds roaring in her ears. Standing, waiting to be noticed. She'd felt angry with him then. Angry and dismayed at having come such a long way anticipating a joyful greeting, an intensely emotional reunion only to have to stand while Ian talked loudly and long—his voice harsher, accent more nasal than she'd remembered—not seeing her. She'd felt something for just a moment that had seemed perilously close to hatred. But then he'd turned. And she'd forgotten the anger, the fatigue. Seeing him. Impressed yet again by his good looks, his tremendous vitality. That a man of such qualities would wish to marry her. Oh God! How could I have been such a complete and pathetic fool?

"She was a good mother," Jimmy said, letting his thoughts surface with unusual freedom. "A fine mother. The house always spotless. I wasn't the sort to walk through the front door demanding my meal. We'd go out to a meal often. I'd ring her from work to say, 'Don't bother with cooking tonight, Mag. We'll go out. You get the kids fed and settled and we'll go out.' I don't know." He rubbed the back of his hand over his forehead. "People change on you and it seems as if it happened all of a sudden. But it was really years in the happening. Years. And you've got to wonder why you didn't take note of this that happened and that that happened that was telling you it was all changing, but you were too busy or too tired to see. D'you like Italian food?" he asked the back of her head.

She sat up holding his handkerchief over the lower half

of her face. Her eyes, red and wet, regarding him with surprise.

"Do you?" he asked.

She nodded, unblinking.

"I know a place. For dinner."

She stared at him a moment longer, then laughed. And at once began crying anew.

"I enjoy shopping," he said, toying with his cigarette lighter. "I've always liked going through the shops. But Mag never liked having me along, claimed she couldn't make up her mind what she wanted to buy with me hanging over her." He lit a cigarette and handed it to her, then lit one for himself. "I like the way you did that," he said, smiling encouragement at her. "I'd give a lot to be able to let loose and cry. It's a good day for shopping. When you're ready, we'll go." He thought for a moment, then asked, "You're all right for money?"

She whispered, "Yes," thinking of all the traveler's checks. Two thick folds of them. Money that had been accruing for years. The checks scarcely making a dent in the remainder of her inheritance and the income from the shop. Money she'd brought along thinking she'd use it constructively for hers and Ian's future comfort. Furniture for the house they'd buy. Small luxuries his salary couldn't provide.

She'd never thought of herself as overly independent, or fiercely self-reliant. It had always been simply a matter of providing for her needs, doing what had to be done. But he'd forced her to see all the differences. Making her independence and self-reliance seem like temporary qualities she'd adapted solely to enrage him. I can't help opening doors for myself, ordering for myself in restaurants, making whatever decisions I do make and accepting the responsibility for those decisions. Mother encouraged me. "Don't depend on anyone but yourself, Lyle. Be your own best friend." I couldn't devalue everything I'd ever been taught in order to become what Ian thought it was proper for me to be. And what was it he expected? Reliance on him. Dependency. Wanting me to allow him to make every decision, regardless of how large or small. Making an increasingly ugly contest out of opening doors, ordering my food; treating me as if I were helpless. I hated it.

"Do you think I'm unfeminine?" she asked Jimmy.

"I wouldn't say so. Not at all."

"He accused me, said . . . so many things. But I couldn't change the way I've always been, done things."

"That's what he expected?"

"It was like a book I'd read once upon a time, or a film I might have seen on the late show. A story, a piece of fiction. Nothing having anything to do with life the way I know it. Having to prove his maleness, his natural superiority. He refused to accept it when I said it wasn't necessary to prove anything at all to me, and got angry that I'd even consider saying such a thing, let alone think it. And his friends. I thought they'd see how badly he was behaving. But they were all just like him. The women, the wives, they all thought I was wrong, too. All of them patronizing me because I was foreign and didn't know any better, didn't know my place, or how things were done. My God! I hated it!"

"There *are* differences," she said urgently. "I started seeing them, so many of them. But I put it down to my tiredness. I wasn't seeing things quite right because I was so worn down from the long flight. But that wasn't it at all, though."

She turned away, gazing at the sailboats in the distance. Feeling the humiliation all over again as she saw Ian sitting up away from her, lighting a cigarette, so coldly saying, I thought you said you'd get the pills.

And herself answering, It seemed to make more sense to wait and get them here. Feeling his coldness penetrating her limbs. "I wouldn't be able to get an American prescription refilled here," she'd concluded lamely. Having been made to feel wrong, inept, stupid, incapable of doing anything right.

"It's like taking a bloody bath with your socks on," he'd said, getting up and going to the bedroom door. Then he'd turned. "When I bloody ask you to do something, Lyle, you bloody do it! Pisses me off you didn't do it. Why in hell d'you think I told you in the first place, because I like hearing the sound of my own voice?"

That had been the second time she'd felt the hatred flaring inside her. Being made to feel so small, so ashamed for having yet again given herself to him with such lamentable eagerness. And him, taking her offerings heedlessly, considering them all but worthless.

"Things are different in America, are they?" Jimmy asked.

"Attitudes," she said, then blew her nose. "Ways of doing things, of behaving. You don't stop every inch of the
way to examine the manner in which you do the things
you do. You just *do* them. Good manners, of course. Con-
sideration for other people. Things like that you do think
of. But being mistreated *because* of what you are, where
you come from . . ." She shook her head, pushing the
hair out of her eyes. "You're not like that," she said,
studying his face. "Others I've seen, met since coming
here, they're not like that. Throwing their weight around,
insisting on running everything, being in command."

"That's what he did?"

"That. And more. Other things." How comfortable you
are, she thought. Comfortable and easy and kind. The way
I'd have liked my father to be. The way he never was.
Other women's husbands I've known who were the way
you are. But no one ever who's been important to my life.

She opened her bag and removed a small mirror. He
watched as she held it up and winced at her image. She
powdered her nose and chin and, with a still-trembling
hand, applied lipstick. He was captivated seeing her do it,
liking very much the way the color added further defini-
tion to her mouth.

"You've a lovely mouth," he said. "A fine-looking
woman."

She looked over at him to see if he was mocking her.
Or mad, perhaps.

"I'm not crazy," he said. "A person doesn't become ugly
just because something ugly's happened to her."

"A fine-looking woman," she repeated. "Don't be offended," she said, her voice still too rough at the edges,
"but I was just thinking you're the way I'd have liked my
father to be. And men I've known."

He laughed. A wonderful sound.

"I'm not offended," he said, reaching to wipe some of
the excess powder from her nose with his forefinger. "I've
had a hell of a lot worse said to me."

She risked touching him. Put her hand on his arm and
said, "Thank you. I think I'm ready now to face some
shopping, if you truly don't mind."

He started up the car saying, "I'll enjoy it. And if you
won't be offended, I was thinking that maybe someday I'll
come visit you in America. I've always fancied seeing it.

Have an old friend in San Francisco I haven't seen since forty-four."

"We'll be friends," she said, meaning it. "I feel so much better. I kept going back to feed the swans, thinking about having to go home. Or dying. Preferring to die. Because it seemed easier than going home."

"No. You'll go home. And it won't be difficult at all."

All the skirts and dresses were far too long for her liking. And the sizes different. But she managed to work out what her size was and found two pairs of slacks, several shirts. And, at Jimmy's urging, bought a pair of low-heeled sandals at far more than she'd have paid at home. The prices were very high. Fifty Australian dollars for a pair of sandals. But what did it matter?

She needed underwear badly but couldn't bring herself to shop for such intimate items in the presence of a man.

"I've got a telephone call to make," he said, seeing her looking into the window of a lingerie shop. "Why don't I meet up with you just over there?" He pointed to a telephone kiosk, then made his way over to it.

In the changing room, nervously eyeing the curtain, she thought—as she did every time she bought new brassieres—of the very first time she'd done it. When the saleslady had pulled open the curtain, cheerily asking, How're you getting on, dear? And Lyle had wanted to hide, positively mortified at being caught with her breasts open to view. Fourteen and so embarrassed. She'd wanted to hide. But where? With the mirror there to show her nakedness no matter which way she turned. Don't be shy, dear, the saleslady had said. It's what I'm here for, to help.

I'll do it myself, she'd managed to say in a small voice.

And the saleslady had sniffed impatiently, dragging the curtains closed, saying, I'll be outside when you're done in there.

It wasn't that she minded having breasts and periods and hair growing in unlikely places. Because she liked the idea of being a woman, of being soft, and, someday, grown up. Capable of having babies. It was just having a stranger see everything about her that was so private.

That first time with Ian when he'd insisted on keeping the lights on while she undressed. Saying, Had an idea you'd look better without your clothes. You do, too. That same feeling all over again. That he shouldn't have been seeing her. Especially since he then turned off the light and did his own undressing in the dark. But seeing had only been the start. There'd been the touching, too. His hands laying claim to every part of her, creating a guilty pleasure and so heightened a sense of self-awareness she'd been utterly unable to involve herself. Experiencing him as a series of shocks. Shock upon shock, building to a point where the final, ultimate shock was like death. To have volunteered herself into pain when she'd thought, hoped there'd be pleasure. Waiting years and years believing love contained only pleasure. Years waiting only to discover that love contained primarily pain and only peripherally a degree of pleasure. That pleasure having to do with the fact that there was someone who wanted her, someone who found her private body of interest, someone who—after that first time—insisted she bare herself to him at every possible opportunity. And she'd obeyed, glad to call it love.

Now, standing in the tiny changing cubicle of a shop in Perth—Australia, I'm in Australia and I know I must go home—fitting a brassiere to her breasts, she carefully avoided looking at herself in the mirror until she was covered. Knowing none of it had been love. A cursory glance to see that the brassiere fit, then her eyes examined the curtain while she quickly dressed—positive someone would come barging in on her at any moment—then brushed her hair back into place.

She was about to leave the cubicle when she stopped and stepped very close to the mirror, studying the face there. Wishing she could love this image of herself. Wishing she hadn't come so very close to finally feeling a fondness for that face, for that body, for that self only to have all of it destroyed. Frown-lines at the top of her nose. And what were supposedly laugh-lines around her mouth. Her eyes, too. And encircling her throat.

Look at you! You're old and foolish and no longer deluded. Go home, Lyle! Check out of the Sheraton, go to the airport and go home! You don't belong here. And you're piling days on top of the decision you know has to be made. All grown up now. At least on the outside. And the grown-up thing to do is go home.

But what will they say?

Who?

Mother and Richard. Penny at the shop. Mother's

friend Will. All the people you so stupidly told all your plans to. You mustn't do that ever again! Tell no one. Don't speak of your life or the people in or not in it. Keep it all to yourself.

Yes.

After I leave here. Never again. But for now, I have someone it's safe to talk to. They'd all like him. Mother and Richard and Will. Penny at the shop. They none of them liked Ian.

She took a step back from the mirror, realizing this was the truth. And she hadn't, until this moment, seen that.

Mother saying, Take your time, Lyle. There's no need to rush headlong into a permanent commitment with someone you've only known a few weeks.

And Richard. Shaking Ian's hand as if the two of them were squaring off before a boxing match.

I didn't see, wasn't seeing. Blind to everything but my own discoveries. Finding out about some of my capacities. Astonished to learn I could become inured to having a man inside my body.

The blood rushed into her face but she continued to confront the mirror.

It's true! I did it. Dozens of times. Something everyone else does. Almost everyone in the world. Why do I think I'm different simply because I was older, because I hadn't ever before. But I'm not different. Not that way. To be put down on my back and open my legs or have them opened for me. That isn't love. God! It's something. And dangerous. But it isn't love.

She felt dizzy and closed her eyes, leaning against the wall. Sick with the knowledge that she'd engaged in activities under the subtitle of love when all the while love had had no part, no place in those activities. She pushed away from the wall and, clutching the lace brassiere, drew back the curtain and returned into the shop.

"I'll have two of these," she said in the new, ruined voice that seemed to have become permanent. "And those, too," she added, pointing out some lace-trimmed bikini pants. "Three pairs."

She paid, received change, picked up the bag and left the shop. And felt calmer at the sight of Jimmy waiting for her by the telephone kiosk. She stood, waiting for him to complete his call, wondering what on earth she thought she was doing buying such outrageous underwear. Lace bi-

kinis and wispy little brassieres that left her half exposed. I
ought to return them, she thought. Intimidated by the
image of how her breasts had looked inside the brassiere.
Wrong, all wrong. Jimmy replaced the receiver and picked
up a paper bag.

"Something for you," he said, holding the bag out to
her.

She looked at him, then at the bag.

"Go on," he urged. "Have it."

She accepted the bag, still looking at him.

"It's a sketchbook. And some pencils. I thought you
might like to have a go at the wildflowers. It's too late for
it now but I thought perhaps tomorrow. I hope they're all
right. I wasn't sure what to buy."

"I'm going to start crying again," she said, lowering her
eyes. Holding her three paper bags. One with clothes. One
with ridiculous undergarments. And one containing something no one else had ever given her: encouragement. She
took a deep breath, cleared her throat, then looked at him
again.

"I am going to buy you dinner," she declared, smiling;
thinking she liked his face better than almost any other
she'd ever known. "And champagne, too."

"Beautiful!" He smiled back. "Never say no to champagne. Fancy seeing the London Arcade now? They say
it's just like the places in England."

"I've never been to London. But I'd like to go. Perhaps
I should buy a few things. For mother. And Richard, Will.
And something for Penny. She's the girl . . . woman who
manages my shop."

"Here, let me carry those for you."

"All right. Thank you." She allowed him to relieve her
of the bags.

"You've decided, haven't you?" he asked.

"It's only been a question of when all along. There's
really no decision to be made. I couldn't stay here even if
I wanted to. My visa has only six more weeks to go. And
six weeks from now, there'll be snow at home. I've got to
go."

"I went to the snow fields once," he said, holding open
the car door for her.

"Where are they?"

"I was in Falls Creek. Victoria. Beautiful stuff," he said,
"snow. The kids went mad. We all came home with

colds." He laughed, remembering it. "Mag had the kids home in bed for a week after."

"Have you ever been to the outback?" she asked. "Or to an opal field?"

"Never. Always wanted to do both, but never have. Still might someday, though."

"I wanted so much to see the Great Barrier Reef. Ian had said we would. But that was before. When I talked about it . . ."

We're not all independently wealthy, he'd said scathingly when she'd raised the question of their going. Some of us have to work for a living.

Offering to pay had been one of her biggest blunders. He had, in turn, actively demonstrated his anger. So that she'd had some trouble walking the day following.

She looked at her watch. After four. They'd managed to use up most of the day. Effortlessly.

"What time do the shops close?" she asked.

"Five-thirty. Plenty of time."

"You're sure you honestly don't mind all this?"

"I'm having a fine day," he said. "Just fine."

"All right," she said. "As long as you are."

"You have my word. I'll tell you the minute I start feeling bored."

Four

———◆———

The place looked awful from the outside. But inside, the walls were hung with huge copper pots and ancient pieces of farm equipment. There was a shelf perhaps twelve feet in length upon which were lined up lovely old serving platters. Brick walls and exposed beams and excellent service. They sat nibbling at a plate of olives, celery, and cheese; having a drink.

Jimmy was having scotch. Lyle had decided on white wine. And they were chatting companionably—she couldn't help remarking to herself on their continued ease of communication—about their afternoon of shopping.

He sat listening, thinking she looked particularly well in her new clothes. White trousers and a blue and white printed shirt, long-sleeved, open-throated.

"What happened to your things?" he asked. "Or would you prefer not to talk about it?"

Her eyes remained on his for a second or two longer, then she looked down at her wineglass. She picked up her cigarette and drew on it, then carefully tapped off the ash into the ashtray.

"He never explained why, but he booked me into the Hilton in Melbourne." She glanced up at him. "I think I told you that already, didn't I?"

"That's right."

She looked down again and went on. "I thought it was a little bit . . . strange. I mean, I'd expected to stay . . . with him. Well." She cleared her throat and took another drag on the cigarette. "That first night I really was so exhausted it wouldn't have mattered where I was. We had lunch, he came up to have a look at the room, told me to have a good sleep and left saying he'd see me the next day. I took a long, very hot shower and went to bed at about four-thirty that afternoon. Slept seventeen hours. Up at eight, I think it was. I could scarcely walk straight." She smiled, remembering. "It was far too early to expect him to call, so I decided to see a little of the city.

"The doorman suggested I go to see Captain Cook's cottage and told me where to get the tram, when to get off. So, feeling very adventurous, off I went. With my camera. And a sketchbook. I felt much better once I was out in the fresh air. And I loved the tram. I loved all of it. The city and the people I saw, the buildings. I went through the park, paid and went in to see the cottage, took some pictures. Then I found a refreshment place and had a cup of tea out on the terrace, did a few quick sketches. I felt so well. The park was so lovely, beautifully laid out. The flower beds and a little waterfall. Have you been to Melbourne?"

"A few times."

"I loved it!" she said again, finding it difficult to keep her eyes fixed on his. "I stayed until eleven or so and then started walking back to the main road. But I'd managed to get myself turned around. And it was getting late, so I took a taxi. I got back to my room, put down my things thinking I might make myself a cup of instant coffee. I think it's so sensible the way all the hotels have hot-pots and everything in the rooms so you don't have to call room service if you want some tea or coffee. The phone rang. And it was Ian, sounding angry. He was down in the lobby. So I told him to come up.

"Where had I been? He wanted to know. He'd been ringing my room for hours, getting worried something had happened to me." Her expression tightened. "I treated it lightly, saying I was used to finding my way around. After all, I'm certainly not a child. He unbent a little. But slowly, stiffly, as if he'd really have preferred remaining angry with me."

He'd wanted to make love. But his body had been angry. His gestures, too, all of it. So angry. Hurting. And afterward, she'd done something she'd never done before—pretended to have fallen asleep. In order to be left alone for a bit. She'd felt him looking at her, could almost feel him deciding what to do. He'd gone into the bathroom, returned to stand over her for what felt like hours. Then she'd heard him pick up her room key and go out. She'd waited a while longer, feeling annoyed that he'd taken her key, then got up and went into the bathroom thinking she'd take a quick shower. Vomiting into the sink instead.

After cleaning herself up, dressed once more, she'd gone to sit on the sofa to await his return and had actually fallen asleep. Still hurting.

"We had an early dinner," she went on. "And he started a very involved explanation of why he'd booked me into the hotel instead of taking me to his flat. I said it didn't matter. Which was the truth because the room was very nice, the hotel food was excellent, really excellent, and I'd have felt awkward staying with him. I've never done that . . . stayed at someone's place. It didn't feel . . . I simply told him it was all right, I was quite happy where I was. Which didn't seem to satisfy him at all. Nothing I said or did was right.

"I'm dragging this out. What happened was we spent the evenings together that first week. Several things happened that bothered me. Attitudes. You and I talked about that. Well, everything I said seemed to annoy him. I don't know. We were starting to argue. I *hate* disagreements. I'll do anything to avoid them. Anything.

"He took me to the theatre and was annoyed because there was a man in the foyer during the intermission who looked . . . talked to me. Ian accused me of attempting a flirtation. Which was absurd. Absurd.

"Then he took me to dinner with some friends and everything I said was wrong. Everything. Everything I *did* was wrong. And he seemed so different. Not at all the way he'd been . . . I don't know. But then, that third week he said he wanted me to come stay with him at the flat. I couldn't understand anything that was happening by that point—what he was doing or saying, or why. And I really didn't want to stay with him. I couldn't help feeling I'd made a mistake . . . misjudged. I thought . . . What did I think?"

As he watched, she seemed to shrink into herself, losing that spark of brightness she'd had upon meeting him in the Sheraton lobby; dressed in the new clothes and ready for the evening. She was shrinking now, her eyes turning inward, hands trembling. He wanted to tell her to stop, felt he'd been wrong urging her to talk it out. Whatever had happened, it had obviously wounded her deeply.

"We needn't talk about it," he began.

She shook her head, took another drag on the cigarette. The shaking gone wild inside her. Everything rattling, lurching. Panic.

"My God!" she said, wetting her lips. "I've always thought of myself as rational. Relatively in control of my life . . . the things that happen. There was no control. No rationality to any of it. I should tell you the truth . . . so you'll understand. I'd never been in a situation remotely like it. He was . . . the first."

She looked about to begin crying again, her cheeks bright red.

"I understand," he said quietly.

"I made a fool of myself." She cleared her throat, feeling the ache, the swelling there. "I compromised. Moved most of my things to his flat but said there were a few last-minute calls home to make, that sort of thing. And I didn't want to run up his telephone bill. It wasn't true. I just wanted to get out of it, but I couldn't, didn't know how.

"That first night I was to stay with him, we were to have dinner with another couple. A business associate of Ian's and his wife. They were to meet us in the Hilton lobby. The wife took one look at me and decided she loathed me on sight. That's never happened to me before. She was small, with a very pointed face, and an unpleasantly effusive, phony manner. I truthfully didn't like her any better than she did me but I felt it wasn't fair to judge on first impressions, better to wait and see, I might be wrong. I wasn't wrong. They'd asked along another man. We were to meet him at the restaurant.

"We went in their car. And sat in the back. I can't bear sitting in the back seat. And he was a terrible driver. Terrible. I felt sick at once. The car screeching around corners. He took a wrong turn and had to go around several long blocks. I wanted to get out and said why didn't we just park and walk back. They all ignored me. And we kept on driving round and round until he'd managed to find a spot fairly near the restaurant. I didn't want to eat or to have to spend an evening with these people. Although the husband really was charming. American. Ian had made the date, he said, because he thought another American would put me at my ease. Or something. I have no idea, really, what he thought. It's just what I *think* he thought.

"The restaurant was very nice. French. I wanted to sit quietly and admire the place. They had some beautiful antique brass pots, with the healthiest ferns I'd ever seen.

And Victorian furnishings, flocked wallpaper. The only person who paid any attention to me at all was the owner. At least, I assumed he was. There were two men running the place. Very, very gay. But not at all offensively so. But really, literally gay. Happy. And gay. I liked them at once. And ordered in French. And the one who was the owner was so nice. We spoke in French—I studied at school, you see—and I began feeling a little better. Then I realized the other three were all sitting there, glaring at me. As if I'd committed the most outrageous faux pas." She shook her head again. "It was awful.

"Then this third man arrived. And the wife began flirting with him in the most obscene fashion. The whole thing was grotesque. I drank my wine, chain-smoked, and simply tried to get through it. Pretending to pay attention to the conversations, but not listening. Still feeling quite ill from that awful ride. Anyway"—she paused to put out her cigarette—"this other man started drinking very heavily. They were all drinking fast, ordering more and more. On their third and fourth drinks while I hadn't finished my first glass of wine. And this man. I think he'd been well on his way to a good drunk when he arrived.

"He started the most incredible narrative about how the C.I.A. was really responsible for the separatist problems in French Canada because he knew that the C.I.A. wanted to get control of the St. Lawrence Seaway and by getting the province to break away from the rest of Canada and become a separate entity, the C.I.A. would somehow manage to establish their own control of the Seaway. Bizarre. I dared to say I thought the idea sounded a little farfetched. And Ian kicked me under the table. Hard. The heel of his shoe caught me on the ankle. I hadn't any idea at all why he'd done it. Except that this—lunatic was someone quite important in business and obviously terribly rich—raving about his new house in Toorak—and Ian wasn't about to have the man offended by me.

"Well, then the food came. It wasn't very good but I wasn't hungry in any case. Still, it was something to do. So I started eating. So did the American husband. He was from Minneapolis. That's in the Midwest. He was a nice man, tried to make conversation with me and seemed to see the difficulty I was having. But I couldn't understand how he could tolerate his wife's behavior. She was the most hateful sort of woman. About twenty-eight or so, with wild, frizzed-out hair. Terribly small and thin. Brittle. In a printed chiffon dress that seemed to be all points. She had what sounded like a dreadfully put-on snobbish sort of accent. The sort of accent they do in those British television comedies. And so bitchy. Stopping every so often—in the middle of a sudden silence like a desert—to say something to me, ask me some preposterous question. Then, shrieking with laughter over whatever answer it was I'd give. As if I were a complete idiot and hadn't she just proven it, yet again, to the satisfaction of everyone present? Asking me about certain American books. Had I read them, what did I think of them? I'd start to respond and then she'd change subjects or attack what I was saying. She admitted to not having read any of the books she'd mentioned, nor had she seen any of the movies . . . God only knows what she was trying to accomplish. The entire evening was horrible and getting worse by the minute.

"After the main course—the American husband and I the only ones who'd eaten anything, the others took two bites and then pushed their plates away—I whispered to Ian that I'd like to leave, go back to the hotel. I didn't feel well. And I wasn't having a particularly pleasant time. He ignored me. Gave me the most indescribable look. As if I were insane not to like his friends and how dare I question his choice of dinner companions. I couldn't possibly leave. It would have created an impossible scene. So, in order to have something to do, I had dessert.

"The third man ordered a bottle of brandy. I've never seen anyone do anything like that before. Oh, with gin or scotch, yes. But not an entire bottle of brandy. They began gulping it down as fast as they could, filling their glasses over and over. All I could think about was leaving, wanting to get back to the Hilton and forget them, the evening, all of it. I was getting a headache. But Ian made no indication he wanted to leave. He didn't actually seem to be enjoying himself. Yet he was working hard at making conversation with them, laughing at that venomous woman's remarks. Arch. I remember when I was very little hearing my mother describe a woman she knew as 'arch.' That's precisely what this one was. Everything she was saying was somehow directed at me, trying to goad me, while her husband sat with an apologetic, yet indulgent look on an otherwise intelligent face. As if to say: I know she's a vicious bitch, but forgive me, I love her. My God!

"This third man. He drank several large glasses of the brandy very quickly, then turned his attention on me. Started saying . . . things. With the most lascivious look on his face. I wasn't, he said, at all the type he'd thought Ian would go for. I didn't look . . . *orgasmic*. I didn't look . . . sexual. I looked, in fact, altogether too antiseptic and well-bred wealthy. 'Are you the orgasmic sort, dear?' the woman said, then laughed. The two of them clutching each other's arms, screeching with laughter. I exploded. I called him a drunk. And told her she hadn't any right to attempt to exercise her dubious intelligence and doubtful wit on me. And asked Ian to take me home.

"He gaped at me as if I'd thrown a pie in his face, wrapped his hand around my wrist—hard, terribly hard— and didn't say a word. Just kept me anchored in my seat and, after glaring at me for a long time, turned to them with a cracked sort of laugh, saying I was just edgy, to ignore me. And they went on with their conversation. I got up to find the ladies' room and went into the kitchen by mistake. The two owners were there. It was quite late by now. And they both smiled at me so eagerly. As if I were a long-lost friend. Asking me how I liked Australia, offering me a glass of wine. It was warm in the kitchen and most of the other people had finished dining and gone. So I had a glass of wine with them in the kitchen and talked to them. The one—the French one—assumed I was with the other American and began talking about Ian. Calling him an 'ocker.' When I asked him to explain, he started telling me about ockers. Beer-drinking, macho types. Football fanatics. You know all about that, of course."

"I know," Jimmy agreed.

"I couldn't see Ian that way. But this man's describing him in that fashion—it seemed to fit somehow. As if Ian had been performing, acting out some role when we'd met. And now that he was home again, it was no longer necessary to continue the performance. I didn't want to leave the kitchen. I felt more relaxed there, warmer than I had since arriving in Australia.

"I stayed too long. But it was so pleasant. And I'd been having such a miserable evening. I felt with these two I was finally meeting people I'd care to know, and I hadn't any desire to go back to the table. They seemed eager, too,

to have me stay, asking me about New York, about where
I lived, telling me how they'd happened to start the restaurant. Asking me how were gays treated in America. They
felt like friends. I was beginning to feel human again.

"And then Ian appeared in the doorway. Livid. His jaw
clenched. Reeking. Drunk. He grabbed hold of my wrist,
asking what did I think I was doing, yanking at my arm.
Humiliating. Forcing me to go back to the table." She
lowered her eyes, her face suffused with color.

Saying, What the fuck d'you think you're doing, out
here *chatting* with those two fucking queers?

They're very nice, Ian. A good deal nicer and friendlier
than your supposed friends. That woman despises me, has
spent the entire evening trying her best to embarrass and
humiliate me.

You're fucking paranoid, Lyle. You know that? They're
just trying to be friendly and the next thing I know you're
out in the fucking kitchen chatting up those two bloody
poofters. Just sit back down at that table and stay there till
I say we're ready to leave.

I think I'll get a taxi and go back to the hotel.

The hell! You're with me. You stay with me.

But, look! We're obviously getting on each other's
nerves. I'll go back to the hotel and . . .

"He wouldn't let me leave. I offered to go back to the
hotel. But he simply would not allow it. I was intimidated.
And I stayed. I shouldn't have. I shouldn't have stayed.
Should have left right then. But I couldn't. It would have
been admitting they'd succeeded, they'd defeated me. Or
that I couldn't control my reactions . . . something. So I
stayed.

"The American drove us back to Ian's flat. That terrible
driving. I rushed into the flat, sick. And Ian went . . .
crazy. I wanted to go to the bathroom. I was going to be
sick. But he wouldn't let me. Finally, I *screamed* at him to
let me go and made it to the bathroom. I've never been
so sick in my life. I just wanted to go back to the hotel
and sleep, forget that any of it had ever happened. But
Ian wanted . . . revenge. It felt like that.

"When I came out of the bathroom finally, I thought he
might let me go to sleep, realizing I'd been sick. That he'd
let me sleep. And we'd talk . . . about everything in the
morning. But . . . he wouldn't."

She was visibly shaking now. Trying to keep her voice

low. Shaking and shaking. Reliving it. The way he'd come at her. Nothing had ever been uglier, more violent. She'd tried to reason with him, deal with the situation logically. But there was no reason, no logic. He was going to make her pay for speaking her mind, for defending herself; for making him look like some bleeding arsehole having her carrying on that way with those two bloody queers. The nightmare. Happening again.

He'd hit her. No one ever had before. His open hand across the side of her head. Once. A second time. Winding both his hands into her hair, yanking her head back so that her voice died with the pain of it. Dragging her down to her knees, he'd forced himself on her mouth.

She covered her face with her hand, trying to catch her breath; knowing Jimmy was watching her.

"I ran out," she whispered, holding her serviette to her eyes. "In the middle of the night. Ran. Managed to get a taxi and get back to the hotel. Up all night. Sick over and over. I have to stop for a minute." She held the serviette over her face with both hands, telling herself, It's over over it's over you're away from that. Telling herself to stifle the building sobs, get control of her breathing. She crumpled the serviette in her hand and lit a cigarette, then doggedly continued.

"I finally fell asleep on the bathroom floor. Woke up with my head between the tub and the toilet.

"Well—" She drew in her lips, biting hard on her lower lip, her eyes on the ceiling, struggling for control. "I took a shower, some aspirin. Got cleaned up. Ordered up some food thinking it would ease the pain in my stomach. I drank some of the coffee, ate several bites of the toast and had to give up. It was only making me feel sicker.

"I tried to telephone, thinking I'd go there, get my bags and bring them back to the hotel. Face him, tell him I was going home. But there was no answer. And I thought, Good. All right. I'd take a taxi to the flat, pick up my bags and not have to see him again. That was better still.

"I didn't know what I was doing, wasn't thinking. I didn't ask the driver to wait. I suppose I thought I'd call another taxi from the flat. I had a key, the one he'd given me. And let myself in. Stepped into the hall and I could feel he wasn't there.

"It was a lovely morning. Sun streaming in through the windows. I stood there in the doorway for the longest time

staring at the way the sun lay in bands across the floor.
Slowly realizing that the sun was shining on my two bags.
And suddenly, I knew I could take the bags, call a taxi
and get out of there. The most unbelievable feeling of
both danger and relief. He might came back at any second. I had to get out of there right away, fast. I ran across
the room and picked up one of the bags by the handle.
And it fell open. I stood there feeling my heart beating so
hard. So hard.

"The bag came open and pieces . . . pieces of things
started falling out. Then I was down on my knees with my
hands in the bag and . . . The other bag was the same.
Everything. And in the fireplace. More. All my needlepoint. The sketches. Even the camera. Everything. All at
once I was terrified. He'd appear and do to me what he'd
done to my things. I ran and ran. For miles. To a main
road. And got a taxi. To the airport.

"I telephoned the Hilton when I arrived here and took
care of the bill. They sent me the few things I'd left in the
room. My hair dryer. Some books. A few other things. I
had my jewelry with me. I always carried it in my bag because it didn't feel safe leaving it in the hotel. That's all!"
she said abruptly. "That's the end."

"I'm sorry," Jimmy said. "A two-pot screamer from the
sound of him."

"What?"

"Can't hold his drink."

"Oh! God!" She let her forehead rest on her hand, staring down at the table top. "I'll never . . . I won't ever be
able . . ."

"I know," he said soothingly. "But that's just the way
you feel right now. And there's sense to that, after all. But
you'll come right. It's not forever. You'll go home and put
it all in back of you, forget it."

"I'll go home and never forget any of it," she said fever-
ishly. "I'll go home and they'll ask me why. And they'll
ask me how I liked it here and what did I see and I'll have
to say I saw the Nullarbor from the plane, and Captain
Cook's cottage."

"You'll show them your sketches of the wildflowers.
And tell them about Perth. And take them all the gifts
you bought today. And tell them you changed your mind.
A woman's prerogative, after all, isn't it?"

"You're right," she said. "Of course, you're right. I don't have to tell anyone what happened."

"Course not."

"God!" she sighed, feeling some of the horror leaving her. "I'm so glad we met. Now that I've talked, told it to you, I won't . . ."

"You'll put it in back of you as I said. And you'll enjoy the weekend. We'll take you to the park. Show you my girls. You like seafood?"

"Yes."

"We'll get you some barramundi. Beautiful fish. And chips. I know a very good place for that."

"Why?" she asked, feeling for a moment as if she might choke to death on his unbelievable kindness.

"Because it makes me feel good. And because I like being with you. Forget the other. Being the rich American tourist you are, you'll just buy yourself another bag and a few more clothes and take yourself home in fine form. Forget it," he said, seriously. "What's the point to going over and over it in your head? I know all there is to know about that. I've gone over Mag and me until there's no sense or meaning. And no answers anywhere. Just decisions needing to be made, that're bound to get made sooner or later."

The waitress came to take their orders.

"Garlic bread?" she asked them.

And simultaneously, they both answered, "Definitely!"

So that Jimmy laughed and Lyle had to smile. And he said, "Another time, another place, I'd've made a go of it with a woman like you."

And since it was another time and another place he spoke of, she accepted it in that way and ordered the champagne. Deciding they both deserved it.

Five

—◆—◆→

For the first time since leaving Melbourne, her sleep that night was free of nightmares and she awakened on Saturday morning feeling stronger, refreshed, and somewhat more optimistic about life in general.

The horror, the shaking were still there, waiting for her to slide back inside them. But she found she could keep them at bay by forcing herself to think of the day ahead. Jimmy would be waiting for her downstairs in the lobby in an hour's time. They'd go to Kings Park. And then he'd said he'd take her out to see his "girls." Lunch. They'd complete their tour of the city and the hills, then dinner.

She brushed her teeth, showered, dried her hair. Then stood naked in front of the mirror, brazening it out, critically studying herself. Not knowing why she was engaging in this exercise. For a few rare moments, though, possessed of an ability to see herself objectively, in focus. Not as she usually did, where her eyes zeroed in on all the flaws, those areas of imperfection. Thinking now that perhaps it was true, she did possibly look better without her clothes. Her breasts and pelvic area startlingly white in contrast to the deep tan she'd managed so effortlessly. As if she were standing there in the bathroom clad in a skin bikini. The thought made her laugh and she turned to reach for her brassiere. That insubstantial piece of lace and elastic she'd bought with so little thought. The brassiere and the lace bikinis gave her a decidedly erotic sensation. As if she were preparing to carry secrets out into the world, beneath her clothing.

Dressed, she stowed the sketchbook and pencils Jimmy had bought in her carryall, picked up her room key and went downstairs to the coffee shop for breakfast. Not nearly so bothered today by the fake aboriginal artwork of the cafeterialike room. She had an omelette and two cups of coffee, smoked a cigarette then went out to wait in the lobby.

For the first time she noticed the display case on the far wall, with geodes and shells and old maps. She stood for several minutes thinking how much she'd like to take geodes and shells and old maps home with her. Making a note of the name of the shop responsible for the display. Perhaps it would be open. The shops closed at twelve or twelve-thirty on Saturdays. A fact that struck her as odd, considering Saturdays were her busiest days in the shop at home. But not in Australia.

Standing there admiring the display, she suddenly wanted to go home. Wanting to see her house, her mother, her brother, the shop. The things that belonged to her, that gave her comfort. People who belonged to her. She glanced at her watch, saw that Jimmy wasn't due for another ten minutes and hurried over to the bank of telephones on the opposite side of the lobby.

There was a Qantas flight leaving Perth the next night at 11:05 p.m. for Sydney. She'd get into Sydney at 6:05 a.m. and leave again at 4:45 in the afternoon, arriving in San Francisco at 1:30 p.m. Leaving Sydney on Monday and arriving three-odd hours earlier on the same day in San Francisco. She booked seats on both flights, then hung up. To look at the information she'd written on the cover of the sketch pad. Feeling nauseated simply thinking about the enormous amount of traveling involved. But it was done. And she was going home. By midnight or so, Monday night, she'd be back in her house.

Shaking again. Ridiculous! she told herself, turning to scan the faces in the lobby, then looking again at her watch. He was late. Maybe he wasn't going to come after all. She walked over to stand at the front windows, watching cars go past outside. Nervous. Unable to help herself. She lit a cigarette, her breakfast threatening to come back. Please be on your way! Don't leave me here waiting, a fool again.

She left the windows and went to sit down, noticing the tremor was back as her shaky hand reached out to the ashtray. She sat back thinking how quickly—how foolishly, probably—she'd formed an attachment to this man. Someone she'd met on a bench. The swans. She hadn't gone to feed them. But others would. The tour buses. The others.

Kind. You've been so kind and caring. Don't let me down, leave me sitting here waiting for a mistaken impression to arrive. Just be what you showed yourself to be. I have to be right just once, not always showing faulty judgment.

"Sorry," he said, rushing up out of breath. "I got delayed in traffic coming back from tending the girls."

"That's all right," she said, getting to her feet, smiling; almost in tears with relief.

"I'd've telephoned had there been a way."

He put his hand under her elbow, leading her out. And she went along, sliding into the car, finding it reassuringly familiar. After only one day. But familiar. Like Jimmy. In his suit and tie. With his clean hands and clean fingernails and dear, battered face. Overweight and comfortable.

"We've a good day for it," he said, starting up the car. "I fixed a picnic." He smiled over at her.

"Wonderful!" She smiled back. "I'm all yours."

"Would that you were," he said inaudibly. Breathing in deeply, satisfiedly. The scent of her perfume and her presence beside him so pleasurable. Mag's opposite in every conceivable way. Shy and quiet and given so infrequently to smiles that when they came he felt rewarded. And wanted to say and do things to generate more of her smiles. Wanting to have her watch his mouth and eyes when he talked, to watch her apply her lipstick, to take her shopping, be with her.

"I wrote down the name of the shop that has a display in the hotel lobby," she said. "Would you mind if we stopped there?" She showed him the address. "Is it out of our way?"

"Not at all. Right close by."

He found a place to park directly in front of the shop and they went in. She was at once captured by the dozens of rock samples, the genuine non-tourist-type curiosities. Sea shells and geodes and maps, polished rocks. Gemstones. No opals. Nothing stamped "Australia" or "Perth" or "Western Australia." No koala bears made in Korea or Taiwan. No shabby-looking kangaroos. No moccasins. No sheepskin coats or rugs. Green snail shells from New Zealand. Huge cowries. Amethyst geodes. It felt perfect. She couldn't contain her enthusiasm. And the woman behind the counter said, "Take your time, my dear. I know just how you feel. I brought a number of my favorite rocks with me from South Africa. You should have seen the customs people when they asked what was I carrying and I said rocks!" She smiled and halfheartedly dusted the top of the glass counter. Jimmy lit a cigarette and stood near the doorway of the small store, having a fine time simply being there.

She wanted to disappear into the hypnotic swirls of the polished rocks, fascinated by their rough nonrevealing exteriors and their contrasting, exotic interiors. And placed one sample after another on the counter, wanting all of them. Knowing she must decide on only a few. Given the option, at that moment, what she'd have most liked to do . . . I'd have this shop, she thought, overwhelmed with sudden greed. To possess these perfectly beautiful, perfectly simple rocks; to know each by name, to be free to touch and admire them.

Finally, she made her selections and paid. And apologized to Jimmy for keeping him waiting such a long time.

"No need," he said. "I'm glad you were able to find so many things you like."

"What I'd like," she said, setting her package down in the footwell of the car, "is to take that entire shop home with me. Transport it in toto, put it in a corner of my garden and spend hours every day there for the rest of my life." She smiled and he was almost able to see her as the proprietor of the place.

She sat on the grass making sketches, one after the other, of four different types of wildflowers growing in clumps, asking, "Do you know the names of these?"

"Those are kangaroo paws." He pointed, deriving great pleasure from the sight of her at work. "I'm not too good on the names. But there's a book. I'll try to get it for you."

"I'd like that," she said abstractedly, using the colored pencils he'd bought for shading, to remind her later of the actual colors. "These would be gorgeous done up in needlepoint," she said, thinking aloud. "A series of flower squares. Or even a rug."

She spent close to an hour in that spot, then they moved to another. Throughout, Jimmy sat watching, smoking, admiring the way the sun shone on her hair and how she pursed her lips slightly when working. And, watching her, he was all at once gripped by an angry melancholy. Thinking, Why couldn't I just once have what I want?

Something, someone for me. There's no future with Mag.
The love for her's been dying for such a long time.

He and Mag hadn't made love in more than two years.
And he felt the need. An aching inside. Wanting closeness
and that quiet time after; whispering, sharing. It seemed to
be so unfair to have nothing to hope for but more of the
same. More impossible confrontations, more one-sided arguments, more of less and less. For what? When here was
someone he felt so close to, so in tune with. Someone he
was happy to make smile.

He wished he hadn't let himself get so out of condition.
At least two stone over the mark. He'd start on his diet
again, he decided, get some of the excess trimmed away.
Thought about the changes he might make, then asked
himself: Why? What for? Lyle would be leaving, going
home to America. And they'd likely as not never see one
another again. Besides, he continued, why would she want
someone like him? What had he to offer? A middle-aged
fat man with some horses, an estranged wife, and two
grown, married kids. Not much to offer.

He'd bought a loaf of crusty bread, a wedge of cheese,
some apples and a bottle of wine. As he spread the things
out on the grass atop the morning's newspaper, she thought
yet again how very kind he was. Thoughtful, considerate.

"This is so nice, Jimmy," she said. "I'll have some good
times to remember, after all."

"That's what we're all about," he chuckled. "Good service, satisfied clients."

He even had a corkscrew and removed the cork from
the bottle saying, "Afraid we'll have to swig it straight. I
couldn't lay my hands on any glasses."

"That's fine." She watched him cut the cheese with his
pocket knife, then reach for the loaf and slice off the heel.

"Fancy this?" he asked, holding it out to her.

"It's your favorite, the heel. Right?"

"That's right."

"You have it. I like the soft inside part better."

They ate, passing the bottle back and forth, the sun fil-
tering down through the leaves. People drifting past. Park
sounds. Birds. The time seemed to her very complete, perfect. One of the very few occasions in her life when the
company and the surroundings and the elements were all
just right. She knew she'd remember the day, think of it

for years. She took a final swallow of wine, passed the bottle back, saying, "I've booked my seat."

"Oh?" He looked up from cutting the last of the cheese. "When?"

"Tomorrow night."

He wanted to say, It's too soon. Stay a time longer! Instead, he said, "I'll see you off."

"I couldn't ask you to do that. My flight doesn't leave until 11:05."

"I'll see you off," he repeated.

Now that we've met, she thought, I don't really want to go. Not yet. I like seeing your face. And the things you do. The way I feel being with you. So often with Ian it was difficult meeting his eyes. My thinking, my views and opinions made him so angry. You don't find my views, my thoughts unreasonable. Still, Ian started out paying very close attention to everything I said, making a show of agreeing. You're not that way, though. I know it. You'd never change the way Ian did. You'd always be just the way you've been from the beginning.

"Where do you see yourself going?" she asked.

"Oh, retirement. A bit of pastureland for the girls. Caring for them. Taking life easy."

"But you're not ready yet to retire."

"I could," he said, having thought it out dozens of times, "turn the company over to Ben. Had enough?" He indicated the food.

"More than enough. Thank you."

"Well, let's get this lot packed away then and we'll have a drive, go see the girls." He carried the trash over to a wire receptacle, then came back asking, "Where do you see yourself going?"

"Nowhere," she admitted. "Sometimes, it scares me. Thinking about it. I think it's why I jumped in with both feet the way I did. With Ian. Desperation. I thought no one would ever want me and I wanted to be wanted. He was someone who claimed he wanted me. What was I waiting for? My chance, so I took it. I thought being married would . . . save my life. Something like that." I'll never marry. I no longer care to, she thought.

"But there were other men, surely?"

"Not really." Boys back when I was sixteen and walking out of step, not knowing what to do with them, or myself; failing to understand why they were there. A few men

later on who couldn't believe I was what I was, that I
didn't wish, at that moment, to alter my status—either
physically or socially. Even in the face of their patronizing
offers. But then I started aging far faster than I'd ever bar-
gained for. And having someone, some man rescue me
into a marriage seemed the idea solution.

"I don't know," she said, returning the colored pencils
to their box. "The truth is I was scared. I didn't want to
be . . . hurt. Physcially. Sexually." Her cheeks turned red
and she paid close attention to carefully putting the
sketchpad and pencils into her bag. "It was safer, I suppose, fantasizing. I'm not sure now I shouldn't have kept
right on fantasizing. Old maids, spinsters, have a perfect
concept of love, you know. Because we've spent our entire
lives rejecting everything else."

"You're not an old maid."

"I am, though, you know, Jimmy." She looked over at
him, her expression totally serious. "Friends, girls I knew,
grew up with, they have teenage children, mortgages,
circles of friends. I don't see any of them anymore. Oh, a
few of them come to the shop. Customers. But I turned
out to be the odd one, the one who didn't fit. I've been
telling myself for years that I didn't mind, I preferred
being on my own to being saddled with a husband and
children and all the rest of it. But I would have liked
something more. Now, I know it's out of the question."

"You talk as if you think your whole life's ended and
all but done with. You're only thirty-five."

"But you talk about retiring, and how old are you?"

"Forty-seven."

"I thought you said almost fifty."

"That is almost fifty."

"No, it isn't," she insisted. "It's forty-seven."

"Does that change something in your mind?" he asked,
bemused.

"No. Well, yes. Maybe."

"What does it change?"

"Nothing. I mean, it changes the way I think of you
somehow. I don't know."

"How do you think of me?" he asked, curious to hear
what she'd say.

She couldn't answer for a moment. She was having the
strangest reaction to him and to the conversation. "As a

friend," she said at last. "As someone special who's happened to me."

"And how do you think of yourself?"

"As a fool."

"Well, isn't that nice," he said. "Makes me out to be a right ass, doesn't it, with a fool for a friend?"

"That isn't what I meant . . ."

"I know what you meant," he said. "I'm just trying to get you to hear how it sounds. Credit me with a bit of judgment, Lyle. A bit of taste, too, maybe. I'd no more want to be out and about with a woman the world thinks of as a fool than you'd care for the reverse. You're no fool. Leastwise not any more than I am. God knows, I've had my moments. But it's not a lifetime sentence I've passed on myself. Don't be so hard on yourself, woman! A mistake's a mistake. That's all."

She stared at the grass. Battling down an impulse to apologize. What was there to apologize for? And why should she?

Her response seemed a little childlike to him. Yet, quickly reexamining his words, he couldn't see that he'd said anything too harsh. Certainly nothing to unduly upset her. But the fact of her cowed reaction made him angry with her, made him want to tell her to stand up for herself and stop being so apologetic about so many things. You're fine, he wanted to say. There's no need to continue on saying "sorry" for sins both imagined and real.

She sensed his anger and continued to look at the grass, wondering precisely what had occurred. Will you become Ian now? she wondered. Then considered the way she was behaving and was, not for the first time, disgusted by her perennial willingness to accept guilt.

"I have this habit," she said, meeting his eyes, "of wanting to hurry into the middle of the ring saying, Blame me. It's all right. You can blame me. Just to keep the peace. I've always hated myself for that. Maybe I did make a fool of myself over Ian. Maybe I did. But you're right. That doesn't make me a fool permanently. So, I'm sorry I said what I did. But it wasn't intended as a reflection on you."

"I know that," he said patiently. "All I was after was to make *you* see that. Let's forget it now, shall we?"

"I don't feel sorry for myself," she said, thinking it

through. "But I do feel sorry for what happened. Don't I have the right to sympathize with myself?"

"Of course you do! Of course! It's just that all that's ended now. And you should remember the lesson of it. But not keep on and on reliving the worst parts. Listen, Lyle," he said, sinking his teeth into it, "I know the whole thing scared hell out of you. First time out and it turns bad, ugly. Now you want to go home, close yourself away forever and never have another go. Never let another man put a hand to you because it'll all turn bad the way it did this time. Am I wrong?"

"It's how I feel," she said, well into the defensive.

"But that's *not* how you should feel," he argued. "One bad experience doesn't mean they'll *all* turn to the bad."

"You're making a case for yourself," she guessed incisively.

"Maybe so," he admitted. "I'm human. I'm attracted to you."

"Is that what it's all been for?"

"Do you think so?" he demanded. "Does it look as if I've been plotting and planning and forcing myself to listen to you just so you'll be grateful enough to bed down with me? Have I touched you? I haven't. I can understand how you feel, respect that. Would you not like to understand *my* feelings, respect them?"

"I don't know your feelings," she said, bewildered.

"Neither do I!" he exclaimed. Then burst out laughing, hearing how silly the whole argument sounded.

She studied his laughing argument, feeling herself responding; the laughter rising. She lifted her head, laughing, and he put his hand on her face, saying, "Whatever happens is fine with me. It's good being with you. I've spent too much time on my own, these past few years. So, it's good."

She touched his wrist tentatively, his hand not altogether unwelcome. It felt good, in fact. But she hadn't any idea what she should do.

"Come on," he said. "I told the girls I was bringing you out to see them."

"Did they say they were looking forward to meeting me?" She laughed.

"Oh, yes. Yes, yes they did."

His hand took hold of hers, pulling her up. And she felt weightless. Light and buoyant, purged. This was real, not an act performed to place her off guard. Real. And she'd go away, leave it behind her. But what choice was there? She had to go home. She had a house, a business, a mother. Responsibilities. She had a residue of lies to dispose of. And resolutions needing to be made that had to do with the rest of her life.

"I wish," she said, "I didn't have to go."

"I wish it, too."

"Do you?"

Sounding wistful, as if his words weren't actually directed at her, he said, "We might've made something of it."

She couldn't respond to that, so lit a cigarette and sat back on her thoughts. Looking out the window. Her thoughts an ineffectual cushion, offering little comfort. Because there wasn't anything to say to him.

Six

---◆---

He pulled the car over in front of a fenced field and got out, calling the horses' names. When they didn't appear, he returned to the car, switched on the radio, handed her what remained of the morning's newspaper and said, "I'll go fetch them. You relax and wait."

She watched as he opened the fence, closed it behind him, then disappeared over a slight rise. She picked up the newspaper, lit a fresh cigarette and began scanning the pages. Tinny music from the radio. Static. Breathing in the fresh, grass-scented air. Her eyes moved over the pages, unseeing.

What do I want? she asked, lifting her eyes from the newspaper. What would make me happy? Would I want to be married, have children—even at this late date—be settled in a life with someone?

The heaviness of permanency frightened her. I don't want to find myself locked inside a day-to-day sameness that goes on and on forever until I die. Dying with none of the questions really answered and nothing very much changed. Children? No. I never did want them or that fake sort of heartiness so many of my friends adapted to cover the panic eating them away from the inside out. But to be me and not lonely. Someone to talk with in the evenings, cook for sometimes. Measures of company, companionship. The same life I've lived for so long. But with a voice to answer some of the questions I might like to ask. And a presence to share the longer evenings and make Sundays something more than just the day for the visit to my mother.

She took her mirror from her bag and looked at her face, trying not to be brought down, as always, by the image presented to her.

Just me as I've always been. Plain, the butt of so many of daddy's nasty, cruel jokes. The comedian trying out his routines on the children. Richard simply dismissed him. Richard so self-contained and unimpressed by him always. But I was the first, the eldest, and thought it was me, my fault that I couldn't find the humor because I was convinced it was there, and it was some damaged wire in my head that prevented me from fully appreciating just how funny he was.

Yet mother wasn't amused either. She suffered him. Because she was the housekeeper's daughter growing up in the rooms over the garage of the house on North Street and aspired to something more. The daughter of an English char lady who decided at an early age that her life was meant to be more than her mother's had been. And so made herself available, attractive; hoping someone would notice and rescue her. Succeeding in developing her natural resources—her charm, her laughter, her poise. Holding her greatest resource in reserve. Her intelligence. Winning the young comic hired for the private party. Determined to help him into success by being his elegant, background wife. Doing it on pennies and good castoffs from thrift shops here and there.

He was never grateful, though. Got everything he wanted. The house in Greenwich. His children at the Greenwich Country Day school. Lyle to Miss Porter's and Richard to St. Paul's. Indian Harbour Yacht Club and the Round Hill Club. All the good things, the right things, the money things. But out of anger. An angry need to prove himself good, better, best. But to whom?

"I don't know what he's after," her mother had once admitted to Lyle when Lyle was fifteen. "I've never pretended to be anything more than what I am. Never. I've simply tried to make life pleasant for all of us. Do my job. And he hates me for it."

The first time she'd heard her mother talk about daddy's hating her, Lyle had argued, saying, "That's not true. He loves you." And her mother had said, "See things as they are, Lyle. Not the way you'd like them to be, but the way they *are*. I did something somewhere along the line that provoked him. Something. Heaven only knows what. But he'll go to his grave hating me. Hating the world."

"Do you love him?" Lyle had asked, fearful of the answer.

"I love you," her mother had said. "And Richard. It's the only love I seem to understand."

My mother who went to night school those evenings daddy was working. Who got her high school equivalency diploma and then her Bachelor's and then her M.A. Without her letting him know she was doing any of it. Financing an education out of the housekeeping money. So that when he died, after a suitable length of time, she was prepared to go out into the business world and try for a job.

And she got one to both children's amazement. She'd had it ever since and was now earning a very reputable salary as one of the few female executives at the corporate headquarters in Stamford of a large Midwest-based manufacturing company.

My mother who, since my father's death, has entertained several men friends; broadened her personal and social horizons. And has grown tall and strong and independent in ways I'd never have believed possible. And she's happy, claims to be content. My mother. Why couldn't I be happy?

I haven't had a husband, two children, or the pain I now understand she endured, living with him. But does that mean I couldn't be happy, content for other reasons? What do I want?

To be valued, not expected to alter in radical ways, to be accepted just as I am. To be given a chance to find out what it is, if anything, I have inside me to offer.

She turned to look out the driver's window and saw Jimmy coming. Running along. In his business suit. His smile brilliant. His hair going every which way in the breeze. And right behind him, his three "girls" trotting along. Three chestnut females, one heavily pregnant.

She got out of the car and stood looking on as he fed sugar cubes to the horses from the palm of his hand.

"Come over!" he called to her. "Come on!"

Feeling very citified and uncertain, she made her way to within five or six feet of Jimmy and the horses. Feeling his excitement, too, his love for the animals. And, amazingly, the horses' response to him. It was beautiful. Her mind clicking. A series of still and moving images that would be with her always. Jimmy running through the field with the three horses. The smallest, youngest of the girls nudging at Jimmy's chest, wanting more sugar. And him laughing, saying, "Off with you! Go on! That's all for today! Go on!"

Right then, that very moment, with the fresh air and the perfect blue sky and the clean grass smell, she thought, I love you. For this, for finding me, for bringing me here, showing me you are precisely what you are, nothing hidden, nothing lurking beneath the surface. Someone capable of love and kindness and generosity, willing to share your pleasures with me.

Not the nervous, breathy anticipation she'd experienced at the first with Ian. But an infusion of something strong and warm and positive. She wished it were possible to remain forever inside these moments, never having to step back outside.

He slipped out through the gate, made certain it was securely fastened, then came around the car to hold open the passenger door.

"They're beautiful," she said inadequately. "They're really beautiful."

"They're good girls," he said, dusting his hands free of sugar before climbing back into the driver's seat. "They make up for a lot." He looked at his watch. "Getting on for five. Close to six by the time we get back. An early dinner?"

"Fine. I'm pretty hungry."

"Me, too."

There was a moment in the car when a decision had to be made. They were parked in the drive at the front of the hotel, sitting looking at each other. Jimmy wanted to kiss her, thank her for a fine day, a memorable day, but was reluctant to frighten her, add to her store of bad memories.

She wanted to know if her failures had been Ian's fault, or her own. And whether she was capable of responding. With Jimmy, everything seemed different. And she hated to have him leave. It was early. Just nine-thirty. He'd be going home—he'd told her about the place—to his done-over room in the widow's house. To make his ritual evening telephone call to Mag.

They both started to say something at the same moment, then laughed.

"What were you going to say?" she asked him.

"I'll see you inside," he said, getting out of the car. Telling himself, Leave it alone. Remember who you are, who she is. Nothing can come of it.

As they walked through the lobby to the elevators, she

was thinking about Ian. Hitting her. Doing the things he had. Wasn't she just asking for more of the same if she invited Jimmy to come up, have coffee? Such a transparent ploy, saying, Come up, have coffee, talk for a while. It's still early. They'd both know what it meant. Come up. When it would be just as easy to retrace their steps and go to the bar for a drink, or to the coffee shop.

They stood in front of the elevators, both trying to think of something to say. An elevator arrived directly in front of them, the doors sliding open.

"Come up with me," she said hoarsely, at once hit by the feeling she'd just asked to be executed. Her face, neck, ears turned to fire.

He looked puzzled, searching for an appropriate response; wanting to go up with her but unsure of her motives or his own.

"We'll have coffee," she said, thinking it sounded like a ludicrous lie.

"You're sure?"

"Yes."

The elevator doors started to close. He put out his hand to stop them and the doors sprang open. He stood with his hand over the door, waiting for her to enter. She stepped inside, nervously pressed the button for her floor, then moved to the rear of the elevator, eyes lowered. As if a crowd might be getting on at the next floor.

"You don't have to, you know," he said, sounding as hoarse as she did.

"I know." She wet her lips, thinking about the woman crossing the Nullarbor. The camel lady. Independent, fierce and strong. Prepared to brave the elements, the treacheries of nature. Simply to go from Point A to Point B for her own satisfaction. No one else's. This is for my satisfaction. And perhaps yours, too. Someone who'd shown himself as sensitive as Jimmy wouldn't suddenly change and become forceful and hard. Would he? She wished she had the courage to look at him, reassure herself. But she didn't, for the moment, have more than the strength it took to leave the elevator and walk down the corridor to her room.

Standing just inside the door of the darkened room, she couldn't bring herself to move one step further, or to turn on the lights, or to do anything. Fear like a sudden fever made the shaking start up again, made her wish she'd never been born.

"It's all right," he said, putting his arm around her, at once aware of her trembling. "Nothing's that bad or that serious," he said, settling her against his chest, stroking her hair. "I won't hurt you," he promised, sensing how much she wanted to prove to herself that she hadn't suffered irreparable damage. "I'd never hurt anyone." He laughed softly. "I wouldn't be able to live with my conscience after."

His hand was very gentle on her hair, smoothing, stroking. His arm secure around her. She began to feel a bit warmer, the turmoil inside abating somewhat as he moved her into the room. Keeping his arm around her, taking her bag and setting it down. The draperies were open, moonlight defining the contents of the room. He put his hand on her throat and she thought wildly, irrationally, He'll choke me, strangle me they'll find my body in the morning when they come to make up the room.

He tilted her head back. Her eyes were closing against her will. Out of fear. He was so near. And she was going to die, knew she would. But his mouth brushed against hers sending a downspiraling coil of response right through the center of her body so that she was obliged to stand very still, waiting to see what he'd do if he'd kiss her more harder what will you do?

His mouth replaced his hand on her throat. The hand where had it gone? She wanted to keep track of all the parts of him know where he was what was he doing doing what? His mouth on her throat like a strand of hair blown lightly by the breeze, pleasure. Her body moved fractionally closer to his.

She wanted to keep her eyes closed, sink serenely into whatever was going to happen and then emerge from it later as someone new to herself. She wanted to be transformed, made capable of receiving and bestowing pleasure without having to feel either minimized or victimized by her own desires.

Reassured by his slow actions, gratified that he wasn't coming at her with the same wet breathiness Ian had. His mouth touching lightly to hers, his hands exerting a slight pressure as they moved the length of her back, then up again. Just let it come out right this time, let it be all right. One more disastrous encounter and I'll go down to the river, past the swans into the water, clutching my handfuls of stale bread and rolls and walk until there's no bottom and no top and my lungs are heavy with the weight of water and finally no more life. It doesn't really matter very much anymore.

Her ears were filled with the rustling, slithery sounds their clothing made as it came away from their bodies and she couldn't bear to look and see how they might appear to each other; simply allowed it to happen, her eyes still tightly closed, terrified to have to see on his face some measure of disappointment. Or to have to look and see how poorly they fit together. She felt his hand tighten on her shoulder, heard him whisper, "Oh!" and opened her eyes, more frightened than before.

"What is it?" she asked.

"You're so wonderfully made," he whispered, awed. "Wonderful. Lovely."

What was he talking about? Did he know what he was talking about?

He had to look at her just a moment longer, absorbing the long slender lines of her body, the unexpected fullness of her breasts, the swell of her hips. Then drew her full into the circle of his arms, holding her the length of his body.

The feeling was exquisite, blossoming. Like some marvelous time-lapse film, feeling herself growing in pleasure; becoming eager. Opening her mouth to further kisses, to the possibility of still more pleasure. Relishing his kisses, the sweetness of his tongue exploring her mouth.

Gently, he laid her down; holding her the best thing that had happened to him in so long. His hand reading the measure of her breast, its softness; her body, her skin filling him to the brim with that ache of need, wanting. He'd forgotten softness and wondered how he could have forgotten something so important, so tremendously important and satisfying. Soft and scented and so warm, yet stiff with reserve and shyness. It touched him.

She felt herself unlocking by painful degrees. Thawing under his hands and mouth. Making a faint, startled sound when he put his mouth to her breast while bringing his hand up the length of her inner thigh. Afraid of the feeling. A mind filled with recollections of barbaric incidents and acts of horrifying subjugation. Yet her body knew no fear. Look at my body! she thought, amazed at her willingly parted thighs, her shrinking nipples and quivering belly. The heat of her body overwhelming as his fingers gently probed, exerting pressure, making their presence felt. She wished desperately she knew what it was she was supposed to feel, where she was supposed to go with what she did feel.

She held him, touched him hesitantly, trying not to squirm beneath his investigating mouth and fingers. Then lay still, disappointed, when he laid himself upon her; knowing there'd be nothing more for her. She allowed him in, bore his weight. It was sweet. Comforting. And near the end even began to be quite exciting. But then it ended. She didn't mind. Because, at least, she hadn't sustained any new injuries; hadn't been harmed at all. And felt quite content—relieved of her monstrous self-consciousness—to cradle his overheated body against hers, accepting his words of endearment and his wearied caresses.

He wanted to explain how he felt intimidated by the knowledge of her prior experiences, but couldn't. How could he say those things? How could he tell her, I'd have liked to be bolder, more assertive, go farther, but I'm afraid to risk arousing your fear while mistakenly believing I'm arousing your passions. And so was annoyed with himself because he'd given her very little and wasn't so much of an egoist as to think that having managed to come inside her was all that was required for her pleasure. Not enough time. He felt inhibited, too, by the time limit set on their hours together. Less than twenty-four hours before she'd leave. What could he hope to accomplish in so short a space of time?

He was stroking her again between the legs. Generating a response that made something inside her twist miserably, heightening. She wanted him to stop but didn't know how to tell him. Feeling a grinding, maddening throb each time his fingers hit her just so, just there. Stop it's wrong doesn't feel right feels strange. She felt he was flint hitting repeatedly against the stone of her body, striking sparks, burning her. Her breathing out of control and the feeling that someone was shouting wildly in her ears.

"Please stop," she whispered, unable to bear the feeling.

And of course he did, at once. And when he stopped her body went instantly cold. The throbbing receding down to a dim pulse. Cold and tired, she longed now to sleep, to be alone. To bathe, try to think briefly, then sleep.

"It wasn't good for you," he said, at length. "I'm sorry."

"It was fine," she lied, thinking of Ian saying the first time was always bad. But every time with him had been an exact duplication of the first time. Is my life to be a series of first times? Is that all there is?

"I'll run along and let you get some sleep," he said, feeling totally separated from her and unable to reconcile specifically why.

"I *am* very sleepy," she said, then felt guilty because she should have been actively assuring him that everything was perfectly all right.

He moved away, collected his clothes and went into the bathroom to dress. Convinced he'd failed because he'd been ill-equipped to appropriately penetrate her fears and reserve. What bloody vanity! he thought, dressing quickly. To believe making love was capable of creating miracles. When the truth of it all was you ran the inescapable risk of destroying what little you'd managed to structure. He couldn't remember when he'd felt quite so depressed.

She wrapped herself in the sheet—her dressing gown among the items Ian had destroyed—and lit a cigarette, sitting back against the headboard. Frightened that he'd emerge from the bathroom armed for a confrontation.

But he came out looking so unhappy, she had to say, "Come have a cigarette with me before you go." He came to sit down beside her and she sat back, surprised at the kindness she possessed. I'm someone who's kind, she thought. Someone who cares. I never knew that about myself.

"It really is all right," she said, looking at his mouth. "You've made me feel much better. I'll be going home more—intact, somehow. I can't really explain it. Everything that's happened these past two days has been a bonus. I hope you'll think of it that way, too."

He puffed on his cigarette, thinking she looked very pretty. With her hair all mussed and her arms and shoulders bare. Very pretty. He smiled, relaxing.

"I'll come by around six tomorrow," he said, "if that's all right with you. We'll have dinner, then I'll take you to the airport."

"That would be lovely."

"I'll go along then," he said, unable to look away from her. Wishing he could stay, could lower the sheet she had so tightly tucked around her, so that he might see her breasts again, put his hands to her breasts, kiss them, kiss her mouth, her thighs. You feel so young, he thought. Slim and soft and young. There'll never be anyone else like you for me.

He kissed her quickly on the mouth, got up and let himself out.

She sat finishing her cigarette, wondering what it all meant. What was the point of becoming excited, aroused, only always to find herself in almost the exact condition she'd been in at the outset? Except for those minutes when he'd caressed her and had created that odd, rather terrible sensation. And the feeling of monstrous incompleteness she had now. She felt strange altogether. Wanton, desperate, in need of something. Sitting in the dark, staring at the light spilling from the bathroom. He'd left it on.

She finished the cigarette and continued to sit staring at the light from the bathroom, reexamining the feeling she'd had. Was it supposed to be that way? My God! My ignorance. I'm so ignorant. It's my body and I haven't any idea what it's supposed to do, feel, be.

She lifted away the sheet and looked at herself, then slid down in the bed and boldly began stroking herself the way Jimmy had. Ignoring the grinding sensation, sensing something stunningly pleasurable just beyond it, if she could just get to it. Forcing herself to keep on. Her body straining, opening. What is it God I should stop it can't be this but I can't stop is this what it is? A melting, anxious need to keep on, on; refusing to see the objective details of this bizarre performance, compelled to get to the end of the feeling. Because it was building, becoming more, becoming the most unbelievable pleasure, and heat. She kept on until everything inside her seized for one molten moment then let go in groaning, spasmodic pleasure. Her body thrown from side to side, her insides electrocuted. Hearing herself making the most embarrassing low moans.

She collapsed and lay gazing unblinking at the ceiling until the interior pulsing ceased and the fantastic heat had gone. Unable to move. Exhausted. She turned her head thinking she'd have a cigarette but couldn't lift her arm. And slid instead directly into sleep.

They talked but didn't really say a great deal. There didn't actually seem to be all that much to say. She was leaving. He was returning to his life. And they'd had a few pleasant days together.

She felt very positive, at ease for the first time in months. And didn't have the time just then to stop and consider the whys and hows of these new feelings. They were simply there. And Jimmy, en route to the airport, smiled over at her saying, "Seems Perth's agreed with you. You're not at all the way you were those mornings feeding the swans."

"I'm very grateful to you," she said.

He misunderstood, thinking she was referring to last night's encounter. But made no mention of it, deciding some things were best left alone.

"I've done nothing," he said.

"No, you've done a great deal. And I won't forget you. I'll write to you when I get home."

"That would be nice. I'd like that."

He'd timed it well. There was just time enough for her to check in, get her seat assignment and then have a cup of tea with him before it was announced the flight was boarding.

He walked with her to the gate, then handed her the package. "Something to look at, take your mind off the travel sickness."

"Jimmy, it's too much," she said, accepting the package. "You didn't have to do this."

"I wanted to," he said staunchly.

She put her free arm around him and kissed him on the mouth, then broke away, unable to speak.

"Be good to yourself," he said thickly, then smiled and hurried away.

She turned to present her bag to be searched and went through the archway, wondering as she did every time if sirens would suddenly go off. But nothing happened. She picked up her bag and the package Jimmy had given her and handed her boarding pass to the attendant at the gate.

She'd taken a pill with her tea at the airport and fastened herself into her seat waiting for it to take effect. Looking around, noting there were only three other first-class passengers. She'd have both seats to herself. Good.

She picked up the package and unwrapped it. *Wildflowers of Western Australia.* A magnificent color photograph on the cover. And inside, "Something to remind you of Perth, Jimmy." She held the book on her lap, fighting down tears. Somehow, on a Sunday, he'd managed to find the book.

He'd done things for her in their brief time together that no one, except perhaps her mother, had ever done or even thought of doing. And there was little chance they'd ever see each other again. But she would write to him, she promised fervently, she would. And try to put into words some of what she'd gained in knowing him.

The pill was starting to work. She let her head drop against the back of the seat and closed her eyes, trying not to smell the jet fuel. Remembering what had happened the night before, what she'd done. That eternal juvenile flush overtaking her cheeks. But a feeling of accomplishment, too. She knew what it was, finally. And she knew something about herself she hadn't known before. She felt a certain affection for her body for having shown itself capable of response. There might even, perhaps, be some future occasion when an opportunity to demonstrate her responses might present itself.

But she wouldn't think about that. She wanted no more Ians in her life. Jimmy? As a friend. As a lover there was something about their being together that had threatened to depress her. Something having to do with haste, and emptiness in the aftermath, and a coldness, too. Their communication having ceased altogether for a time.

They were taxiing down the runway. Her hands grew damp, her stomach went tight in anticipation. The two first-class flight attendants were offering champagne, orange juice, drinks. She refused, not wanting to be distracted from the takeoff. She always had the arbitrary notion that if she dared remove her attention from what was happening to the plane, it would crash. How stupid! she chided herself. As if she were piloting from her seat and the safety of everyone on board were contingent on the fixing of her attention to the sound of the engines and the condition of the runway.

Once airborne, she anxiously watched the No Smoking sign, waiting for it to be turned off. It flickered, went off, and she dived into her bag for her cigarettes. Lit one and lowered her seat back. Dramamine always made her very thirsty and, at the same time, somehow gave cigarettes a better, more satisfying taste than ever. She refused the second and third offers of drinks, passed up dinner and enjoyed the cigarette, thinking it was a pity she was flying at night. She'd miss a second viewing of the Nullarbor.

She was grateful, upon arrival in Sydney, that she'd thought to book a room at the Hilton for the day. Because she was exhausted. And dreaded having to face the flight out later in the afternoon. Her baggage having been checked through, she took a taxi into the city, went up to her room and slept for five hours. At noon, she donned her bathing suit and went down to the pool for the last bit of sun she'd have until next summer at home.

She ate a large meal poolside, admiring the view up there on the twentieth floor, swam for a while, then returned up to her room to shower and dress, leaving the bathing suit in the wastepaper basket in the bathroom. There was no point in dragging a wet bikini along.

She checked out, made a quick tour of the shops in the arcade beneath the Hilton, bought several things, then returned upstairs and took another taxi back to the airport. Having, in advance of the taxi ride, taken a double dose of dramamine. She was prepared to be shaken, bounced and generally jarred. And sat in the Qantas first-class passengers' lounge waiting to be told to board; longing for sleep, dry-mouthed. There'd be no more traveling for a good long time to come. In just under six weeks, she'd traveled more and farther than she probably ever would again in her lifetime. The irony of it all—she smiled to herself—was that she'd seen almost nothing of the country; met very few of the natives and had only a few souvenirs to take home.

Thousands and thousands of miles traveled—more than half the earth's circumference—to come face to face with certain of life's harsher realities and many of her own. Taken in hand, by a dear, gentle man and sent on her way with a dozen or so wildflower sketches and a full-color book of photographs. And the obstinate memory of her solo performance.

The lounge hostess touched Lyle on the shoulder saying, "Your flight's boarding now, Miss Maxwell."

Lyle thanked her, gathered her bag and several pack-ages together and dizzily went out of the lounge, making her way to the gate. Feeling an eager leaping inside. Thinking, Home. I'm going home.

Part Two

Seven

———◆———

She was aware of the cold, but so fatigued she didn't really feel it. Paid the driver and let herself into the house feeling only a tremendous sense of accomplishment at having made it home. Leaving her things in the kitchen, she went through to the living room to turn on the heat, then stood looking at the room. Penny, true to her promise, had been looking after the plants. They all appeared to be larger, healthier than before.

In the kitchen, piled on the table, were stacks of mail she skimmed through while waiting for the coffee to finish dripping. Longing for coffee. Not having had one really good, strong cup her entire time in Australia. Bills, magazines, a couple of catalogues. At the moment, her priorities were a cup of coffee, a shower, a telephone call to her mother, and then bed.

There was no cream, of course. She found some Coffee Mate at the back of the cupboard and stirred it mechanically into the coffee, finding herself staring fixedly at the counter top. She sat down with her cup, deciding to telephone before showering. Because she knew once the hot water hit her, she wouldn't be able to open her mouth again, let alone speak. She dialed her mother's number, then thought to look at the time. After eleven. Her mother answered.

"Were you sleeping?" Lyle asked.

"Lyle? Where are you?"

"Here. Home. Did I wake you?"

"No. I was reading. When did you get back? Are you back? I'm so surprised."

Lyle laughed, then wondered why. "I'm back," she said meaningfully.

There was a pause, then her mother said, "Don't hate me for it, but I'm glad. Aside from everything else, I've missed you. And I simply couldn't see that working out."

71

"Well, it didn't," she said tiredly.

"Did you have a good time, though?"

"No. But I'll tell you about it when I see you."

"I'm sorry to hear it," her mother said. "Richard and I were just talking about you tonight. Both of us wondering when we'd hear from you. I expected a letter. Come to dinner tomorrow night. I'm dying to see you and I want to hear all about it." Another pause. "Are you all right, Lyle?"

"Tired. I don't suppose you've talked to Penny."

"This week. When I was in to sign the checks. She wanted to know if I'd heard from you. We've all been waiting."

"I'm sorry. I just couldn't."

"It wasn't an accusation, dear. You do sound tired. Get a good night's sleep and call me at the office tomorrow."

"Why?"

Her mother laughed. "Because I'll enjoy it. I really have missed you."

"Me, too."

Lyle hung up and lit a cigarette, sipping at the coffee, staring again. She forced herself to stop and went through the mail for the second time as she finished the coffee and smoked out the cigarette.

Frances put the phone down saying, "Lyle's home."

"I gathered that."

They both laughed.

"Seriously," she said, amused by the way he always let his reading glasses ride on the very tip of his nose. "I'm glad. She'd have been miserable married to that pretentious, arrogant boob. God! He was awful. Why don't you wear those if you're going to wear them? It always looks as if any minute they'll be sitting on your upper lip."

"It's bad enough I'm getting old," he said, removing the glasses altogether, "without giving in to the fact that everything's wearing out."

"They can't do your eyes much good just hanging there."

"We're going to be up for hours now," he said. "I might as well get something to drink. Want anything?"

"No. Thank you." She was thinking about Lyle. Wondering how she'd take it. The changes. Lyle never seemed to properly absorb things, but rather recorded the details of what she'd seen or been told and filed it all away in some remote place for future reference. Frances frequently wondered what was responsible for Lyle's inability to focus, her shy lack of substance. And hoped—less with each passing year—Lyle might grow out of it. Whatever "it" was.

Oh, a lot of it, Frances was quite sure, had been Jack's fault. Forever making the child his straight man, teasing her mercilessly. As if her shyness goaded him beyond all reasonable levels of father/child behavior. And he'd picked away at her relentlessly, succeeding in driving Lyle deeper and deeper into herself. So that by the time he'd died, when Lyle was twenty-three, she'd been as staid and somehow dried-out as someone of fifty. Damn the man! He'd harmed everything in life he'd ever touched. And it seemed Lyle was his major beneficiary. Never mind what he did to me, she thought. I was always able to cope, to deal with him. But not her. She couldn't.

Will came back carrying what looked like a scotch and water and kicked off his slippers before perching on the side of the bed, taking a sip of his drink. She watched him, liking the way he looked in his red pyjamas with the white piping.

"You've got style." She smiled. "I have to admit it."

"What did I do now?" he asked, setting down the drink and climbing back under the blankets.

"Nothing. Is that scotch?"

"Hmmm. Want some?"

"No. Yes. Just a sip."

He handed her the glass and retrieved his book. Another tome concerning the world of finance. He read them the way she read historicals. Just as fast and hard as he could. And retained great hunks of material, able to quote verbatim entire paragraphs. It might be a bit boring from time to time, but his brain was anything but boring. She loved him without reservation.

"Worried about how she'll react?" he guessed.

"I wouldn't say worried. Curious. I'm dying to know what happened."

"You'll live till tomorrow. She'll tell you then."

"Would you mind having dinner out somewhere tomorrow night?" she asked.

"Oh, sure. What time'll it be safe for me to sneak in the back way?"

"About eleven. Lyle usually starts wilting by ten."

"Nice way to talk about your daughter."

"It's just that I'm a realist by nature. No point in deluding myself. Lyle *does* start going limp at the edges by ten."

"Okay. I'll be home by eleven."

"Just because I see her weaknesses doesn't mean I don't love her," she said quietly. "I do. It's just that I've stopped hoping for the impossible."

"I'm not criticizing you, Fran. God forbid! Remember me? I've been there." The open book lay face down across his lap, the glasses once more riding the tip of his nose. "It's just that Lyle has some lovely qualities. Strengths. You never talk about any of that."

"They can't be doing your eyes one bit of good sitting way down there."

"No response?"

"I'm aware of all Lyle's qualities," she said, reaching past him to take another sip of his drink.

"Talk about my glasses," he said, "riding my nose. And you with these nightgowns." He slipped his hand in over her breast.

"God! Your hand is cold," she complained, setting the glass down. Then smiling, said, "Don't take it away," as she plucked the reading glasses off his nose and put them down on the night table. "I'm too wide awake now to sleep."

She looked out the window at her car sitting in the driveway, thinking she'd have to get the oil changed, have it winterized this week. The snow tires. Before the temperatures really started dropping. There was a substantial layer of fallen leaves cloaking the car and the lawn. Leaves everywhere. She turned on the outside spotlight to watch them drifting down. An overture to snow. It felt as if she'd been away for years.

She wandered through the downstairs rooms making mental notes to herself. Order a cord of wood to be delivered. Arrange to have the leaves raked. An appointment to have the oil burner cleaned. Groceries. Get her fur coat out of storage. She thought of writing it all down but didn't have the energy and stood instead in the living room comforted by the sight of all the things she'd collected and arranged during the years. The books. And the stereo she'd bought. Last year's Christmas present to herself. Yawning, she turned out the lights and went up to shower.

Item for the list: dig out the electric blanket. The sheets were cold. The weight of the sheet and summer blanket insufficient. She groaned, climbed out of bed and went over to the rattan chest in the corner to get two more blankets. Threw them on the bed and, achingly tired, got back in.

She smoked a last cigarette, eyes on the ceiling, thinking about tomorrow. The drive down to Greenwich in the morning, stopping at the post office to check the box for mail, then on to the shop. Anticipating Penny's surprised greeting. Hoping Penny would like her gift. Wondering if an Australian cookbook was such a good idea when she didn't even know if Penny liked to cook.

Imagine working with someone for more than four years and not even knowing if the woman liked to cook! She'd have to begin paying a little closer attention to the people and things around her.

Penny hugged her. "You're so *tanned!* I had a feeling you might be back when I went to check the box and it was empty. Did you have a great time? How was it?"

"Interesting," Lyle said noncommittally. "How's it been here?"

"As usual. You know."

"This is for you." Lyle handed her the cookbook.

"Isn't this great!" Penny said. "I think the loose pages are such a good idea. I'll have to have a look through it tonight and see what sounds good. Thank you, Lyle. I'll go put the coffee on."

"It's made."

"Oh, good. I could use a cup. It's freezing out this morning."

Penny went through to the back of the shop to hang up her coat, put her handbag in the filing cabinet and pour herself a cup of coffee. Cup in hand, she went back out to lean against the counter, thinking, Now's as good a time as any. Might as well get it over with.

"I'm glad you're back," she said, sensing something different about Lyle, but unable to put her finger on the difference. "I wasn't sure what to do and if I didn't hear from you this week, I was going to write to you."

"About what?" Lyle finished lighting her cigarette and put the package and her lighter down on the counter.

"Jim's being transferred," she said, her eyes on Lyle's. "To Indiana."

"When?"

"He's leaving next week. I've got to be going fairly soon. To find another house. Ours is already sold."

"How do you feel about that?" Lyle asked with atypical directness. "Are you glad to be going?"

"Mixed. I just got used to being here. It seems he invariably gets transferred just about the time I start feeling at home somewhere. The kids are furious because all their friends are here and they won't know anyone there. And it all sounds too rural and small-time to suit them. But they'll adjust. I'm just sorry to leave you on such short notice."

"Well, I hate to lose you. But I understand."

"I know it was a bit of a liberty," Penny said, "but not knowing when you'd be back, I thought I'd better go ahead. So I put an ad in a couple of the papers. Here and in the Stamford *Advocate*. There was a pretty good response. I was quite surprised. I made a list of the names and numbers of the ones I thought were the best."

"How many?" Lyle asked, feeling unreasonably panicked. More changes. Drastic ones. She wanted to go home, pretend she hadn't yet arrived back.

"Four. Three women. And this one man. He seemed the best of them, to tell the truth. He's young. He's got an interesting background, and some credit courses at the School of Visual Arts in the city. I put a star beside his name," she said, pressing the no-sale button on the cash register, lifting out the drawer and removing a slip of paper. "I liked him," she said, handing Lyle the paper. "He's clean-cut without being creepy. And he's bright. The others were all right, you know. But he really made an impression. I'm sorry, Lyle. I hate to leave you up in the air, but there's not a hell of a lot I can do about it. Jim's screaming because I've stayed as long as I have. He wanted me to go two weeks ago but I couldn't do that to you."

"When are you leaving?"

"Saturday. I thought I'd finish out the week."

"Well"—Lyle wet her lips—"I appreciate that. I really do."

"I'm sorry." Penny touched Lyle on the arm. "It seems kind of like a dirty trick. Sometimes, when I think about it, this whole system, I can't help thinking how crazy it is. I mean, the people who've bought our house are being transferred in from Chicago. They've sold their house in Chicago to some people who're being transferred out there from upstate New York. Jim's negotiating on a house for us in Fort Wayne and the people who own it are being transferred to San Jose. If you stop and think about it, it's scary. Like a great big checker game with all of us moving here and there. I just wonder what would happen if we all said, No! and refused to move."

Lyle looked at the list of names. She felt suddenly tired. Even more than the night before. Why was there always something? Some sort of problem every inch of the way. "I'll be sorry to lose you," she said finally, seeing the upset on Penny's features. "I might as well get on the telephone right away."

"Call Jess Kelsey. I really think you'll like him. If I didn't hear from you, I was going to hire him."

Lyle moved to the rear of the shop, then stopped and turned.

"Thank you for taking care of the plants and the mail. All of it. I'll call him."

The voice on the other end sounded so fresh, so young. And so enthusiastic. "I can come down right now," he said. "To tell you the truth, I've been waiting in, hoping to hear."

"I just got back," Lyle explained. "If you wouldn't mind . . ."

"Half an hour," he said. "You'll know me. I'll be the one with the white carnation." He laughed and hung up.

Lyle returned to the shop. "Are you sure about this kid?" she asked Penny. "He sounds like a joker."

"He's got quite a sense of humor. But he's also got some very good ideas. And, well, you'll see for yourself."

"How old is he exactly?"

"I forgot to ask," Penny said rather sheepishly. "He looks pretty young. But he did two years in Viet Nam, so he can't be all that young."

"How old, do you think?"

"Looking at him, I'd say twenty-four or -five. But talking to him, I'd have to up that to maybe twenty-eight or -nine."

"At least he lives in town," Lyle said distractedly.

Thinking that if he did work out, he'd be able to pick up the mail, open the shop in the mornings the way Penny always had. The traffic could get pretty heavy on the turnpike in the early morning and quite often it took her twenty-five or thirty minutes to cover a run that should have taken only ten or fifteen. And she liked having the shop open right at nine-thirty.

Unexpectedly, it occurred to her to add one more item to her mental list: a trip to the gynecologist. She'd missed her annual checkup. She'd also never filled the prescription Dr. Wojeski had given her for the pills. She'd gone along thinking she'd see another doctor in Australia, get a prescription there. My God! she thought. What if I'm pregnant? Jimmy hadn't used anything. She hadn't even thought about it until this moment. And was terrified by the idea. Of course there were always abortions, but she could barely stand having her annual checkups let alone the idea of an abortion.

"Is something the matter?" Penny asked.

"No, no. I was just thinking of something." Counting frantically, trying to remember the dates. She'd had a period just after arriving in Melbourne. Another was due, was late. She wanted it to start that minute, at once. And went to the back to pour herself a second cup of coffee, willing it to happen. A customer came in. Penny went to help. Lyle settled herself at her desk with the books, trying to fix her attention on the sales for the previous month. Mrs. Wallace had the books right up to date, as always. And Lyle's mother had, with her power of attorney, paid all the bills. The figures were a little off, she saw. The profits down a bit. But then late September and all of October were always slow, never good times. November usually picked up and December was always very good. Satisfied, she put the books back in the filing cabinet and got up to have a look at the racks in the stockroom. Just to see how the stock was holding up. Not that Penny wouldn't have ordered to cover shortages. But just habit. And a need to move.

The bell at the front door went off again and she went through to the front knowing Penny was still busy with her customer.

My God! she thought, knowing at once it had to be him. He's just a kid. I can't trust someone who looks like

that to run my business. No, wait! she warned herself.
Don't prejudge! Wait!

"I'm Jess." He grinned, extending his hand. The woman
at the counter with Penny turned around inquisitively. He
seemed to be filling the shop with laughter.

She gave him her hand and her name, then said, "We'll
talk in my office," and led the way to the rear of the shop.

"I'm crazy about this place," he enthused, following her.
"It has all kinds of potential. Penny told me you do all the
designs. Some of them're really excellent."

"Thank you." She indicated he should be seated, prick-
ling slightly at that "some of them." Not that she thought
everything she did was a masterpiece. But she only put the
best pieces into the shop. There were a lot she discarded.

"Do you know anything about needlepoint?" she asked
him, lighting a cigarette.

"I'm going to learn." He smiled at her, positive he was
going to get the job. Intrigued because she wasn't at all the
way he'd thought she'd be. She'd sounded a lot older on
the phone. Not like someone with good legs and what
might be an altogether dynamite body. Not like someone
with the capacity to blush or capable of turning him on.
He couldn't understand it, but he was crazy about her at
first sight. Liking her hair and her hands. "I've got all
kinds of ideas," he said.

"Where were you employed previously?" she asked,
hating how officious she was sounding.

"I had a job working for my father. It was no good. We
grate on each other."

"What sort of job?"

"A handout," he said truthfully. "Driving one of the
trucks. Delivery."

She couldn't imagine him driving a truck. He didn't
look at all the type. He was, as Penny had said, clean-cut.
With a very appealing light to his eyes. And that engaging
smile.

"What courses did you take at the School of Visual
Arts?"

"Painting and drawing, a photography course, and one
in graphics. I did three semesters. I would've stayed but my
money ran out. And I couldn't get a grant."

"Where did you go to school?" she asked, wishing this
conversation were less official and more relaxed. But she
did have to know, have to ask.

"St. Paul's. Yale."

"My brother went to St. Paul's," she said automatically, without thinking. "But he's quite a bit older than you. Did you graduate? From Yale, I mean."

"I got drafted. And after, I didn't feel like going back."

She understood precisely what he meant. Not the specifics, but the feeling. It was the feeling she'd had this morning when Penny had said she'd be leaving.

"Why would you want to work in a needlepoint store?" she asked. "Why would this appeal to you?"

"Because it's quiet, for one thing. There's no machinery."

She pushed her chair back somewhat from the desk and crossed her legs. "I can't afford to hire someone who'll be moving on in three or four months," she said.

"Listen, it's the only thing that's appealed to me in ages. I've always liked this place, the stuff you have. A lot of my mom's friends come here. I didn't say that to pull any political number," he added quickly. "It just happens to be the truth. I don't know," he said, looking thoughtful. "I want some peace. Something to do that makes a little sense. Your things are beautiful and this place makes sense to me."

"How old are you, Jess?" She asked the question. Her face, like neon, lit up red.

"Twenty-nine," he said, smiling. Loving the way she blushed. It didn't go with her voice, or her hard-line questions, or the shape of her face. "You thought I was eighteen, right? Man, it's all I get! I can't help the way I look." The smiled faded and he leaned toward her. "Listen, I really want the job. I'll work like a slave, do anything that needs doing. I need something I can handle that doesn't mess my brain."

"I take it you're not working now?"

"No. I could start right now, if you like. Let me try. I've got a lot of good ideas. *Good* ideas. I've been to the library and checked out all the books on needlepoint, even tried a few designs."

"Don't beg," she near-whispered. "Don't do that."

Their eyes met. She put out her cigarette and opened the top side drawer of her desk. "Fill this out for me," she said, her voice gone peculiar. "Help yourself to a cup of coffee, then go out and work with Penny. She'll tell you what to do. I've got to get to the bank."

"You won't be sorry," he said, again extending his hand. "I know I come on like a flake sometimes. But I'm not. A flake, I mean. And I'll work my ass off for you."

Somewhat reluctantly, she shook his hand, then stood up and reached for her coat. "Take your time with that," she said as he reached for one of the pens on the desk. "And please, don't talk about your ass to any of the customers." She smiled stiffly, having halfway choked on the word ass. He grinned at her and pulled the application over in front of him.

On her way out, she stopped to talk to Penny. "Get him started. Show him the stock and the prices. I'll be back in half an hour."

She didn't really have to go to the bank. There was nothing that couldn't wait a day or two. But she needed badly to move, get out into the air, find room for her thoughts. She walked up Greenwich Avenue trying to unravel her many reactions to Jess Kelsey, to Penny's imminent departure, to her own return home. She felt very unlike herself. Peculiar, disoriented. Thinking, I'm crazy, hiring him. He'll be gone in a few weeks and I'll be back to putting ads in the paper, trying to find someone reliable, dependable, to help run the shop.

I'm crazy.

And I don't understand half of what he says. More than half.

I'll work my ass off.

My God!

Why isn't this damned body bleeding?

Tired. I'm tired.

I shouldn't have hired him.

Eight

On her way back from the bank she stopped in the drugstore to buy a box of Tampax. As if making the purchase would coerce her body into performing properly. She pushed the Tampax to the bottom of her bag, then returned to the shop. And tried not to think about the possibilities of pregnancy, abortion.

She sat at her desk listening to Penny and Jess talking out in the shop, trying to concentrate on work. Failing. After Saturday she and Jess would be alone together in the shop every day. She'd never before worked with a man.

Feeling herself sliding into negative areas, she reached for the telephone to call her mother.

Her mother's secretary said, "She's in a meeting, Miss Maxwell. I'll have her get back to you."

Lyle hung up. Impressed, always, by her mother's importance. An assistant, a secretary. A large office. A voice that contained confidence, had control. The telephone rang a few minutes later, and after their conversation Lyle had the feeling she'd been talking to someone she'd encountered dozens of times—like the pharmacist in the drugstore and the man behind the counter in the deli—but hadn't ever really begun to know.

The feeling was reinforced upon seeing her mother, embracing her in the large foyer of the house on Lake Avenue. Holding this stranger, her mother; breathing in the familiar scent of Blue Grass. Thirty-five years of breathing it in, her senses saying, This is mother! Aware of the textures of cheek and hand and mouth; reminded again that she was taller than her mother and totally unlike her physically, facially, and in every other way. She hugged her mother hard, holding her close for long moments; eyes closed, unnerved by all the mood swings and changes of the day.

Frances wasn't prepared for the intensity of the embrace or for the anxious look to Lyle's eyes. Nor was she prepared for the feeling she received instantly, upon seeing Lyle, that something of great significance had taken place.

"You're positively black!" Frances exclaimed, carefully extricating herself and leading Lyle by the hand into the living room. "You look so well! I love what the sun's done to your hair."

Vaguely, Lyle touched her hair as she looked around the room. The brass fan in front of the fireplace and the two wing chairs. The drop-leaf side table, the tuxedo sofa. The needlepoint rug, candlesticks on the mantel. The portrait gone from above the mantel. A watercolor woodscape in its place.

"I put it in the attic," Frances said, following Lyle's eyes. "I decided the charade had gone on long enough. And I was sick to death of having Jack glowering at me every time I walked into the room. Drink?"

"Whatever you're having," Lyle said, still staring at the woodscape. "That's very good," she said, moving closer to the painting. Fine technique, wonderful simplicity.

"It is, isn't it? Will bought it for me."

"How is Will?" Lyle asked, lowering herself onto the sofa. Wondering if she'd start bleeding and ruin the upholstery. She'd be happy to pay for reupholstering the sofa.

"Fine, fine!" Frances carried two scotch-and-waters over, set Lyle's down on the coffee table, then slid onto the sofa beside her. "What happened, dear?" she asked. "You look shell-shocked. Do you want to talk about it?"

"Are there cigarettes in here?" Lyle asked, opening the box on the coffee table, helping herself to one; lighting it, then straightening, looking at her mother. Surprised again by her mother's youth, her aura of health and vitality, her good looks. "My God!" she said, giving voice to her thoughts. "You're so good-looking! You really are!"

"What *happened*!" Frances repeated, convinced now Lyle had been well and truly traumatized. She couldn't remember Lyle's ever having said anything even remotely similar, nor openly admiring anything or anyone.

"He hit me, abused me, destroyed all my things. I ran away and got myself rescued by a fat, middle-aged man who was very kind, so kind. I'm trying very hard not to think about the fact that I might be pregnant. Penny's leaving on Saturday and I hired a kid today, a man. To replace her. I'm sure I shouldn't have done it. Why do I have the feeling I've never seen you before in my life? Have you been wearing that Blue Grass for thirty-five years? I didn't think it'd been around for that long. Do you suppose I'm having a nervous breakdown?"

Frances knew her mouth was open, that she was staring, but she couldn't do anything about it. She was too stunned. After a moment, she took a hefty swallow of her drink, then returned the glass to the table.

"I can't absorb all that in one go," she said. "Could you bear to elaborate just a little for me?"

"I probably *am* breaking down," Lyle said, carefully studying her mother's eyes and mouth. "I started out this morning feeling really quite optimistic. Before the morning was out, I was back to wishing I'd walked into the river. I've been carrying around a box of Tampax all day as if it could save my life. I'd die if I had to have a baby."

"You don't *have* to have babies nowadays," Frances said reasonably. "You know that as well as I do."

"Knowing something's one thing. Actually doing it is something else altogether. Have you ever had an abortion?"

"No."

"Well, would you have?"

"Absolutely. If things had turned out that way. Definitely."

"Really?" Lyle said. "That's interesting. I didn't know that about you."

"You find you do what you have to do."

"I suppose you do. He was Mr. Hyde." Lyle smiled, amused by that. "Dr. Jekyll warmed me up for the kill then turned me over to his associate. It was an absolute nightmare. Jimmy said I'd forget it. I don't know why people think you can just walk away and forget the absolutely worst thing that's ever happened to you."

"Jimmy?"

"In Perth," she explained. "I ran out, took a taxi to the airport and got on the first plane leaving. It happened to be going to Perth. It's the most beautiful place on earth. Did you know there are palm trees in Australia? They never mention that in books. I was so surprised. And the cities are so big. You think everything's going to be small, tiny old-fashioned towns with a few people in bustles wandering around. Sydney was *enormous*. Six million people.

It's far bigger than New York. I mean the size of it. It went on and on forever. And all the houses have red-tiled roofs. It's what you see first from the plane. Miles and miles and miles of red-tiled roofs. Everything would've been all right, I think, if Penny hadn't had to hit me with that first thing. Of course, when else could she have told me?"

"I knew," Frances admitted. "She's been very nervous about it, worrying when you'd be getting back."

"Why didn't you tell me last night when we talked?"

"It didn't occur to me."

"Oh! You didn't like him, did you?"

"Not the least bit, no."

"Why?"

"Because he wasn't a particularly nice person. He seemed to be trying too hard to make an impression. It surprised me that you didn't seem to see it."

"Obviously, I didn't. Do you suppose everyone saw it but me?"

"I don't know. It doesn't matter now, does it?"

"I guess not. It's just that I feel so damned stupid, making such a fool of myself that way."

"It hasn't hurt you," Frances said, picking up her glass.

"Of course it's hurt me!" Lyle said sharply.

"I don't think it has. I don't mean to say that you're not *hurt*. By the experience. But it seems to have improved you, I think."

"How? What does that mean?"

"Well, you're talking about it. You're talking, period. That's a major change. I've spent a lifetime trying to drag information out of you. It's really a refreshing change to have you volunteering some. In fact, it's a little astonishing to think that I'm sitting here having this conversation with you."

"Oh!" Lyle put out her cigarette and immediately lit another. "I hadn't realized I was that bad. Well, yes, I did. I did."

"You've changed, Lyle. It may have been the worst thing that's ever happened to you, but it seems to've shocked you right into the world. I honestly can hardly believe this is you."

"Neither can I. I'll probably be myself tomorrow."

Frances laughed. "Wait awhile. Give me a chance to know and enjoy this you."

"You're laughing at me."

"A little. But not unkindly. With you, really. Not at you."

"I don't care. I can't keep up with anything. Nothing looks quite right. Not as if things have been moved. Not like that. But as if someone's changed the lighting, or the perspectives. I did bring you something," she said, setting her cigarette on the lip of the ashtray, then reaching for her bag. "Several somethings, as a matter of fact. I hope you like them." She took three tissue-wrapped packages from the bag and put them in her mother's lap. The act struck her as being extraordinarily intimate. I'm putting packages in this woman's lap, she thought. Just as if we know each other and I have the right to do things like this.

An amethyst geode. An antique ivory apple with a silver stem and leaf, on a heavy silver chain. And a packet of tobacco.

"That's for Will." Lyle indicated the tobacco.

"These are lovely," Frances said, admiring the necklace. "You've always had superb taste. And this"—she held the rock in her hand—"is fascinating. It'll make a perfect paperweight for my desk. It's very dear of you to think of Will."

"It's hand-blended. There's a tiny shop in the arcade under the Hilton in Sydney. The nicest man. He made up the blend while I watched."

"If you can stay for a bit after dinner," Frances said, "you'll be able to give it to him yourself when he comes home."

One beat, two, three. "Home? Did you get married?"

"No."

"Oh! When . . . How long?"

"He moved in just after you left. You're shocked."

"No. No, I'm not. I think that's fine. He's a very nice man. Why shouldn't you, if that's what you want? You deserve someone nice, like Will."

Frances put her hands either side of Lyle's face, leaned forward and kissed her on the mouth, then sat back beaming at her. "I'm happy to have you home, dear. And don't hurry back to your old you. I like this you a lot better." She looked surprised and very pleased. "I mean that, Lyle. Don't go back in. There's no law written that says you have to be shy and afraid and insecure."

"I still am all those things."

Frances withdrew her hands, still smiling. "But to a much lesser degree," she said, looking again at the geode.

As if he'd known all along she was going to tell Lyle, Will let himself into the house just before ten. And, laughing, a bit angry, Frances said, "I should have known not to trust you."

Lyle got up to hug him and give him the tobacco. She'd always liked Will. Tall and grey-haired with penetrating eyes and a mouth always upturned, as if he were permanently riding the edge of amusement. He'd been the family lawyer. Now, it seemed, he was in the family. In his late fifties, he always appeared impeccably dressed but invariably with something small, something almost unnoticeable that was not quite right. A bulge in his pocket where he'd crumpled his handkerchief and jammed it in. Or a tiny burn on his trousers, the result of his pipe-smoking. Just a little something that rendered him somehow more human. Watching him open the package of tobacco, Lyle tried to imagine Will and her mother upstairs together in the bedroom, making love. She could see it all too easily. And turned very red.

"You're looking so well, Lyle," he said. "Hand-blended. I'll have to have a pipeful right now." He kissed her on the forehead. Bending slightly to do it. He was very tall. "Thank you very much," he said, smiling.

"I'm going to help you load the machine," Lyle told her mother, "and then I'm going to go home. I'm still not caught up on sleep."

They went out to the kitchen while Will busied himself cleaning his pipe bowl.

"Never mind the dishes." Frances took hold of Lyle's arm. "Just stand still for a minute and talk to me. Is there a real chance you're pregnant?"

Turning bright red once again, Lyle looked down at her mother's hand on her arm.

"There's a chance. But it was only . . ."

"What?"

"Two night ago. Or three. I'm mixed up with the time change." My God! Am I actually having this conversation with my *mother*? Talking about my having made love to some man. Talking about it to my mother?

"Tell me something." Frances released her arm. "You

don't have to, of course, if you'd prefer not to. But was Ian . . . Was that the first time?"

An agony of embarrassment. But she nodded, wishing desperately she had a cigarette, something to do with her hands, somewhere to direct her eyes.

"I thought so," Frances said softly. "Are you going to stay away from men forever now, because of it?"

"I don't want to think about it, about any of it."

"Obviously, you're not, are you?" Frances thought it through. "You said you slept with the other one. The one you think may have made you pregnant."

"Mother, please."

"Lyle, I'm not passing judgment on you. I'm not probing for details, either. All right," she said, seeing how tortured Lyle looked. "Richard's coming up for the weekend. I was hoping you'd come with us for dinner Saturday night."

"Yes."

"He's anxious to see you. We both missed you."

"I really have to go home," Lyle said, hoping that what was happening was what she wanted to be happening. A slight twinge, a cramping just above her groin.

"You're not running away because you're embarrassed, are you?"

"No. I'm tired."

"I know," Frances said sympathetically, placing her hand on Lyle's cheek. Overcome by a feeling of tenderness for her. "How long was the flight?"

"Thirty-odd hours altogether. I'm sorry to fade out on you but I feel as if I'm going to fall on my face. Are you going to marry Will?"

"I have no desire to remarry. Why?"

"Just curious."

"It makes a difference to you?"

"No" she said slowly. "Not in any negative way. Anyway, why shouldn't you have what you want? You've earned it."

"Have you ever stopped to consider that you've earned something, too?"

"I've been thinking about that. I just don't feel as if I have. Some moments, I do. But then, I feel . . . I don't know. Undeserving. I don't know. I have to think about so many things and I'm too tired right now."

"You're embarrassed because you think you've said too much."

"No. Yes."

"Don't be, Lyle. I mean it. I can't tell you how good it is to know your thoughts, hear what you have to say. For the first time in thirty years I have the feeling you're familiar. Don't you know there's nothing you can't tell me? I'm not going to judge you. I'm not in any position to. Especially considering my own life right now. Just because I'm your mother doesn't mean I can't see you as being separate, someone outside of me. And there has to be someone for all of us. To talk to, confide in. I'm just embarrassing you more," she realized.

"I'm trying not to be. I just can't help it. I start saying and doing things, feeling a certain way. Then I stop myself."

"*Don't* stop yourself! It's not a breakdown. It's just life."

"I have to go."

She hurried to the bathroom upon arriving home. Hoping. Disappointed. And went to bed imagining the worst, seeing an image of herself bloated and grotesque, waddling through dreams that were too ominously lifelike. She made herself wake up, got out of bed and went to the bathroom. It had started. Dizzily relieved, she got the box of Tampax. The remainder of the night's dreams unremarkable.

Jess was spraying Windex on the counter tops when she arrived in the morning. Polishing the glass lovingly, grinning at her, saying, "Hi! Coffee's made. And I picked up the mail, too. Penny had to go somewhere, said she'd be right back. I like your coat. Is it mink?"

She said, "Good morning," and continued through to the back to her office. Bothered. Not sure if it was his babyish face, or his compliments, or his enthusiasm that bothered her most.

He'll never stick with it, she told herself, hanging up her coat before sitting down to go through the mail. He's not serious. He's too young. Too good-looking. I should've called the women on the list. I should've interviewed the others.

The mail contained nothing of interest. She reached for a scratch pad and began making up the list of things to do. The car, the leaves, the gynecologist. She didn't feel like working, didn't even want to be in the shop today. Not with that baby-faced boy out there humming to himself as he went through the shop polishing the glass. She chewed the end of the pencil, trying to remember what else had to be added to the list. She couldn't think.

"How do you take it?" he asked, appearing in the doorway.

"What?"

"Your coffee?"

"With cream," she said, then thought to add, "Thank you."

"Coming right up!" he said cheerily, gratingly, returning seconds later to set a mug down in front of her. Hovering by the desk as she picked up the mug, took a sip of the coffee.

"How long have you had this place?" he asked.

"Nine years."

"Have you ever thought of changing things around?"

"What things?" she asked, tensing.

"Just rearranging, making the place more interesting."

"Did you have something in mind?"

"A few ideas," he said. Thinking, She hates me. She positively hates me. "I was thinking about it last night."

"Such as?"

"Well, the window, for one thing. Instead of having a whole bunch of stuff all jammed in there, why not have just one really fine-looking piece. With the wools arranged sort of to one side. And scissors, needles. I could show you. It sounds weird trying to describe it."

"You want to change the window."

"Could I?"

"Jess, you're not here to do displays."

"I thought I was here to do everything." You don't hate me, he decided. You're just scared shitless of me. What the hell for? I'm not scary.

She couldn't respond to that for a moment.

"If you don't like the way I do it," he said, "I'll put it back. It's early. There's no one even out on the street yet. Let me do it. And if you hate it, I'll junk it."

"All right," she said unenthusiastically. "Go ahead. I don't care."

His expression became clouded. "You should care," he said. "A good window can bring in a lot of customers."

"I said you could do it."

He opened his mouth to say more but decided the timing was all wrong. "I'll let you know when it's finished."

"Yes," she said distantly.

What was he trying to prove? she wondered. And why did she want to fight him? If he wanted to take on more than the job required, wasn't that a good sign?

She cleared the desk top, got up and cut some 12-point Penelope, taped the edges, then sat down preparing to copy the first of the wildflower sketches onto the canvas. She'd finished the pencil outlines when Jess reappeared in the doorway saying, "You want to come have a look?"

"You did it that quickly?" she asked, feeling crowded as he leaned across the desk to look at the canvas.

"Listen! That's really nice!" he said. "Different. I like that."

"Thank you." She wanted him to move, wanted to look at the damned window and then get back to work.

He moved out of her way, hurrying past her to hold the door open so she could go out into the street. Telling himself to slow down, cool it a little. She's not the type of lady you push too hard, Jess. Just lay back a bit. Get it fixed in your head that you scare the lady, Jess. You really honest to God scare the living shit out of her.

It was very effective. He'd found some lengths of yellow fabric in the storeroom and stapled them around the entire lower half of the window. Stapled one large, geometric design she'd done ages ago and forgotten about to an easel, then he'd draped skeins of wool over the easel and at the foot of it. An inviting basket of more wool in the same colors, with a pair of scissors tossed down. A threaded needle, a pair of glasses—where had he found those?—and a lace handkerchief. It looked exactly as if someone had stepped away for a moment but intended to return. To put on the glasses, pick up the handkerchief and begin work on the canvas.

"It's very good," she said, chilled, anxious to get back inside into the warmth.

"You really think so?"

"I do. It's excellent. I don't know if it'll attract any new business but I like it."

"I've got all kinds of other ideas," he said eagerly,

knocked out by her fairness. Whatever else you are, he thought, you don't mess around with giving the credit where it's due. I get off on that.

She stopped in the middle of the shop, turned and looked at him. "One at a time," she said, forcing herself to smile at him. "I'm only good for one idea a day. Will you put the things you took from the window back into stock?"

"Oh, sure," he said, visibly deflated. "Sure."

"I'm an old lady," she said. "Old ladies can't be rushed."

Old? He stared at her retreating back. What kind of trip was she on? Old. He shrugged and began clipping the canvases onto the hangers, putting them back on the rack. Thinking he was going to have to talk to her about bins. The racks were dumb.

Nine

◆◆◆

Saturday, the shop was crowded with customers from the moment the front door opened until closing time. She'd hoped to take Penny to lunch, give her the gift. But there wasn't any way on earth Jess could have coped singlehandedly with the volume of customers. Particularly since a lot of the regulars insisted Lyle serve them personally.

Locking the front door, finally, she said, "We'll have a glass of wine, Penny, and a few quiet minutes before you go."

Unable to think of any legitimate way to disinclude Jess, she went back to get the bottle of white wine from the small refrigerator, three paper cups, the envelope with Penny's check, and the gift. They were all exhausted and not in a particularly festive mood. Standing against the counter with their wine.

"This is just something small," Lyle said, giving Penny the package.

Penny smiled, set down her cup and removed the gift wrapping.

"Something small! This is gorgeous!" Penny lifted the gold chain out of its box and at once fastened it around her neck.

"It suits you," Lyle said, cowed by her own generosity. She never knew how to respond to peoples' reactions to the gifts she gave them. "I hope you like it."

"I *love* it! Thank you." Penny kissed her on the cheek, then turned to Jess saying, "Isn't it gorgeous?"

"Really!" he agreed. "Dynamite!"

He was watching Lyle, trying to read her. She talked and acted as if she were going on eighty. And he couldn't make that out. She's not that much older than me, he thought, noticing the self-conscious way she accepted Penny's thanks. Noticing, too, the avid way she smoked her cigarette. Her eyes. Her mouth. Thinking, You wouldn't be bad at all if you just thought you were better. And was mildly jolted, realizing that that had to be it: she just didn't think a whole hell of a lot of herself.

They finished the wine. Lyle stood by the front door. Jess said goodnight and went out. Then Penny stopped in front of Lyle saying, "I'll stay in touch. I just can't believe I won't be coming in on Monday morning. I left my keys on your desk. Thank you for the necklace. It's really too beautiful."

"Send me your new address," Lyle said, not knowing where to look. "I'll miss you."

Penny hugged her, stepped away, said, "Bye," and was out, running through the rain toward her car.

Lyle closed and locked the door, turned off the lights in the shop, went back to her office, sat down, laid her head on her arms on the desk and began to cry. Penny had been more than just an employee. She'd been a friend, someone to talk with, someone who'd looked after the shop, and the house, the plants, the car while Lyle had been away. And now she was gone. Someone she'd get a Christmas card from for a year or two or three. And then, one year it wouldn't come and that would be the last of Penny.

She lifted her head, took a tissue from the box on the filing cabinet and wiped her eyes, blew her nose. Startled to hear the front door opening. Jess calling out, "It's only me." He came into the office, asking, "Are you okay? You looked kind of down and I thought I'd come back, make sure you're all right."

"I'm all right," she said brusquely, wondering what he wanted. He seemed always to be wanting something.

"You're mad 'cause I cared and came back," he said. "Why?"

"What I don't need at this particular moment is an inquisition or an analysis of my feelings."

"How d'you know?" he countered. "Maybe you do."

"If I do, it's not your place to do the analyzing."

"My place? What does that mean, *my place*?"

"Exactly what it means. My God! What do you want?"

"I don't want anything. I'm just trying to be a friend."

"I . . ."

He held up his hand to stop her. "Okay!" he said, his smile gone. "Don't say it! You don't want me coming around being a friend. Message received. Over and out. Sorry if I stepped out of 'my place.' Have a nice weekend. I'll see you Monday." His eyes remained on hers a moment longer, then he turned to go.

"You have a good weekend, too," she said weakly, to his back.

His footsteps continued on through the shop.

"God!" she cried and pounded her fist on the desk. "God, *God*!"

He heard it as he was closing the door, but kept on going, shaking his head as he yanked up his collar against the rain, heading for his car. Standing for a minute looking at her car parked a few slots down from his. Even the car was like her, somehow. Subtle styling and conservative color, but expensive and mechanically excellent. Not too old. A seventy-four or -five Mercedes 280. Right smack in the middle of the line. Not the bottom-of-the line diesel. But not the top of the line 450 SEL. Just right there, bang in the middle. He had a sudden desire to kick one of the fenders, add a human touch to the machine. Thinking, what's the matter with you, anyway? I wasn't trying to do some big number on you. But you acted as if I were.

Still. The way she'd cried out. He could relate to that, knew that feeling. It was saying, No more. When does it quit? Leave me alone, I can't handle anything more.

So, okay. I can dig where you're coming from.

He got into his car, floored the accelerator, then switched on the ignition. Bingo! He patted the dash affectionately, turned on the wipers, then reversed the old Mustang out of the lot.

It was wonderful to see Richard. She just wished her mother had bothered to mention that he'd be bringing along a female friend. Lyle felt uncomfortable. Tried not to, but couldn't help herself. It was so obvious she was the odd woman out. Her mother with Will. And Richard with his beautiful girl. All his girls were beautiful. Always. So New York and so young. Lyle was reminded of that dinner with Ian. The American from Minneapolis and his obnoxious wife. That third man. She wanted so much to relax and enjoy the evening, but she couldn't. All she could think of was getting home, having a long hot bath, something good perhaps on the late show and then sleep. Sunday to herself.

"Come on and dance with me," Richard invited, pushing his chair from the table. "Come on, Lyle. I'm not going to take no for an answer."

She smiled, unable ever to resist Richard. And took his hand, walked with him to the crowded dance floor. My brother, she thought, as he led her into the dance. Tall and good-looking and possessed of charm, brilliance. Never appearing with the same woman twice. Showing up time after time with one impossibly beautiful girl after another.

"You're all shaken up," he said. "I hear you had a pretty rotten time down under."

"What did she tell you?"

"The bare essentials. That it didn't work out."

"It was a disaster," she said, looking over his shoulder at another couple on the dance floor. The way they were looking at each other. Their eyes.

"So what happens now?" he asked, steering her out of the path of yet another couple so that she was very aware of the strength of his hand on the small of her back. And aware, too, of a strange, dull ache at the base of her spine.

"Nothing. Business as usual."

"What are you looking at?" he asked, turning his head to see.

"Sorry," she said automatically. "I wasn't really looking at anything."

"Come into the city next weekend," he suggested. "Stay at the apartment. We'll go see a play, or the ballet. Have dinner out. I'll put you on the train Sunday."

"I'll have to let you know."

"Why don't you let me know right now?" he coaxed, smiling. "You can't have filled your social calendar in the couple of days you've been back."

"I don't feel like doing anything," she said truthfully. "I don't even really feel like doing this. I'd rather be home in a hot bath."

"With a rubber ducky!" He laughed. "Jesus Christ, Lyle! Why're you so determined to be an old fuddy-duddy? You're thirty-five, not sixty. According to all the books I've read, you're at your sexual prime, Miss Brody. You should be out having a blast, not thinking about hot baths."

She laughed with him, thinking for a moment of Jess. Over and out. Message received. I was wrong, cruel, rude.

I shouldn't have treated him that way. I haven't the right
to treat anyone that way.

"Too bad you're my sister," he said, his hand directing
her to the right. "I could set you straight in about a
week."

"You think so, do you?"

"I know so. It's just that incest isn't a popular number."

"Are you *serious*?"

"Maybe twenty-five percent. I don't think I'm that super
hot. But you've got a terrific body, you know. And you
can move it. Now, don't go all stiff! Just do what you were
doing. You can't stand it, can you? One compliment is
worth a thousand agonies. Most women *like* hearing that
kind of thing. But not you. Why don't you invest in some
clothes that do something for you? Unbend a little and let
your life happen."

"This sounds too familiar," she warned.

"Okay, so we talked about it. Frances and I happen to
agree when it comes to you."

"Why do you always call her that instead of Mother?"

"Because it's her name."

"It jars me."

"You jar easily anyway."

"Maybe I do. I can't help it."

"You should try to stop."

"And what about you, Richard?" she counterattacked.
"Advising me. I've never seen you with the same woman
twice. What's that all about?"

"Living the safe life," he said a little too cleverly.

"But it's the truth, isn't it?" she said. "You're not doing
very much better than I am. You just happen to be doing
it differently. But it's really the same."

"I hear Penny left," he said.

He wasn't going to go into it. "Today was her last day,"
she said, wearied of everything.

"Did you get someone else?"

"A bo . . . man. He's a kid, really. I don't think it's going to work out."

"Why not?"

"He's the type who wants to start changing everything."

"And that's bad?"

"Would you mind if we go back to the table, Richard?
I'm honestly not in the mood."

"Not for a minute," he said, keeping hold of her, his

face serious now. "Do you want to tell me what happened, Lyle?"

Richard. My brother. Why have I felt for so long that you're older and wiser than I, when suddenly tonight I know that's not the case? Believing you to be less susceptible to life and more in control of it. You're not, though. Any more than I am.

Seeing you in my mind as a little boy, climbing the maple at the back of the house. Singing, "The Teddybears' Picnic." Your legs smeared with dirt and scabby at the knees. While I sit on the back steps and watch you disappear into the leaves.

She let her head rest against his shoulder, allowing him to lead her; her eyes closed.

Seeing Richard's face contorted in little boy's anger, waving clenched fists. And Daddy's casually cuffing him across the side of the head, saying, Get out of my sight! Dumb fucking kid.

Her mouth close to his ear, she whispered, "I don't want to talk about it, Richard. I feel old and tired. I know it's boring and everyone's sick of me, sick of hearing me say it. But it's the way I feel." I'd give anything, *anything* to be here, right now, held by someone who loved and wanted me, Richard. Just loving me, wanting me. Not promising to spend the rest of his life with me or tape me up in legalities. None of that. I'll die dreaming, die of the dreams. I don't know how to stop even though I know I should.

She lifted her head and opened her eyes.

"Your friend's very beautiful," she said, examining his face; seeing faint traces of her father there. But minus the mouth's hardness or the eyes' spitefulness.

"She's all right. Not as attractive as you are, though."

She laughed. Loudly. "You're demented, Richard! She's *beautiful!*"

"You're more attractive, more of a woman," he persisted. "Half the men here have been watching you."

He realized at once it had been the wrong thing to say. She stiffened, the blood rushed into her face.

"That's *good*, Lyle. It's *nice*. You're supposed to go all buttery and say, 'Thank you.'" She shook her head, her hand damp inside his now. "Okay," he said. "The second thousand agonies. I wish somebody smart would come along who'd be able to convince you."

"What about you?" she asked. "Is someone ever going to be able to convince you to give up your 'safe' life?"

"Let's face it," he said bitterly, "neither one of us is ever going to stand still long enough to get caught. I'm sorry if I pushed it too hard. Will you come in next week-end?"

"Another time. Ask me again."

She escaped just before ten. And drove home through the rain breathing as if she'd been under water and had only just surfaced.

The telephone was ringing as she came through the door and she picked it up to hear a male voice saying, "I just wanted to say that I'm sorry if I said the wrong things. I didn't mean to offend you."

"Jess, I was rude. *I'm* sorry. How did you get my number?"

"From Penny. Are you going to be bugged because I'm calling?"

"I'm not 'bugged.' I just don't understand you, what you want."

"I told you. I'm trying to be your friend."

Still in her wet coat, she sat down at the kitchen table with the telephone and lit a cigarette.

"Why?" she asked at last, feeling somehow defeated.

"Because I like you."

"I'm old enough to be your mother."

"Oh, bullshit!" he said impatiently. "What is that thing, anyway? My *mother*! What're you, thirty-three, -four?"

"Almost thirty-six." Why am I bothering to talk to you?

"Okay. Almost thirty-six. I'm almost thirty. You started a heavy sex-life at the age of six?"

She laughed.

"See!" he sounded pleased. "Hey! Did I catch you in the middle of something or something?"

"I just got in."

"Oh! Okay. I'm not keeping you from anything, am I?"

"Only a hot bath and bed."

Jesus! It got him! Picturing her naked in a tubful of water.

"At ten o'clock on a Saturday night?" He sounded astonished.

"Is that so amazing?"

"Yeah, kind of. D'you want to do something?"

"What?"

"Do something. You know. A jigsaw puzzle or back-gammon or Scrabble or something."

"Are you asking me to invite you here?" She couldn't believe any part of this conversation.

"I was kind of trying to invite myself," he said. Naked in a bathtub.

"No, Jess. No, thank you. I appreciate your calling . . ."

"Maybe another time, okay?"

"Goodbye, Jess." She put down the receiver and continued to sit smoking her cigarette, listening to the rain slanting against the windows.

Sunday morning, she watered the plants, then got dressed and drove into town to get the Sunday *Times*. She wrote to Jimmy in the afternoon, ate an early dinner then sat down to watch *Sixty Minutes*. Halfway through, she fell asleep and awakened with a start at four a.m. Wide awake at once, she switched off the set and went into the kitchen to make some coffee. The rain had finally stopped.

After drinking the coffee, she pulled on an old raincoat, rubber boots and gloves and went out to walk along the beach. The sand sodden, littered with debris. The tide out. She sat on her heels on the sand and watched the sunrise, smoking a cigarette, seeing lights going on in the houses nearby. Monday morning.

Why is it that sometimes, inside, I'm still sixteen and find the same remarkable newness, freshness to everything around me that I did then? And other times, I'm eighty-seven and it's all a rerun of a film I've seen thousands of times. There's supposed to be more. Isn't there? And if there isn't, why do Mother and Richard keep telling me there is? Jimmy, too. And why is there still something in me that so badly wants that something more to material-ize? I should be able to be satisfied with what I have, the me I am, not wanting more. But, my God! To have some-one to share this sunrise, or to wake me when I fall asleep in the middle of a t.v. show. I've got to stop wanting. Got to stop. Accept the fact that there's nothing more. There's only me. And I don't see the point to any of this. What's the point? The shop, working. For what? What's the point, really, of my being alive? There has to be some reason. Has to be. I just haven't found it. And neither has Richard. Never mind all that other business. Telling me

I'm more attractive, more of a woman. Should I have told him he's more attractive, more of a man? It makes no difference to either of us. Neither of us seems able to change the patterns we've woven.

She finished her cigarette, got up and walked back to the house, planning to get in to the shop early. Pick up the mail. No, Jess would do it. Jess.

Do you want to play Scrabble, backgammon, do a jig-saw puzzle? My God!

He was already there when she let herself in. Sitting on the floor, surrounded by canvases.

"What are you doing?" she asked quietly, closing the front door.

"Sorting this stuff out. You ought to have a sale, unload a lot of these."

"We have a sale every summer."

"Have one now. You'll get rid of all of it. November's a perfect time for a sale. Next week's November."

"And what else?"

He looked up at her. "Don't sound that way." He looked wounded.

"What way?" You mystify me, she thought. Utterly, totally.

"As if I were torturing you. They're just ideas. I'm not trying to force you to do . . . it's just . . . ideas. That's all."

"What ideas?"

"You ought to get rid of the racks. And these things." He held up one of the hangers. "Get bins. Five or six of them. Group the pieces according to size so people don't have to go through everything in the whole store to find something the size they want to do."

"And?"

"And maybe give classes here one afternoon a week. Teach people how to do different stuff, different stitches. Fix up the whole place. Make it cleaner, less crowded, airier."

"And?" She felt as if she were suffocating. Drowning again.

"Some advertising. A little catalogue, maybe. Do a mailing three or four times a year. And other things. Lots of things."

"You want to change it all," she said, her voice reduced to a whisper by incipient tears. "Make it yours."

"I don't at all," he argued. "I just want to make it better. Look at these!" He held up several canvases. "These're terrific! But it'd take somebody a year to plow through all this stuff to find them. And you don't need glass cases. They're so out of it, so old-fashioned. Get a good-looking butcher-block table, some bins. And put a radio in here, some music. Lighten it up, make it easier. It's all so fucking *heavy*!"

She wanted to say something, couldn't, was going to be sick. Fled through to the back and into the tiny bathroom to vomit into the sink, tears flooding her eyes. She straightened, ran water into the basin to clean it, then rinsed her mouth with cold water. Her stomach ached, her head hurt. And that dull strange pain at the base of her spine. Give him the damned store! Just *give* it to him! Hand him the keys, go get in the car and go home! He cares more about changing it than you do about owning it.

She opened the bathroom door to see him standing in the doorway opposite, his face pale and frightened.

"You okay?" he asked, his hand reaching out to her.

"What do you want?" she asked. "What? I can't . . . I don't know how to deal with you."

"Why do you have to feel that way, think about 'dealing' with me? I'm not threatening you. I don't understand you. I'm not trying to make the place mine. Nothing like that. I'm trying to make it *yours*. If you don't want to do any of it, you don't have to. Ideas, that's all. Just ideas. Because I like being here, working with you."

"I don't want to teach classes," she said slowly. "I despise teaching. And I do do mailings. Twice a year. As for the rest of it"—she turned her head to look into the body of the store—"I . . ." She wet her lips, trying to think of what she wanted to say. He put his hand on her arm and she jumped. He whipped his hand away, his eyes gone wide.

"You want me to quit?" he offered soberly.

She blinked, then shook her head. "No. I just can't . . . move so quickly."

"Will you let me do the bins? I can make them. Just some plywood and two-by-twos."

"All right. Go ahead. Just please," she said. "Please, don't . . . swear."

"Okay. Sorry. Want me to get you some coffee?"

"No. Thank you. I'll get my own."

The front door opened. He said, "I'll go."

He moved away and she exhaled painfully, then removed her coat, poured a cup of coffee and sat down at her desk. Pulling the wildflower canvas over in front of her. Opening the book Jimmy had given her, to look at the colors. Lifting her head at the sound of Jess's laughter out in the shop. Some woman's laughter accompanying his.

Who are you what do you want?

Ten

———◆———

Within a week, he'd made the bins, brought them in, arranged the canvases in them according to size and was urging her to get rid of the glass counters. He was right about the bins. They were sensible, practical, good-looking.

"But what would I do with the counters?" she asked him.

"Sell them. Put an ad in the Stamford *Shopper*. They'll be gone in a flash. People'll buy anything, you know, if they think they're getting a bargain. Like the canvases. What you do is you take off the old price stickers, put on new ones marked five dollars more than the original price, slash that out with a nice red pen and show the price at ten dollars off. You're actually only knocking the price down by five dollars but it looks like ten."

"That's dishonest," she protested.

"The hell it is! That's business. You don't want to *give* the stuff away."

"But what will we do for counter space?"

"I told you. A nice big butcher-block table. For what you'll get selling the counters, you'll have enough for the table and a couple of dynamite plants. Now that we've cleaned out the front window, there's plenty of light coming through. Some green right over here would be great."

She looked around, dismayed. With all the light coming in, the walls showed themselves badly in need of painting. The old carpeting looked shabby and badly worn. Everything looked old and dirty. Depressing. It was nine years later and she hadn't seen the disintegration happening. She could hear Jimmy talking about the changes, about being too tired, too busy, too whatever to notice them taking place.

Jess was watching her, anticipating her reaction.

"Do you honestly prefer it this way?" he asked quietly.

"No."

"Then, let's change it. One weekend and we can have it painted, cleaned up. And I was thinking if we knock that partition down back there, we could rig up a kind of loose-weave screen so that people coming in could see you working. It looks so good, you know, you working away down there. The only thing that would really cost anything would be the carpeting. And that's a legitimately deductible item, taxwise. I can see it!" he enthused. "All clean white walls, the plants and butcher block, some grass-green carpeting. You know?"

"Is that everything?" she asked.

"Well, no."

"You might as well give me all of it."

"The rest is just small stuff. Like a big coffeemaker so the customers can have a coffee while they're browsing or whatever. And a couple of tall stools in front of the butcher-block counter. Give the place the feeling of a studio. People work here. That's the feeling you want to give. I don't know about you, but there's something that gets to me walking into a shop where there's a feeling of creativity, activity."

"We'd have to close for several days."

"No. The way I figure it," he said eagerly, "I'd get started here on a Saturday night after closing. Once we've sold the counters, of course. Arrange to have them picked up either that Saturday night or Sunday morning. I can paint the place over the weekend. Then the carpet installers come first thing Monday morning. The table, stools, plants and everything get delivered after that. Some odds and ends Monday afternoon and Tuesday you're all set to go."

She lit a cigarette. Stalling, trying to visualize his plans. She couldn't fault them. He'd come up with excellent ideas.

"I'll make the arrangements, do it all," he added hopefully.

"All right," she said, drawing hard on her cigarette. Wondering if he'd start trying to make her over once he'd completed the shop to his satisfaction.

"Terrific! You'll see! It'll be terrific!"

"Yes, all right."

"I'll phone up and put an ad in right away for the counters. And I know a place where I can get the butcher block wholesale. I'll get some estimates on the carpeting."

He went on and on. She nodded, not hearing. Seeing only his face, alive with excitement. His mouth moving, moving. His eyes searching hers, wanting her to summon up a matching eagerness. A pair of women came into the shop and she fled back to her desk, relieved. Picking up her brush, continuing to paint in the colors on the *banksia*. Pushing herself into the delicate task of laying the color down within the grids so that when the wool was worked into the canvas, the details wouldn't be lost.

Let him do it if he wants to. There's nothing in it that can harm me. He's trying to be constructive. It will be an improvement. Brightness, light. Fresh colors, more comfort. What is his life that he's home alone on a Saturday night? Someone young and good-looking home alone on a Saturday night wanting to play Scrabble or backgammon, interested in jigsaw puzzles. Games.

She remembered to call and make an appointment with Dr. Wojeski. Then hung up and lit a cigarette, appalled at the idea that the doctor might commence his examination, then look up at her with a leer, having discovered the significant change in her status. Seeing him down there between her reluctantly parted thighs, smirking at her. God!

And what was the point of refilling the prescription for the pills now when the need for them was gone? Still, why not have them? No one could predict what might transpire. In any case, she was due for a checkup. Was the examination different when you were no longer a virgin? She wrapped her arm around herself, furiously smoking the cigarette; imagining new and different medical humiliations that might now be perpetrated upon her.

Her mother had made an appointment for Lyle, when she'd been sixteen, to have an examination. And Lyle had gone along to see Dorothy Chambers, her mother's gynecologist. For months after she'd mentally cringed and groaned every time she recalled the pain of that rectal examination. "Why did she *do* that?" she'd asked her mother. And Frances had calmly responded, "I don't suppose they do internals on young girls."

She'd stayed away from doctors of all sorts for the next fifteen years, the memory of that painful and humiliating experience all too fresh in her mind. Until the year she was approaching thirty-two and started having periods that lasted longer and longer until she bled nonstop for six solid weeks. And greatly alarmed, got the name of Penny's gynecologist and went along to see him.

With some tablets—she never risked asking what they were—to take four times a day for a month, her body righted itself and her periods returned to normal. But Dr. Wojeski insisted she come in for annual checkups, Pap smears. She loathed every aspect of these visits, but made the appointments and kept them. And here she was, about to go again.

She sat down in the waiting room, looking at the assortment of magazines on the table. *Redbook, Ladies' Home Journal.* Pamphlets on You and Your Baby. *Parents' Magazine.* A very young, very pregnant girl wedged into one of the armchairs. An elderly woman accompanied by a young black woman, both on the leather sofa. A bowl of candies on the receptionist's hatch.

Her name was called and she got up, her stomach in knots.

She emerged feeling gooey from the lubricant. And in shock at the pain. Always forgetting how awful it was having him shove his hand up inside her body, moving it here, there.

On the way home, she stopped and finally got the prescription filled. Then put the pack and its two refills in the medicine cabinet, rearranging several items on the shelf in order to make room. And took the first pill that night as if it were a cyanide capsule.

The same day the ad came out, Jess sold the counters.

"Didn't I tell you!" he crowed. "We'll have plenty for the table and the plants, even a little toward the carpeting."

"That's fine." She detested these confrontations, when he caught her as she came through the door in the morning and threw his enthusiasms over her like a net.

"What's the matter?" he said, his hand touching the sleeve of her coat. "You look pissed. Did I say something?"

"I'm not . . . 'pissed.'" God! The things you say! "When were you planning to begin the miraculous transformation?"

He smiled. "You make it sound like a religious experience," he teased, wondering if she knew she was getting a line between her eyes from drawing her eyebrows together all the time. "I thought this weekend. If that's okay with you."

"It's okay with me." She moved past his hand.

"Hey! I grabbed a peek at your desk. Those flowers are really beautiful! Really!"

"Thank you."

"Do I have bad breath, or B.O. or something? Something even my best friend won't tell me about?"

She stopped and turned around, regarding him wide-eyed.

"What?"

"Maybe it's the garlic," he went on. "I'm big on garlic." He held his hand over his mouth and breathed into his palm.

"What are you talking about?"

"Maybe it's the leprosy," he said, unfastening his shirt cuff, pushing up his sleeve and examining his arm. "Or the heartbreaking psoriasis."

"*What?*"

He dropped his arm and smiled at her. "What is it about me that turns you off so hard?"

"You don't . . . I'm not . . ."

"Want to come help me paint this weekend?" he offered, giving her a winsome smile. "Just to show your good faith?"

She had to smile. He was a little crazy.

"All right," she said. "Now, may I be excused? I have work to do."

"Yes, ma'am." He grinned, buttoning his cuff. "Just so's I know you-all ain't got no kind of hard feelings against me."

"You're crazy." Her smile growing.

"Yes, ma'am!" He nodded vigorously. "Right on, ma'am! You want some coffee?"

"I'll get it," she said, unable to stop staring at him for a moment. Was he trying to make a fool of her? Or encouraging her to make a fool of herself? "Thank you."

"Okay, ma'am!" He gave her what appeared to be a military salute, then went around behind the counter to continue removing everything from inside it.

Friday morning, Dr. Wojeski's nurse called.

"The doctor would like you to come in," she said. "Could you make it this morning?"

At once alarmed, Lyle asked, "Why?"

"Doctor would like to talk to you."

"About what?"

"It would be best if he talks to you."

"What about?"

"Shall I put him on?"

"No. All right. When should I come?"

"Now?"

"Yes, all right. Now." She dropped the phone, picked it back up and replaced it properly. Stricken with panic. Feeling the way she had racing out of the flat in Melbourne. I'm going to die. He's going to set a time limit on the rest of my life. Oh, God! I don't want to die.

She grabbed her coat and bag and frantically beckoned Jess away from his customer. Seeing her blanched features, he excused himself and rushed to the rear of the shop.

"What's wrong? What happened?"

"I've got to leave. I don't know if I'll be back. Can you take care of everything? Can you manage?"

"Sure. No problem. What's coming down?"

"Nothing! I have to go."

She rummaged through her bag for her keys, found them, and went flying out. Jess watched the door slowly swing open after her and went to close it, standing watching as she went running to her car. She'd left something in the air. Something large and cold and very nearly tangible. He could feel her fear like a sudden drop in temperature. And wished he knew what had happened.

"I want to do some tests," Dr. Wojeski was saying. "I'd like to put you in, get going on it right away." Knowing Lyle, if he gave her any chance to say no, she'd say it. And probably never come back to the office.

"Now?"

"Right now. I'd like to take you over, get you admitted myself."

"What have I got?"

"It may be nothing, Lyle. Or it may be something. Quite often the smears come back positive and it doesn't mean a thing. But I want to be absolutely sure."

"What if it's all positive? What does it mean?"

"Let's cross that bridge when we come to it. If you're ready, I'll take you over."

She was absolutely terrified, feeling like a small child, alone in her private room with its yellow curtains and splendid view. The color television set. The room cold, cold. She put on the hospital gown as she'd been told to do. Wanting to cry. Telling herself not to be ridiculous. It could all be nothing. But things were happening so fast.

She was barely into the gown, feeling the draft catching her from nape to knees when they came and began taking blood samples, preparing her for the tests. They handled her, held her open, peered into her with the aid of a shiny blue machine Dr. Wojeski called a colposcope. Snipped tissues, sent them to be biopsied. Tests, more tests. Throughout, she contained her tears and terror.

"We won't have any results until tomorrow night at the earliest," her doctor told her. "There'll be a few more tests in the morning. Relax and don't get yourself all worked up."

And she was left alone in the now overheated room. With a bandage gracing the back of her hand where they'd taken the arterial blood sample. And a burning pain inside. A Band-Aid across the fold of her inner arm. More blood. She was presented with a tray of food. She didn't even bother to lift the lids but pushed the tray away from her and chain smoked, her eyes fixed on the Channel 4 news. Arson in the Bronx, Murder in Queens, Bank Robbery in Brooklyn. She moistened her lips repeatedly, trying not to think about any of it. The name tape on her wrist. *Lyle Maxwell.* She buried her right arm under the blankets and smoked with her left.

She couldn't think. Not at all. Just dozed off and on all night. Watching television, smoking. Waiting. Hoping Jess had coped with the customers, done the night deposit. Dismissing him from her mind. Thinking she'd call her mother. When I know I'll call her I don't want to talk not to anyone what are they going to find what do I have?

Dr. Wojeski came in at 6:45. Right in the middle of a documentary that had managed to capture her attention. She had to switch off the set. She knew by the way he sat down on the bed instead of in the chair that he was going to tell her something dreadful. All the waiting about to end. A day and a night and a day. Waiting.

"I'm sorry, Lyle," he began, his eyes very damp looking.

"What have I got?" Her heart had stopped altogether. Her breathing, too.

"Cervical carcinoma."

Her hand under the blanket was clenching, unclenching; the nails raking her palm, digging in.

"Am I going to die?"

He smiled sadly and took hold of her left hand. His hands were shockingly warm against her cold skin.

"You're not going to die. But you're going to have to decide."

"What?"

"Two choices. A course of radiation treatments. Or a radical hysterectomy, removal of the pelvic lymph nodes."

"My God!" Her lips were so dry they were splitting. "A choice?"

"The side effects of the radiation can be very unpleasant."

"You're saying I should have the surgery."

"It's your decision."

"And if I don't do either?"

"You'll die." He said it so effortlessly, talking about her life, her death.

"I see."

"If you decide on the surgery, I'd like to get it done at once," he said, warming her hand, chafing it as if it wasn't attached to her.

"At once," she repeated. "All right."

"I'll need you to sign a consent form," he said. "I'd like to consult with the surgeon, set you up for an O.R. in the morning."

"The morning. Excuse me." She freed her hand and reached for her cigarettes, lit one, then drew so hard on it the smoke burned her split lip. "And if I don't, I'll die."

"I'm not going to play it down, minimize any of this," he said softly. "It's a big surgical procedure. But once it's done, that's the end of it. You'll stay in for two weeks, rest at home four to six weeks and that's that. You'll be up again and good as new."

"Not quite," she said.

"Well, no," he said. "Not quite. I am sorry. But the surgery's a wise decision."

"Okay. In the morning."

He released her hand and stood up. "I'll have the nurse

bring you the consent form to sign. And some medication to help you sleep. I know it's rough. I know that."

She nodded stiffly. He left and less than two minutes later a nurse came in with the form. Lyle signed it and, without a word, the nurse left.

Fast. So fast.

She picked up the telephone and gave the operator her mother's number. When she heard her mother's voice, she suddenly knew it was all real.

"Mother?" She wanted to say something, but couldn't. If she tried to talk, she'd start crying.

"Lyle, what is it? You sound terrible."

"Just wait a second," she whispered, swallowing, trying to get her voice to perform. Is this happening? Is it real?

"Where are you, Lyle? I tried to reach you at the shop and Jess said you went tearing out of there yesterday morning and he hadn't seen or heard from you since."

"The hospital."

"Here?"

"Yes."

"I'll be there in ten minutes."

Disconnected. Buzzing. Lyle replaced the receiver, lit yet another cigarette and tried to watch the tag end of *Sixty Minutes*. My mother's coming it'll be all right I won't think about it the car I'll have to do something about the car I can't leave it in the doctor's lot for two weeks. Why am I worrying about the car? They're going to cut me apart, take everything out. Cancer. I've got cancer. Oh god my god is this everything or is there more am I going to die anyway?

She recognized her mother's footsteps. Heard them clicking down the hallway. Knowing the sound. And sat up slightly higher, reaching to turn off the set with the remote control. Tensing as she groped for words, feelings. The door was open and Frances stepped into the doorway, stopped, then came over to the bed and sat down. Lyle simply fell forward into her mother. Into her arms, her Blue Grass, the sound of her voice.

"Your Dr. Wojeski was on his way out as I was coming in. I'm sorry, Lyle. I'm so sorry."

"Did he tell you I was going to die?" Hiding her eyes against her mother's shoulder.

"You most definitely are not," she said firmly, her hand stroking Lyle's back. "Definitely not."

"I'm so scared." Her voice tremulous, breaking. Her arms going around her mother, holding on; unequal to any of what was happening.

"I'd be, too. I would be."

"I never wanted children," Lyle said. "It isn't that."

"I know, I know."

She kept her eyes closed and allowed the tears to slip out, her body shaking, cold. "It's just that I don't want to die," she whispered. "When it was my choice, that was different. Something I could do or not do. But not this. Not cancer. God!"

"I'll stay with you," Frances said, too aware of the terrible vulnerability of Lyle's naked back. She'd have liked to draw the gown closed, but couldn't.

"My car's still in the doctor's lot." *Why in the hell am I worrying about the damned car?*

"I'll take care of it."

"And the shop."

"I'll take care of that, too."

She suddenly sat away from her mother, her eyes large. "Don't say anything to Jess! Not about where I am. Don't tell him anything! Say I had to go away, out of town. Anything. But don't tell him!"

"All right, Lyle. Is there anything you want? Your own robe, nightgown?"

"Yes, yes." She looked at her hands clutching her mother's arms. She couldn't let go. "I'm so scared," she whispered, telling her hands to let go. They refused. Frances gently broke her hold and placed both her hands in Lyle's. "You're not going to die, Lyle."

"No."

"You'll be all right."

"Yes."

Frances drew her back into her arms. Her hands stroking again, soothing, calming.

"I love you," Lyle whispered. "Love you." *Why do I have to wait to be dying to tell you something so important?* "I love you!"

"I know, dear. I love *you*. I'll be here. There's nothing to be afraid of."

"Yes."

"Nothing!"

"Yes." I want to go to sleep now wake up with all of this over finished go to sleep and wake up seven years old again to play with my baby brother and never have to grow up grow old have diseases, men who push themselves inside me hit me force themselves into my mouth choke and gag me make me want to die. Only to live through all that and be told I could die, after all, simply from living. Is it because I was a virgin and should have stayed that way upset the chemistry of my interior by letting him break his way into me? Is that why?

Eleven

He let himself in, then stopped, hearing the shower going. She's back, he thought. And felt suddenly high. And as suddenly confused, not knowing quite what to do. She'd probably freak altogether finding him in the house. But he could explain that. He went toward the steps and, about a third of the way up, stopped, hearing the water go off. What to do? He turned, able to see between the railings directly into the bedroom, the bathroom beyond. He froze, hearing the sound of the shower curtain being pushed back. A glimpse of her naked, just a glimpse before she wrapped herself in a large towel. He tiptoed backwards down the steps, moved to the front door, opened it, slammed it.

"Mother? Is that you?" Her voice drifted down the stairs.

"Hey! You're back! It's me!"

"Oh, my God!" she whispered, madly dropping the towel, grabbing her robe. "What are you doing here?" she called out, wishing she hadn't left the bathroom door open. Wishing she was able to move faster.

"Is it okay to come up?" he asked, already halfway up the stairs. It was registering now, what he'd seen. Red, raw-looking. A scar down her belly.

"Do you always just let yourself into other people's houses?" she demanded, belting her robe too tightly.

"Before you go crazy," he said, leaning on the banister, "I've been looking after the place, the plants, your car and all. I didn't know when you'd be coming back and your mom asked if I wouldn't mind."

"Oh! I see. I'm sorry. I didn't know."

"Where'd you go?" he asked, for a moment purposely ignoring her obvious discomfort. She was so thin! Christ! A couple of weeks and she'd lost all her roundness.

"Would you mind waiting downstairs?" she asked, anxious to put on a nightgown, finish drying herself.

"Sure! How about some coffee?"

"Thank you. I'll be down in a few minutes."

He smiled at her and went skipping down the stairs. Putting the pieces together as best he could. Some kind of operation. One of those female numbers where they take out all the gear. Or something. He got out the coffeepot and filled it with water. Thinking about her body. Skinny as a stick. Like a kid's. With breasts. He hadn't thought she'd have much in the way of breasts. What was it with her, always doing that number about being old? She'd looked about eighteen, coming out of the shower. He wished it had lasted longer, so he could've had a really good look.

While the coffee was perking, he took off his jacket and watered the plants. Positively hung up on the idea of getting a look at her, touching her breasts. She was taking a long time. Probably mad as hell. He was crazy about the house, had jumped right in when the mother had asked him to do it. Dynamite lady, Lyle's mom. He remembered her. Remembered one time caddying for her old man at the club and seeing her at the bar, waiting. A great-looking lady. And that was Lyle's mother. Small world, man! But boy the old man had been a real prick. Telling all his rotten jokes, yukking it up with the foursome.

He finished the plants and went back to the kitchen to put the watering can away.

Having him in the house made her so nervous she could scarcely function. She hurt herself getting the robe off, the nightgown on, the robe back on again. She finally managed to get it all done and stood listening, hearing him moving around downstairs. Glancing over at the door, satisfying herself it was closed and locked. But it didn't help much. She couldn't help feeling he could see through closed doors and clothes, could see her standing naked. Already exhausted from being on her feet for too long, she longed to lie down.

She quickly dried her hair. Taking ages, nevertheless. Maybe he'd get fed up and leave, she wouldn't have to see him. But no, as she came creaking down the stairs, she could hear him fussing with cups, pouring coffee.

She sank down on the sofa, catching her breath.

"What kind of operation did you have?" he asked, carrying in the coffee.

"How do you know I had any kind of operation?"

"First of all, you're in your nightgown in the middle of the day. And second, I could tell by the way you came creeping down the stairs. When my mom had surgery, she did that same number. Hey! You're supposed to be stretched out. I'll run up and grab a pillow and stuff." And went off before she could respond. Returning to make the sofa cosy, insisting she put her feet up and rest against the pillow, then covering her with the afghan from her bedroom.

"Okay," he said, putting the cup of coffee into her hands. "What was it?"

Why don't you leave me alone what are you trying to prove? "Cancer." She spat out the word then waited to see his reaction.

He wasn't ready, couldn't absorb it. "*Jee-sus!*" he said softly. She wasn't going to die, was she? He didn't think he could handle that. He couldn't just sit there, had to move, got up and walked halfway across the room, came back, walked away again. "Cancer? What kind of cancer?" He took several steps toward her, then stopped. Looking fearful.

She wanted to put the cup down but her experience in the past two weeks had shown her that certain moves were exceedingly painful. And reaching out sideways, stretching, was one of those. She had to do it in slow stages. And hated the idea of having him see her do it. So continued to sit holding the cup, looking anywhere but at him.

"Is it over?" he asked. "Or just starting? Tell me! I really want to know."

"Why?" She looked at him.

"*Why?* Because I care is why. What's the matter with you?" he asked, confounded by her. "You tell someone you've got cancer and you expect that person to nod and smile and say, that's nice, lovely weather we're having. Are you terminal?"

"No, I'm not terminal. I don't have it anymore. They say."

"You don't sound too convinced."

"It's a little hard . . ." her voice trailed off.

"You don't have it anymore," he repeated.

"That's right. They took everything out."

He came back and sat down. "Why didn't you want me to know you were in the hospital? Wait a minute." He held up his hand. "I'm getting the picture. You didn't want me coming to visit. Right? Sure, that's right. You thought I'd get the word and come charging over with flowers. I would've. What's so awful about that?"

"Please, I'm tired . . ."

"Okay." He lowered his voice. "Okay. I'm really sorry. You don't have to believe it or even listen, but I'm sorry. I think it sucks. Shit! That really *sucks*! How long d'you have to stay at home?"

"Five or six weeks." Sucks?

"I'll get your stuff and like that," he offered. "Groceries, you know. Papers."

"Jess." She wet her lips, defeated by him. "What . . . ?" She gave up. He made absolutely no sense to her.

"You have to eat," he said reasonably. "And you're not supposed to go galloping around, up and down stairs, hanging over the stove or making beds or any of that. I know all about it. I told you, my mom . . ."

"I can manage," she interrupted.

"Hey!" he said. "*Let* me! It won't kill you. I'm not a bad cook and some people think I'm even pretty good company. I'll bring over my cassette player for you and my Scrabble set, we'll play backgammon. Come on. You'll go squirrelly all by yourself here, living on toast. That's no good. Especially with Thanksgiving coming up in another week."

She closed her eyes. I want to let you I should say something but I don't understand you or what you want why you keep offering.

"What?" he asked, alarmed. "Something hurt or something?"

She opened her eyes. "I'm just tired."

"Don't *do* that!" He smiled. "Really threw a scare into me, the way you did that."

He waited for her to say something, react, something; but she simply sat there looking at him. He wanted to say something heavy, something profound and meaningful.

"I'm crazy for this house," he said. "Right on the beach and everything. How long've you had this place?"

"Eleven years." She sighed.

"Probably got it for peanuts compared to the market today. Prices around here are insane. I guess you know that, though. I was looking to rent a place up here but there's nothing under four-fifty a month. So, I'm still hanging out in the apartment over the garage at my folks' place. It's not bad. Considering." The screaming room, he called it.

She couldn't hold the cup any longer and turned cautiously to set it down on the coffee table, wanting a cigarette but she'd left them upstairs. She sank back against the pillow, resigned to having him watch her.

"Hey! I didn't tell you about the shop. Wait till you see it! Everybody's been freaking out. It's fantastic! No kidding! We've been really busy, too. Sold all the sale stuff. Had a few people interested in buying those two wildflowers you did."

"*No!*" she almost shouted. "They're not for sale!"

"I know that. I know."

She couldn't take any more. And got up. Too quickly. So that it hurt, everything pulling straining. Dizziness and nausea.

"What're you *doing*?" he asked, jumping up, seeing her eyes going out of focus. "You shouldn't be jumping around that way."

"Please!" she said faintly. "Leave me alone!"

The stairs. She'd go back up, lie down, breathe deeply until the sudden pain went away. The floor felt peculiar under her feet, wavy, like sand and the stairs miles away.

"What're you doing?" he asked plaintively, seeing her reaching out for the banister like someone caught in quicksand. "Oh, shit!" he said. "I never in my life saw anyone go to so much trouble to avoid me. You look like you're going to pass out. Are you going to pass out?"

His voice roared distorted in her ears, a wall of black closing her off, the floor of her mouth filling with bitter liquid.

"I knew it," he said, racing over to catch her as she began to crumple. Slipping one arm around her back, the other under her knees. Scooping her up and carrying her back to the sofa. "What did I ever do to you?" he said. "Or maybe it isn't even me. Is that it? Look at that! Out like a fucking light!" He settled her head on the pillow and covered her with the afghan. Her face had gone an odd color under the residue of tan. "Killing yourself to get away from me." He straightened and went upstairs to her bedroom. Found her cigarettes and lighter, a book on the bedside table that had a bookmark in it. He stopped in the bathroom, opened the medicine cabinet, spotted the pills.

Well, he thought, opening the packet to see one pill missing, at least now I know you don't hate men altogether. He returned the pills to the medicine cabinet and continued on downstairs, placing the cigarettes close to the edge of the coffee table and the book nearby, all within easy reaching distance.

"Don't move your ass from that sofa," he said, knowing full well she wasn't hearing him. "I come back and find you moved, I'll whup you good." He smiled and dropped down beside the sofa, looking at her face. "You're so stupid," he whispered. "I wouldn't do any kind of number on you. But somebody did, huh? You look like a kid, you jerk." He touched her still-damp hair. "Where d'you get that 'old' shit from? Anybody ever tell you you have this incredibly great mouth?" He touched her lower lip. Split. The upper lip, too. "You need some Chap Stik or something." He looked at her throat, then at her hand, picked it up, studying it. "Pretty hands," he said, gently setting down her hand. He stood up, got his jacket and let himself out.

She wet her lips, tasting peppermint. And opened her eyes, touching her fingers to her mouth. They came away sticky.

"Kissing Potion." He laughed. "I couldn't lay my hands on any Chap Stik, if you can imagine that. An entire drugstore without any Chap Stik. But that should do the trick. You'd better be hungry because I've cooked up enough stuff for the entire Russian delegation."

"What time is it?" she asked thickly.

"Just about five."

"What about the shop . . . ?"

"New deal. Wednesday's we're only open a half day."

"God!" She let her head fall back and lay staring at the ceiling.

"After dinner," he said, "we're going to play backgammon."

"I don't *play* backgammon."

"I'm going to teach you. I'm very good at teaching."

She turned her head, smelling woodsmoke. He'd lit a fire. She'd never brought Ian here, he'd never seen the house. She hadn't wanted to bring him here. Something had warned her not to; because if it was simply a trick or some sort of game he was playing, she'd never, after, be able to live here. It had always been her place, hers alone. And now this boy, this kid, this—whatever—was making fires and cooking dinner.

"You passed right out, you know that?" he said, lightly accusing. "That was so goddamned dumb I could hardly believe it."

"All right," she said. "Okay! *All right!*"

"All right what? What're you talking about?"

"You're here. I can't do anything . . . *Okay!*"

"You know," he said, "you think I'm crazy." He dropped down in front of her to eye-to-eye range. "But I'll tell you, I think *you're* crazy. I mean, you just had major surgery. Right? And you're so fucking—what? I don't know what the hell it is you are, but you're so into it, you'll practically give yourself a relapse just so you don't have to stay in the same room with me. Is it personal or just general?" He hung there, waiting for an answer. "Oh, *shit!*" he said miserably, hurting for her. "Don't cry! If it's really getting to you that bad, I'll split. I don't want to be responsible for messing anybody's head. I'm just trying to be *nice.*"

"I know that," she sobbed, covering her eyes with her hand. "I know you are."

"Stop fighting me for a while," he said, daring to touch her hair. "Somebody's got to help out. That's all. And I'm good at that stuff."

"Just stop *swearing* at me," she hiccuped, still hiding behind her hand.

He laughed and withdrew his hand from her hair. "You clown! That's not swearing! That's just talking. When I start swearing, I promise you'll know the difference. Here, have a smoke while I get the salad finished." He put a cigarette between her fingers then went back to the kitchen.

She wiped her eyes on the sleeve of her dressing gown and raised herself to a sitting position before lighting the cigarette. Asking herself, Why am I fighting? I don't even know what I'm fighting or why. Just that I don't know how to deal with him, can't understand so many of the things he says. Afraid he thinks of me as . . . something. What? No one does the things he does. Not without a reason. Motives. But I have to accept, can't fight because I haven't any strength. None. God! More frightening than anything else to be so weak, so completely powerless. Feeling the pain there where nothing exists anymore. Nothing inside. Everything severed, the edges sealed. Empty.

He cleared the coffee table, preparing to bring in the food, noticing her distraction. Her eyes fixed somewhere over there. She didn't see him. She was thinking about the babies. Trying to understand how they could have put her there, next to the new mothers. Listening to them coo and cluck over the babies. The sounds of infants wailing. She'd been desperate to escape the mothers, the infants, the nursery nurses. They daunted her. And her mother saying, Was it the truth? Did you really not want one of your own?

Answering, I don't know the truth. About anything. I'll never know. *I don't know.*

It might have been something like all those stories, those fables she'd told through the years about being satisfied with her life as it was. Alone. With her shop and her house and holidays like Christmas and Thanksgiving she spent with her mother and brother and Will. But alone. Lying, claiming she found satisfaction in a life that hadn't any relationship at all with the cache of dreams in her head. All actively spinning, complete to the minutest detail. Images of lovers and glowing, perfect days spent in the company of one who loved her. No problems, endless sunshine, perfect weather.

Jess was standing there with a tray, waiting for her to tune back in.

"Soon's you land"—he grinned—"we can dig in."

"Sorry," she said absently, accepting the tray. Staring at the plateful of food. Her hand over her mouth. Just staring.

"Is there a bug in it?" he asked, sitting cross-legged on the floor in front of the coffee table.

"What? No. I don't think I can eat this. It does look very good, but I don't think I can."

Daddy screaming the length of the table. You'll sit there all night until you finish that food. But she couldn't. So she sat in the dining room, the whole house dark, the food congealing on the plate. Couldn't. Their voices upstairs.

Shouting. You're a sadist, forcing always forcing. She's a child. Children don't care for the same foods adults do. Why can't you leave her alone? Why? The rage in his voice. Barking at her. You go down there and I'll put you through the fucking wall, Fran. Leave the son of a bitch kid, she can sit there all goddamned night but she's going to eat that food. What d'you think you're doing? You're not going down there. I am, Jack. This is cruel. Lyle's a good little girl. She doesn't deserve this. And neither do I. I don't understand why you have to devil her so, why you can't leave her alone. Half the reason she is the way she is is because you never give her a chance to relax and just be a little girl.

Sounds. Struggling. A loud echoing smack like the sound of a gun being fired so loud in the silent house. Her mother running down the hall. Familiar footsteps. Running. Then another sound, noises in the hallway. A door slamming. More noises. Muffled. A cry. Doors slamming open. Footsteps. Running. Coming down the stairs. Her mother trying to fix her hair with a trembling hand, a quivery smile. Saying, You go up to bed now, dear. You don't have to eat that. You go up. Richard's already asleep.

I wanted to say, *Turn around*, my heart beating so hard he was right behind you in the doorway right there his face purple. Turn around he'll kill you.

Go ahead, Lyle. Go to bed.

I *told* you not to interfere!

Go on, dear. *Go on!*

Fleeing. Shrinking past his figure in the doorway, then away up the stairs. Stopping at the top, terrified of what he'd do. Crouching in the dark, watching him pick up the plate of food, put his hands into it. A handful of food smearing it over her face into her hair pushing it into her mouth. Mother's fists swinging colliding making no impression flies pestering a bear. He threw the plate at the wall. Terrible words, terrible saying those things to Mummy don't hurt her. Crying at the top of the stairs, gripping the railing, don't hurt Mummy. Fucking bitch. Cunt you cunt. Falling to the floor with a big thud. Then the awful silence heavy breathing he was killing her killing her the sounds she made pushing at him trying to get him off his body moving up and down on hers killing her

crushing her until Mummy died she died went all still not
moving she was dead just the sound of Daddy breathing so
hard and Mummy not even crying anymore dead.

Creeping into the linen closet to hide knowing he'd kill
her now and Richie, too, filling her mouth with a pillow-
case so he wouldn't hear wouldn't find her crying and crying and if Richie was sleeping and stayed very quiet he
couldn't kill Richie. The dark and the house all silent he'd
come up and try to find her. She'd go down in the morning and Mummy would be dead on the dining room floor
her clothes all pushed up.

But in the morning the closet door opened and there she
was looking just like always with Blue Grass and her hair
all clean. Did it really happen? How could it have happened if she was here with her perfume, no smell, no food
in her hair not dead? Darling, what are you doing in here?
Gave me the fright of my life finding your bed empty
come out of there, Lyle. It's all right, dear. Come, come.
Her hands reaching Mummy not dead.

"Hey! Come on. You've got to eat just a little. I can't
believe how thin you got in just two weeks."

"I'd like to go upstairs," she said, her mouth dry.

"You're running away from me again," he said sadly.

She turned her head slowly to look at him. This man.
Not a kid. Not a boy. A man. He was. Over six feet tall.
With thick black hair, black eyebrows and lashes, deep
blue eyes. The whitest skin, very red lips, color in his
cheeks. Wide shoulders, long legs, narrow hips. A man. If
I don't eat you'll push my face in the food smash the plate
to prove you're stronger. She wet her lips, realizing she
couldn't go on fleeing from him. He'd keep on stopping
her.

"Eat," he said. "Just a little. Please?"

"It does smell good." She gave him a small smile. It
made his lungs expand hopefully.

"It *is* good." He beamed at her. "Have I ever lied to
you, lady?"

She shook her head.

"You've got the goddamndest smile," he said. "Really!"

She picked up her fork, tasted. "It *is* good," she said.
And smiled again. As if to show him she did know how,
after all. He leaned all the way over the coffee table, all
the way over to kiss her softly, lightly on the mouth. She

remained motionless until he was safely back on the floor, eating again.

, What's going to happen oh I know what's going to happen and you'll go off disgusted because I'm empty inside, stripped. Isn't that what's going to happen? Isn't that why you're here, really? Isn't it?

Twelve

—◆◆◆—

The shop was totally transformed. The entire feeling and atmosphere of the place lightened, brightened; altered. She stood looking in, wanting to cry. Because what he'd done, what he'd created was so evidently a work of love. And she felt unworthy, not equal to being the recipient of such a gift.

"It's beautiful," she said, looking around, trying to take it all in. "Just beautiful. You were right." She let her eyes fall on him, finally. "Everyone likes it?"

"They love it. They come in, have a cup of coffee, hang around and wind up spending twice as much money. Wait till you see the books. Mrs. Wallace was oohing and aahing over them last week. She and your mother with their heads together like a couple of proud hens."

She sat down on one of the new stools. He'd even painted the cash register. With white enamel. God! What does it mean that someone like you would come here wanting to be here, wanting to put so much of yourself into something that isn't yours? Her body was filled with odd darting pains she doubted would ever completely leave her. And the sight of the place made her chest hurt, as if something were trying to take root between her breasts and was determined to succeed.

"You're remarkable," she said. "And the sales are up?"

"Have a look for yourself."

"I don't know . . . what to say . . . how to thank you." Her eyes wandering over gleaming surfaces, new textures. More than merely decoration. He'd created art. It made her grieve for the loss of the talent she might have nurtured had she had any belief whatsoever in her own possibilities.

He tapped her on the shoulder, caught her attention, pointed at his mouth. She looked confused.

"Here!" he pointed again at his mouth. "That'll say it all nicely."

Her face took fire. But she did it. Put her closed lips against his for the briefest moment. Then withdrew.

"That wasn't so bad," he said very softly. "Was it?"

She didn't answer, couldn't.

"I'll get your stuff then take you home," he said, going to her desk to collect up the wildflower sketches, the canvas. "There's one other part to the thank-you," he said, returning.

"What?"

"Dinner Saturday night. I'm taking you. You're allowed, aren't you?"

"You don't have to . . ."

"D'you have any jeans? No. You wouldn't. Something easy, okay? Just slacks, or like that. Comfortable. I'll close up and come get you." He kept talking as he took her by the arm, directed her out, into his car. Saying, "One of these days we'll have to get you some jeans. You'd be good. Saturday we're going to celebrate."

"What are we celebrating?"

"Who knows? Surviving four weeks housebound without going bananas. Whatever you like." Celebrating the fact that you're starting to stop fighting, letting some feeling happen. Letting me get close to you. If you'd just let me show you, tell you what it means how it feels getting close to you.

During the following Sunday's dinner with her mother and Will and Richard, who was with yet another new girlfriend, she suddenly found herself wondering about Jess. What was he doing? Did he spend time with his family? Or was he alone at that moment? She hated the idea of his being alone. Perhaps she should have asked him along. Her mother wouldn't have minded. Her mother liked Jess, said so often.

"He's charming," she'd told Lyle on her visit to the house the previous week. "There's something about him. I can't define it. Or even put it properly into words. Something . . . pure. He is what he is. Nothing more, nothing less. Gifted. He's also," Frances said carefully, "very fond of you."

"That's ridiculous. I'm his employer."

"I won't debate the point."

I should have invited him along, she thought now. He's probably alone. Why does it hurt, the idea of his being alone? He is, so much of the time. And that doesn't make sense. Someone young, and so good-looking. No sense at all. Always off home early, never staying later than ten or ten-thirty.

Forcing her to become accustomed to on-the-mouth kisses as a ritual goodbye. Closed-mouth kisses that felt safe to her. So she gave them, accepted them. Feeling a small shock of surprise and pleasure every time. Constantly wondering why, what, how? Wondering.

Upon arriving home that night, she telephoned him. Overheated, heart triple-beating; listening to the ringing, ready to hang up. Then hearing his voice. She said, "Hello," sounding a thousand years old. And he said, "Hey! You're calling me! Wow! This is the first time you've ever called me."

"I just wanted to know how your day was."

"I went to see *Star Wars*. That's a very good flick. Have you seen it? How did the Sunday dinner go?"

"Oh fine, fine."

"This is one very big occasion," he said. "You called me."

"Well, yes." She groped for words. "I'll—um—talk to you tomorrow."

"Bet your sweet life you will. Sleep well."

"Yes."

She put down the receiver. Hands dripping. Mouth quivering, caught midway between laughter and despair. Am I completely crazy, phoning him? But they were going out to dinner Saturday. He'd asked her. So it was all right to telephone. Wasn't it? Just a friendly thing to do. God! Everything I ever knew is changed.

He took her to Boodle's. Noisy, crowded. They sat side by side on a banquette and she was so unbearably aware of the pressure of his thigh against hers that she could scarcely swallow.

"Food no good?" he asked her.

"Oh, no. I mean, it's fine. Very good."

"Then eat it. You're still way too thin. Eat up. We're going dancing after this."

"I couldn't," she protested. "No."

He was shaking his head. "Dancing! No arguments.

When you take me out, you'll get to pick the places and the action. Tonight, I'm taking you. Dancing. Eat up."

Dancing. Dancing?

They drove up the turnpike and she wondered where on earth he was taking her. Grateful that he drove well. As if he knew how sick it made her being thrown about in a moving vehicle. He pulled off the turnpike at exit 13. Darien?

"There's nothing here, is there?"

"Sure there is," he said. "You'll see."

Up the Post Road, cutting through the A & P parking lot. To the Plankhouse.

The place was packed. A blast of hot, thick, smoky air hitting them as they came through the front door. Singles lining the bar. Everyone watching the dancers on the small dance-floor. And the duo up on the stand. Soft rock blaring out of huge speakers. Jess elbowed his way through the crowd, his hand tight around hers, making a pathway through. Finding two seats vacant at a table at the far end of the room.

"Mind if we share?" he asked the two young women already seated there.

They shook their heads, moving their things.

She sat down feeling ludicrously out of place. Everyone looking so young. And so desperate, somehow. Their eyes constantly moving, scanning the crowd. And the two girls sharing the table, devouring Jess with their eyes. Hungry eyes. Whispering to each other. Casting strange, hard, almost angry looks at Lyle. She knew they thought she didn't deserve to be there with Jess.

I'm too old to be here, she thought miserably. People are staring. Trying to understand why someone as young and vital as you are out with someone as old and unremarkable as me. She felt as if she'd started sagging, wrinkling, aging at a tremendously accelerated rate.

"What would you like to drink?" he asked, leaning very close to her in order to make himself heard over the music. She was overwhelmingly tempted to touch him, assure herself he was real.

"White wine?"

"Fine."

He ordered, then sat back, smiling at her. Liking so much the way she looked, the softness of her face. Everybody else looked to him to be composed of sharp lines and sudden angles; harsh corners, jutting knobs of bone and vibration.

She was grateful the music was so loud. It was close to impossible to talk. She lit a cigarette and looked at the people, very aware of Jess watching her.

The waitress set down their drinks, went away.

"Want to taste?" he offered, holding his glass out to her.

"What is it?"

"Cognac."

"No, thank you."

The music stopped. People left the dance floor. The duo started something slow. He held out his hand. Quietly said, "Come on. Dance with me."

Wanting to say no but powerless again. He had her hand. She had to get up, go. Move with him into the middle of that small area where he gathered her up, drew her in against his body; whispering, "I knew you'd feel good. I knew you would." She couldn't speak. Stunned with pleasure just to have him hold her, feeling like some biblical lost soul adrift on a sea of illicit joy. Turned to a feather, to follow his body moving hers; aware—unable to ignore it—of his response to her. There. Locked so close she couldn't possibly escape the evidence. Had no desire to. Incapable of moving even fractionally away from him. Breathing deeply, then unable to breathe at all for long moments. The smooth softness of his cheek, the warmth of his neck. His lips against her ear, whispering. His words causing her eyelids to flutter closed because it didn't seem right or fair that he would want to say the things he was saying, not to her. Not when she'd dreamed always of the man who'd take her dancing. The man who was as tall as Jess and as hard and held her this way, but whose hair had gone silvery, into wings, and whose voice was sonorous with depths of wisdom and maturity. Not this. Not this voice, whispering, this body holding her.

". . . want you, going crazy wanting you I know you can't, not now. You know you want me, too. I'm waiting and I want you to know I'm waiting. Jesus you feel so good move so well. I know you can't stand it hate it I won't say any more but just for a minute oh Jesus, Lyle the way you feel don't put me down I can't help the way I feel, just go with it, go with it . . ."

It couldn't be real, couldn't be happening. It was all just part of the dream, the dream continuing. She kept her eyes closed, allowing him to take her wherever he chose. Dreaming.

At ten-thirty he looked at his watch, tossed down the last of his cognac and signaled for the waitress. "I'm going to take you home now." He smiled, running his forefinger over the back of Lyle's hand.

He saw her to her front door, gave her another of those fraternal kisses on the mouth then went loping off down the walk. She went inside quaking with emotion, battling against it. And when she finally lay down to sleep with her eyes closed, she heard his voice again whispering in her ear. Want you want you feel so good want you. It made her empty insides ache.

Sunday morning early, he showed up with the *Times* and a bag of croissants.

"I came for breakfast," he announced, depositing the paper on the sofa. "I came to cook it. And play some backgammon. You're getting too good."

She looked flustered, unsure. He wanted to open his arms, close them around her. He wanted to photograph her. With the lace of her nightgown showing at the neckline of her robe. All softness. Her hair disarranged.

"I had an idea," he said, going out to the kitchen, opening the refrigerator door. "I think it's a good one, too. Want to hear?"

"What?" she asked, lighting a cigarette. Trembling.

"You know those wildflowers you've been doing? You know how everybody keeps wanting to buy them? Well, what I've been thinking you should do is make them up into a book. Do a dozen plates. I could do the photography. We could both work on the illustrations and the text. Not that you need a whole lot in the way of text. But it'd be dynamite. Really! There's nothing else like it on the market. I know. I checked." He put four eggs on the counter. Then, on second thought, reached in for two more and a package of cheddar. "So what do you think?"

"I wouldn't have any idea where to begin." That crowded feeling between her breasts again. Roots taking hold, tendrils winding themselves around her lungs; squeezing.

"We can get format ideas from some of the other books," he said, getting out butter and a package of bacon, the orange juice, cream. "Just go through a whole bunch of them, pick out what looks like the best stuff, then adapt it to suit our book. A dozen full-color plates of the finished pieces. Then black and white plates with the color codes. It's different, unusual. And they're beautiful. People could either do them up as individual pieces, frame them or make them into pillows. Or use all twelve together to make a rug."

"That's a lot of work, Jess. I mean, I'd have to do all the canvases. Then color code them. Then actually work them up. It would take me months to do that many pieces. Not to mention blocking and finishing them."

"What else've we got to do that's so exciting?" he said. "The shop's all finished. Business is great. You don't want to teach classes. I think it's a terrific idea. And I'll help you with the needlepoint. I've already done one piece. It's kind of messy because I had kind of a hard time figuring out how to reverse on basket weave. But I've got it down now, so we could both work on them."

"But that's only part of it," she said. "I haven't any idea how one goes about getting something published."

"Let's get the thing done first. Then we'll worry about finding a publisher."

"It does sound interesting."

"Something to do on long winter evenings," he intoned. "While the winds are blasting the clapboard and creating blowbacks in the fireplace. Want to try?"

"Okay. All right."

"Great! I'm going to make a soufflé. Like soufflés?"

"Where did you learn to cook?"

"I fool around with it when I get home from work. Keeps me off the streets and out of trouble. I've been thinking about trying one of these ever since I saw that set of soufflé dishes you've got."

"They were a Christmas gift one year," she said. "From Mother. I've never used them."

"Well, ta-da! Get out the big one and we'll christen it."

She got down the dish, then said, "I'll get dressed."

"Too bad," he said, succeeding in further flustering her. She turned and went off.

After that weekend, they seemed to be constantly together. At the house in the evenings, doing the wildflowers. And the weekends. He took her to the movies, to dinner, to walk on the beach. He was always there. And always gone before eleven at night. She had no idea what was happening. Except that she was learning to enjoy his company, to savor his wit, appreciate his cooking. And to depend upon those chaste hello and goodbye kisses.

There were no formalities. Nothing planned. At the end of the fifth week, she returned to work. And each evening one or the other of them closed up the shop. They said goodbye and she drove home to Westport, he to his garage apartment in town. Within an hour he was at her door. With a pizza, or a bag of hamburgers, or groceries. Or, having located her store of boldness, she'd pick up the telephone, dial his number and say, "Come over. I'll give you dinner. I need some help on this illustration."

She no longer even dared question what was happening. She thought perhaps it might be friendship. But she couldn't quite believe that. Love was out of the question. Impossible. Still, it was so good having him arrive to share meals with her, share work with her, share time. So good to sit and watch his hand move, working on the illustrations. Or having him clicking away with his camera. He never seemed bored in her company and she thought he was possessed of admirable patience to tolerate someone like her. Someone older, slower, less inspired, less imaginative, less everything.

The week before Christmas, Frances called.

"Is Jess going to be alone over Christmas?" she asked.

"I don't know. Why?"

"Why don't you bring him along, dear? No one should be alone on Christmas."

"Are you sure?"

"Of course I'm sure. Aren't *you* sure yet?"

"Sure about what?"

"He's in love with you, Lyle. Don't you know it?"

"Mother! That's absurd!"

"I'll tell you something even more absurd," Frances said.

"God! What?"

"You're in love with him, too. The two of you are very sweet together."

"This entire conversation's ridiculous!"

"I agree. But he's decent and kind and caring. And he's not another Ian. Although I strongly suspect you think he is. Can't you tell the difference, Lyle?"

"Mother, I'll *ask* him," she said impatiently, anxious to be done with the conversation.

"Richard's bringing another new girlfriend. I don't know where he finds them."

"Maybe he uses a modeling agency."

Frances laughed appreciatively. "I must remember that. That's very funny. Let me know about Jess, will you? For place settings."

"I *hate* this conversation!"

"Naturally, you do. Call me back and let me know."

Jess said, "Great! I'd love it. Whose idea was it?"

"My mother's," she admitted.

"And not yours," he chided. "I hoped it was yours."

"It wasn't."

"I'll get even." He smiled and ruffled her hair. "We're going out Christmas eve," he announced. "Dancing."

Somehow, the timing seemed ominous. She had her office visit with Dr. Wojeski on the 22nd and he said, "Everything looks fine. Good as new." He gave her a prescription for estrogen, told her she could recommence her sexual life. She wanted to slide out of the chair and hide behind his desk. "Of course," he went on, unaware of her tremendous discomfort, "if it doesn't feel right, or if there's pain, don't keep on. You're going to be aware of certain differences. But don't be bothered. You'll get used to it."

God! She escaped the office and breathed in deeply the biting cold air outside. Certain differences. What? She had no idea what he was talking about, didn't care to know. Hurried back to the shop to help Jess with the crowd of customers all doing last-minute gift-shopping.

"How did it go?" he asked her in a quiet moment.

"How did what go?"

"Your checkup."

"Fine, fine." She fled to help a customer. Was everyone keeping tabs on her medical comings and goings, the state of her body? My body my God! He didn't mean it couldn't have, all the things he said that night and now he was going to take her dancing again. She attended to the customers, refusing to think about any of it. All just dreams, part of other dreams. Every time he caught her eyes or smiled at her or in passing put his hand innocently on her shoulder or her arm, everything in her started; shocked. Frightened.

He took her to Pancho Villa's and introduced her to Mexican food. She loved it, burned her mouth on the hot sauce, ate too much and drank a second glass of wine. To cool her mouth, she told herself. To cool her body heat.

Out to his car, back to the turnpike, down to exit 13. She shrank inside, knowing they were going back to the Plankhouse.

He ordered drinks, held out his hand to her, led her onto the floor. And reeled her in. Smoothly, easily, fluidly. Brought her all the way in so that his cheek lay against hers, his arm encircled her waist, his hand enclosed hers, his chest a warm wall. Forcing her to be aware of her own body, her breasts flattened against his chest, her hips aligned with his, thighs and knees touching. She felt dizzy, distraught, unable to focus. Her eyes closing heavily, the music pulsing in her temples, their bodies moving totally in tune. And in her ear, his voice whispering.

". . . love holding you I can feel your nipples they've gone hard you smell so good we're not going to sit down we're just going to stay here dance every dance so I don't have to let you go do you know how pretty you look you do look so pretty and your hair's so soft . . ."

It made her palsied with nervousness. It made her dreamy, avid. She felt as if she might blow apart, half of her going one way, half going the other. She couldn't speak at all, couldn't smile, couldn't think. Aware only of the different textures. Of his hair, his cheek, his neck. Of his collar, his sweater, his hand, his trousers. Hardness, softness. And the quivering, racing response inside herself. Fear was like a chorus of screams in her head.

At ten o'clock, he paid the check. "I'll take you home now," he said. "Are you finished with that?"

She looked stupidly down at her drink, nodded.

When they got outside, it was snowing. He laughed. Happily, like a child. Grabbed her hand and ran with her through the snow to the car. "Man, I *love* snow! I knew it'd make it for Christmas! What's the matter, Lyle? Are you okay?"

"Fine. I'm fine." God if this is a game a trick I don't know what I'll do if you're playing with me don't do this to me.

Her teeth chattered, her stomach lurched and bounced throughout the ride. She hurried out of the car, desperate to get inside, to get warm, to get back inside of herself. Forgetting him for a moment in her haste. But how could she forget him when he was there, coming up the walk after her, coming inside, pushing off his boots as she unzipped hers. Taking her by the wrist, pulling her upright. Strong, she thought. My God! You're strong.

He kissed her on the mouth. She did as she always did: received it.

"Kiss me," he said. "Really kiss me." His arms tight around her, his mouth covering hers, urging her mouth open. She kissed him, tossed directly into a furnace kissing him his tongue in her mouth urgent she couldn't break it make it end going on until he was holding her up moving her into the living room kissing her blind, deaf, witless.

His mouth left hers and he began taking her out of her fur coat, unfastening it; his hands going to the buttons on her cardigan, then her blouse while she frantically tried to get her mouth to make words. "Wait! I *can't!*"

"Yes, you can," he said, determined.

"No! Jess, you're so . . . *young!*"

"Oh, Jesus, Lyle! So're *you!*" He pulled at her clothing, his hands here, there, in back of her. Plucking her hands out of the way, not to be deterred. Exposing her breasts. Exclaiming, "See! *Young!*"

"No, I can't! I haven't bathed! No!"

"Good! I want to taste *you*, not your soap."

"God! *Jess!*"

"No!" he insisted, yanking down the zipper on her slacks. Taking his hands from her only long enough to throw off his jacket. Then he had her by the hand and was towing her up the stairs. Her clothes hanging open, her free hand trying to hold everything closed. Ushering her into her bedroom, then stopping with such a weary-sounding sigh, saying, "Just stay here, stand still. Don't move!" as he removed his clothes right there in front of her, took everything off, then advanced on her. "I can't wait anymore," he whispered. "I just can't stand it." Taking away her cardigan, pausing to touch her throat, his eyes moving over her face. Then her blouse. Clothes piling up on the floor.

"Jess, it's no good! I can't! Please, I can't!"

The lace brassiere. He pulled her hands away.

"You're perfect," he said softly. "Jesus! Perfect."

His hands on her breasts, his mouth again covering hers.

It isn't right it's no good I can't.

Impatiently tugging at her slacks, getting them down around her hips, the tights, too. Everything caught at her hips. Kissing her, his hand slipping down over her belly, down between her thighs, fingers sliding over her. She threw her arms around his neck, pressing herself against him. Scared to see, to feel, to have it all turn out emptiness and loneliness afterward.

He got the last of her clothes off and put her down on the bed, lay on top of her.

"You're so good," he said, looking at her breasts, her shoulders; his hand smoothing her breast, going around and around it. "Don't think about it, Lyle. Let it happen. I want you, want to feel you, touch you." And then he slipped away off her, his hands skimming over her, up and down her belly, following the scar down, easing open her thighs, his hand moving up and down her inner thighs. His cheek against her breast, then his tongue touching her throat. His head moving, hands dragging slowly down the length of her body, around, under. Lifting her.

"I dreamed about this," he said, "doing this." And kissed her there.

Oh my God don't do that what are you doing? She twisted, seeking to get away. He held her down, held her still, his mouth moving.

She wanted to hate it, couldn't. He was taking her directly past that dreadful gritty feeling and beyond, into pleasure. How could anything so grotesque feel as good as this? Terrible pleasure. Mortifying pleasure. Firing her up, rendering her liquid. Removing her from herself and plunging her directly into the heart of performance so that it didn't matter what did it matter? She was compelled to go where he led, letting it happen it was what he wanted and she couldn't stop it happening. Clenching her teeth with pleasure, wanting him inside her. He was making her feel as if having him inside would be good, would be right. She had no idea what to do, couldn't touch him, longed to touch him. But then he stopped, coming down on top of her again, kissing her mouth.

"That's what you taste like." He smiled. "Good."

Then, delighting in her astonishment, he turned her, put her down on her belly and held the hair away so he could kiss the nape of her neck, downy; taste it with his tongue, take his tongue across her shoulder blades, down the length of her spine; down into the heat. Lifting her. Tasting, touching. Savoring her, filled with a kind of delirium at finally being able to fill his hands with her breasts, their softness; to take his hands and mold them to her waist, her buttocks, undergoing a kind of madness in at last having succeeded in displacing her fear.

She clutched the sheet with both hands, ashamed of her pathetic little cries. Then past shame, he was lifting her more, up onto her knees and so easily, without pain, so easily, he brought himself all the way into her and she was somehow astride his lap, impaled. While his hands played her out, drew her attention away from the echo of Dr. Wojeski's voice telling her there would be certain differences and there were, she *was* empty inside, he was striking nothing. Moving inside her organless body. Yet there was pleasure. How could that be when there was nothing left to provide it? But still it was there, happening, all of her tensing, getting closer, closer, his hands stroking, knowing. His mouth in the curve of her neck, his chest damp against her back. My God! she thought, frenzied. Nothing, no part he hadn't claimed. His fingers rhythmically pressing, hand gently kneading her breast, tongue on her neck in her ear. She was madly rising and falling a strangled cry her fingers digging into his knees; sobbing while he held her steady, kept it happening until his arms were wrapped around her middle and his head lay on her shoulder and she rested dissolved in his lap, hearing him whispering, "Jesus I love you I love you Lyle so much I love you."

Thirteen

◆—◆—▶

He took her caution, her reserve, her shame and embarrassment, and discarded them; wrapped them into a crumpled, untidy package and burned them. Refusing to accept less than everything she had to give. Telling her, "Don't feel that way! Just enjoy it! You're terrific!" Insisting that she accept satisfaction, pleasure, as her due. Held her down over his mouth, covered her breasts with his hands. His expression rapt. How could he look that way, doing what he was doing? But never mind never mind God the feeling, the *feeling*! Her body no longer her body but something capable, beyond her wildest fantasizings, of pulsing, convulsive response.

He cooled her down, then fired her up; handling her with effortless ease and strength, whispering, "If you hate it, we won't," stretched out beneath her, urging her carefully down on him. Asking, "Is it all right for you?"

"Yes."

"Hate it?"

"God! No!"

"Come here so I can kiss you. It feels good?"

A hiss, "Yes."

"Jesus! You're so much. I'm not hurting you?"

"No, no."

"And it's good?"

"Hmm, yes."

"I love you so goddamned much. Do you know that?"

She hadn't words or answers or thoughts. Because he could hold her hard, plunging deep hard and she was astounded to discover she wanted all this, wanting hardness. Yes yes yes hard.

Things she'd never done, never dreamed of doing, never knew could be a part of dreaming. And willingly accepted instruction, accepted praise of her previously unsuspected

139

aptitudes. Until it seemed as if she'd always known and was performing naturally, spontaneously.

"I really should go home." He looked at her clock on the bedside table. "It's late."

"Stay with me. I've never had . . . anyone . . . stay."

He looked uncertain. She wondered why.

"I want so much to have you stay, to hold you." *If I open my arms, let you go, tomorrow it will all be reduced to a fantastic fantasy. Something I dreamed.*

"Okay!" He held her face between his hands and kissed her. "Let's take a bath."

"All right."

She wasn't thinking, tossed in bath oil. And he laughed at the sight of the bubbles. They sat face to face and he said, "You should see yourself. You look so surprised. You're so pretty."

"I'm not pretty."

"Oh yes you are! And when you come, you're beautiful." He lathered his hands, made soap patterns on her breasts. "I love it," he said, "the way seventy-five percent of everything I say turns you fire-engine red right to your hairline."

"I can't help it. I'm a puritanical old maid."

"Bullshit! You know what blew me away?"

"What?"

"That day I came in, to meet you? We went back to the office and talked, then you kind of moved your chair back from the desk and crossed your legs."

"I don't understand."

"Lady, you've got great legs! And these perfect breasts! Man, I don't think I can leave you alone. Want to do it all all over again?"

"I'm a bit sore," she admitted, agonized at having to talk about it. "I'm not used . . . I've never . . . God! I wish I could talk about things as easily as you do."

"What've you never?" he asked. "Didn't you go with other guys?"

"Just one, really. And one other, once."

"Good! I'm glad. I get all the prizes."

"I mean, I don't even know what to do . . . how, I mean."

"Hey, you know all you need to know. It's all there. Every bit of it."

"No. I've never known . . ." Her eyes fixed on a point on the far wall.

"When'd you break up with that guy?" he asked.

She wet her lips, dragged her eyes back. "Break up. It ended in September. It only started in May." God! May and now it's December and I've gone from not having ever to my third man. How can I be doing all these things?

"The other guy was before that?"

"There was no one before any of it."

"You mean until this year . . ."

She couldn't bear to have him say it aloud, put words to it.

"I was a thirty-five-year-old virgin," she said. Wanting to look away from his eyes but unable to.

"Jesus! That's heavy. I'll have to think about that. I'll really have to think about it."

"Why?"

"Because it means something, makes a difference. Something. I've got to think about it."

I don't understand you or what has significance to you or why I'm so anxious to have you stay. I should be hiding somewhere. It's the feeling I have—wanting to hide. But unable to. Because if there's a chance of having more of you, I want it.

"Man, you've had one bitch of a year, haven't you?" he said, taking stock of all she'd told him and a lot she hadn't. "That's rough. Very rough."

"You think so?" she asked, fascinated by the things he said and thought and did. Like watching some rare, exotic creature perform.

"I think so. Don't you think so?"

"I've tried not to think about it."

"Okay, we won't talk about it anymore now."

He kissed her goodnight, settled her comfortably with her bottom in his lap, kissed her shoulder, then closed his eyes. Hoping like hell it'd be cool, but unable to help feeling it was a big mistake staying with her. Too risky.

She lay just on the edge of sleep, waiting for it. Her brain reeling over this reality. He was here. They were together. Sleeping in her bed. How on earth had this happened? But don't question it, she told herself. Don't. Her eyes closing, she sank down into sleep. Smiling to herself at discovering she could actually fall asleep with him in the bed beside her.

She was dreaming a terrible dream. Violence and torture. Screams. Dreadful screams. Her brain slowly emerging from the dream, her body rising up out of it. The screams louder. Not in the dream but real. She opened her eyes, feeling the violent movements in the dark. He screamed again. And her heart exploded. What was happening? Was he having a nightmare? She put her hand on his arm. His arm flew out, catching her across the middle, knocking her backward. She groped for the light switch, her eyes huge as she looked at him. Curled into a sweating knot, his body rocking. Crying out.

"Jess!" She again put her hand on his arm, shaking him. "Jess! What is it? Wake up, Jess!"

He came out of it with a jolt. His eyes snapping open. Staring at her blankly, suspiciously, for several seconds, then his features slowly relaxed, his body untensed.

"Jess," she said hoarsely, very frightened. "You were screaming."

"Oh, Jesus!" He covered his face with his hands and lay that way for several minutes while she sat beside him trying to get herself to come away from the fear. Those screams. He uncovered his face finally and reached out for her, bringing her down beside him. Saying, "I'm sorry. What did I do? Did I hit you, hurt you?"

"No, no. Just frightened me."

"I'm sorry." He looked deeply unhappy, remorseful. "It's why I wanted to split home." He smoothed the hair back from her face. "It happens all the time. Close my eyes, drop off and they're all over me, dropping down out of trees, climbing in windows, coming out from under my bed."

"Who is? What are?"

"V.C. Jesus! I didn't hurt you, you're sure?"

"No. Really. I'm all right. What's V.C.?"

"Viet Cong."

She drew in her breath sharply. And cradled his head to her breasts. Not understanding, but sensing the terror, knowing it somehow. His screams the most shattering sounds she'd ever heard anyone make.

"I'm sorry, Lyle. I'll go home, let you sleep."

"No, no." She held on to him. "It's all right. Go back to sleep. I want you to stay."

"I can't lay that on you."

"You're not doing anything to me," she whispered, so many things making sense suddenly. "I think it's what you're doing to *you*."

It always starts out this way, he thought, comforted nevertheless by the smooth cushion of her breasts. And ends up with them saying, Yeah, Jess, why don't you go home. But this time I want to stay, want to be with you.

She felt his arms tighten around her, then relax.

"Does it happen every night?" she asked softly, her fingers in his hair.

"Every time the goddamned lights go out. Honest to God, I'm sorry!"

"Go to sleep. Sleep." Stop apologizing, you don't have to. Is that how I've always sounded to the people who've had to listen? Saying, sorry, sorry over and over when their caring has made it unnecessary for me to be apologetic. You're here, this is happening and all at once, because you screamed, because of experiences you've had I can't begin to guess at, I'm happy to comfort you, hold you; willing you to go to sleep in my arms. Because after all the countless gifts, in countless ways, you've given me, the very least I can do is hold you, try to soothe you.

He slept again and, after a time, she did, too. Coming awake once, near dawn. Identifying the sound. He was grinding his teeth. It registered as noncritical. She returned into sleep.

"Do you know that it's ten o'clock," he whispered into her ear. "D'you know you have the most enticing ass I've ever seen? D'you know that I want you to wake the hell up, go do your morning bathroom gig, then come back and stretch out here with me so I can make love to you? When the hell're you going to wake up?"

She lifted her face out of the pillow and blinked at him.

"Surprise, surprise!" He smiled. "I'm still here and I still love you. Just can't believe a bit of it, can you?"

She shook her head.

"Go on," he told her. "I'll zip down and make the coffee. Merry Christmas!"

Her mouth glued shut from too many nervous-anticipation cigarettes, she got up and walked dopily into the bathroom. Emerging with well-brushed teeth, well-scrubbed body to stop on the threshold, amazed at herself. Walking around completely naked. Having slept naked and made love very very nakedly for most of the night. She smiled, feeling giddy, and climbed back into bed, reaching for a cigarette.

"How can you smoke first thing in the morning?" He gave her her coffee. "Rot your guts out."

"Tastes good." She smiled again, turned into a grinning idiot.

"So do you." Another idiot grinning back at her. "Man, will you look at that color go!"

"I told you, I can't help it. I've never done any of this before."

"Yeah. Funny how you don't seem to get red in the face watching me march around here in the altogether."

"I like looking at you," she answered truthfully.

"Ditto, lady."

"God! How *can* you?"

"Easy. You've got everything just exactly where it's supposed to be."

She took a sip of the coffee, then a drag on the cigarette, her eyes on him.

"Really," he began. "I'm sorry about last night."

"I understand, Jess."

"I wish *I* did."

"What happened?"

"Right near the end, I got captured. I was lucky. Not like some of the guys. Jesus! Some of them." He shuddered. Coffee splashed on the bedclothes. "Oh, shit! I'll clean it up."

"Leave it," she said, her hand on his arm. "How long did it last?"

"Four months, three weeks, two days. Then we were traded or something. I don't know. I just know they came waving and shouting, shoving and that was it. None of us could believe it."

"What were you?" she asked. "I mean which service."

"Just the army. I was nobody special. One of the noncoms."

"You hate talking about it," she realized.

"Yeah."

"I know how that feels."

He studied her eyes. "Maybe you do."

"I have a present for you," she said, feeling foolish again. So graceless and inept in so many many ways.

"Well, where is it?" The unexpected always turning him too flip, too cool so that it sounded as if he didn't care when he cared so much the only way to handle that kind of thing was to play if offhandedly.

"I'll get it." She put down her cigarette, her cup, then was suddenly seized by embarrassment at the idea of having him watch her.

"You're not getting it," he said, his hand under the blankets coming to rest on her buttocks. "There's no hurry."

"No, I'll go," she said, rendered totally receptive by the touch of his hand. If she didn't get up, go, she'd never move again. She got up, went to the closet, reached up to the shelf and pulled down a large box.

"The view from here's just dynamite!" he said.

"Don't!" Red-faced, she carried the box back to the bed, set it down on his lap.

He ripped off the wrapping, tossed the paper over the side of the bed. Impatiently lifting the lid, parting the tissue to discover half a dozen wrapped packages inside.

"The old small box inside the bigger box trick!" He laughed, gleefully attacking the first of the packages. While a voice in his head was saying, Oh, man! I'm not ready for this. Too much, too much. Doing this for me.

"Oh, terrific!" he exclaimed, getting the box open to find fleece-lined leather gloves inside. "Man, do I need these!"

"I know. I noticed," she said quietly. "Open the others."

Keeping the one glove on, he went on to the next package. A fine wool scarf. Then a suede billfold. Heavy woollen socks. A bottle of Cardin cologne. And a silver watch with a black alligator strap.

He sat surrounded by the gifts, the torn wrappings, the boxes. His eyes filling. His chest hurting.

"What is it?" she asked. "Have I offended you, Jess?"

"You haven't offended me." He sniffed and gave her a watery smile. "You just knocked the hell out of me. I can't believe you."

"I had such a good time shopping. I've never bought presents for a man before. I couldn't stop. You're sure? I know it's a lot."

"Damned right it's a lot. Goddamned right it is." He pulled off the glove, lifted the blanket, causing everything to slide to the floor, reaching for her. Bringing her up against him, his hands trying to transmit all the feelings to her through her flesh. Resting his forehead against her shoulder for a moment. Then he took a deep breath and lifted his head. "I can't even think of one good thing to say, I'm so knocked out."

A little awkwardly, she slid down so she could kiss him. Telling herself, I don't care how it looks there's no one to see but you and you say you like what you see is it true?

The kiss at once evolved into something else. She was caught in it with him, sent wildly into blind action. Her hands possessed of a new greed, anxious for the feel of him; hands roaming over his body, entranced with his body. My sexual prime. She wanted to stop and laugh and laugh. This is my prime. God! Yes.

Complete madness. Body curved to body. I can do this I want to. Tentatively caressed him first with her hands, then with her mouth. Silk he was smooth perfect. He made an indescribable sound that induced her to do more, more; finding an extraordinary pleasure simply knowing he was pleased. He drew her up, took his hands the length of her thighs, opened her, buried his mouth against her. She wound herself around him, quivering with lust and this new greed. To give, receive. He stopped her, laid her down, his hands holding her underneath. She reached, led him in. Exhaling slowly when he lay inside her finally.

Holding her poised, bolted to him. Her body rolling against his, gone into this rhythm they created in intense heat and devouring kisses. Heat welding them together, fire; striking cries in her throat, mute. He's making it happen again it's happening more make it more. Oh god I want to tell you I love you I do so much my god so much if only it were safe to say I love you because I do I've never loved anyone in my life so much.

"You look marvelous!" Frances hugged her at the door. Then turned to hug Jess too. Sensing a major change. "You look marvelous, too!" she told him. "Come in, come in!"

Will in a red wool shirt and grey flannel trousers, loafers, pipe in hand, coming forward to embrace Lyle, shake Jess's hand. Smiling, fatherly. Irrationally, she wanted to tell everyone she loved them. All of them. Even Richard's latest beauty queen. A blonde, this time. With an impossibly pure complexion and round blue eyes.

Looking precisely like a doll. Only the cellophane missing. But when she moved, you could hear it rustling.

"Jess!" Richard heartily shook his hand. "I've been hearing about you!"

"Hey, baby brother!" Jess laughed, comfortable from the word go with these people. "Dynamite, man! Great to meet you! I've just got to get something from the car. Be right back."

"Lyle." Her mother beckoned to her. "Come get some eggnog."

They went out to the kitchen. Frances got two glasses, opened the refrigerator for the eggnog, poured.

"Admit it," she said. "Tell the truth! Was I wrong?"

"No. No, you weren't wrong."

"You look so happy. I've never seen you look so happy."

"I'm scared to be happy."

"It's Christmas, Lyle. Be happy today. And when tomorrow gets here, be happy tomorrow. Take the days as they come."

"I'm trying."

Frances reached out to touch Lyle's cheek. "You look happy. It suits you. Try to *be* happy."

Lyle picked up the two glasses and carried them to the living room just as Jess came in with an armload of presents.

"Don't think I don't know how to arrive!" He grinned. "I've had some training at elf school, you know." He dumped all the packages under the tree. "Course I get the good part. I get to play Santa." He peeled off his jacket, shoved the new gloves into the pocket and went back to the hall closet to dispose of them.

"Eggnog." Lyle handed him his glass.

"Happy days!" He held his glass aloft, then drank.

She couldn't stop staring at him, tried to stop, feeling they could all see right through her. Transparent, clumsy. Incapable of hiding anything or of keeping secrets.

"Why don't we get this going?" Will suggested from the wing chair, Frances perched on the corner edge of his seat.

"Really?" Jess looked around at everybody.

"Sure!" Richard said. Feeling strange. Knowing, seeing. Lyle had gone ahead and done it. She'd found someone. And here he was. He looked at her, seeing her watching

Jess. Like a child at a magic show. I want it too, he thought, feeling it twist inside him. I want it, too. How do I do it? How did you?

Jess distributed the presents. Much laughter and quiet excitement. She watched, trying to make herself believe all that had happened, all that they'd done together. And the many times he'd said, I love you. All of her wanting to believe, yet unable to commit herself; scared to. He might invite her into different territory and reveal a totally new face. Remove the mask and show the maggots underneath. But I want so much to believe you, she thought, captivated by his smile, his ceaseless enthusiasm. I want to believe in you more than I've ever wanted anything. But why me? That's what I can't understand. Why not a little blonde doll like Richard's latest friend? Or a brunette, a redhead? Someone young and . . . She heard his screams again, saw his knotted, sweating body; saw the terror in his eyes when they'd opened. And suddenly had the insight into why.

Because I understand. I do. Perhaps, instinctively, you've moved close to me because you sensed I'd be sympathetic. But how did you know that about me when I didn't know it about myself? How would someone young and pretty and accustomed to flattering adulation and indulgence react to your screams, your cries and moans?

But I don't want to be a pillow, the sponge that collects all your tears. You wouldn't do that to me, would you? No, no. Weeks and weeks, months of trying to get me to see, to know you. I'll never ask anything of you, Jess, except that all this be real and not something cleverly fabricated to surmount my defenses for purposes entirely beyond my comprehension.

He was smiling at her and she smiled back, still caught in her thoughts.

"I'm starting to feel kind of stupid sitting here holding this." He was pushing a small box at her.

"Oh! Sorry!" He placed the package firmly in her hand, then continued distributing the other gifts.

Absently, finding it hard to connect with present-tense because her thoughts at that moment held so much appeal, she unwrapped the box. Her fingers registering softness, she looked at what she was holding. A small velvet box. Her fingers smoothed the velvet. She reached for the wrapping to read the card. "For you, from me." From you? She looked over at him. His head at an angle, reading out a gift tag, tossing another box at her. "That's for you, too. Hey!" He laughed, picking up the next box. "This is for me. From Frances. Wow! Thank you!" He leaned toward Lyle, whispering, "Will you open the damned thing! I'm waiting to see your face."

She lifted the lid.

"I wasn't ready last night. I had it planned for now because I didn't think about staying. Otherwise, I'd have given it to you this morning."

Diamond earrings. Two small perfect stones.

"What d'you think?" he asked.

"I think . . ." She stopped and wet her lips, trying to catch her breath. "I think they're so beautiful. But, Jess, how . . . ?"

"What are you two up to?" Frances asked.

"Look!" Lyle said, holding out the box. "What he's given me." Her head was filled with light, her body electric with awareness of the significance of the entire exchange. He'd made a public declaration, done it with diamonds and platinum. And she'd publicly acknowledged his declaration. It was real. Everyone knows now, she thought, uncertain how to deal with this. But you do love me you do I believe that you do.

Fourteen

———◆———

"I'm not going to stay."

"But it's silly to drive all the way back to Greenwich. And the roads are bad."

"Don't tempt me."

"I'm not trying to tempt you. I'm *asking*. Stay!"

"Lyle, it's not fair. I hate putting you through it."

"Don't say that. I don't think it and neither should you. Anyway, what's the point? You'll get up, get dressed, go out in the cold, drive home, then turn around and come back in the morning."

He smiled, resting his cheek against hers.

"Want me to be here in the morning?" he asked, touching her earlobe.

"I feel as if I want you to be here all the time."

He lifted his head. "Do you?"

"Yes."

"Really?"

"Yes."

"Why do you look like it's torture saying it?"

"Because it feels like torture," she said.

"Come over here and tell me why." He held his arm up so she could slip into its circle. To lie skin to skin the profoundest pleasure. She longed to be able to absorb this miraculous closeness into her pores.

"I don't know why," she lied.

"Sure you do. All kinds of reasons why. What went down with that guy?"

"I was going to marry him."

"And?"

"Jess, I can't! I despise thinking about it let alone having to talk about it."

"Okay," he said equably. "Tell me something else."

"What?"

"Anything. I like listening to you." He had the palm of

his hand on her hipbone, liking its prominence. And the
soft rise of her belly.

"It's hard to think when you're doing that."

"I'll stop."

"No."

"Okay, I won't stop. Tell me."

She turned onto her back, lit a cigarette, folded one arm
under her head, looking at the ceiling. His hand trailing
over her breasts, down her side, back to her breasts.

"You like my mother. And Richard. Don't you?"

"A whole lot."

"Isn't it funny?" she said, leaning over to tip off her ash.
"Someone you know your entire life long, yet it takes
something—I don't know—something outside that happens, to make you see that person clearly all at once. She's
amazing. For years, while my father was away on the
road, she went to school. Never told him, told us not to
tell him. She went every day. I could never see the point
to it. After all, your mother was supposed to be your
mother, not anything else. But she did it. And she's managed to get where she is. On her own. By herself. In spite
of him.

"She's always defended me, been supportive of whatever
I wanted to do. And I've just gone along accepting it,
never questioning. Then. That day I came home from the
hospital. Remember?"

"I remember."

"That day, I remembered something I'd forgotten, or
buried, for years. Years and years. I didn't want to
remember it. But it started . . . something started it coming back to me in Perth. That afternoon with Jimmy. But
I remembered." She leaned over again and put out the cigarette. Her arm back under her head. Her other hand
touching her lips. Deeply distressed by the memory.

"He was a hateful man, my father. God! Jack Maxwell,
king of the comics. I could never relate the funny man on
t.v. to the angry one who'd come storming into the house,
shouting—always shouting—about something. And she
was always calm, always . . . contained. As if allowing
herself to react to the things he did and said would be
diminishing her own image of herself. I can see that now.
It's what she's always had—a feeling for her self. What
I've never had. What he did, what I saw . . . I couldn't eat
my dinner. Just couldn't eat it. Brussels sprouts and baked

yam and some kind of meat. We had a cook then and she used to serve up our plates, Richard's and mine, drowned in gravy, onion gravy. Brown. It used to make me gag. Eight years old." She shook her head. "I had on a middy dress. Navy, with a red star on each side of the collar. I loved that dress. I don't know why that sticks in my mind, but it does. Anyway, I was pretending to eat. And Richard mashed up his brussels sprouts and tried to hide them behind his potato. When my father was home, mealtimes were always misery. As if he saved up all his grievances with my mother to hit her with them at dinner.

"I couldn't eat. And finally he said I'd have to sit at the table all night until I did. So I sat there. Richard had to go to bed. He was little, only five. Daddy couldn't do the same things to Richard. But I had to sit there. They had a terrible fight. Terrible." It was coming back. So real. The huge empty dining room. The push-door to the kitchen. The hallway behind. That long table and the coldness of the house. "She said he was being sadistic, forcing me. He began hitting her. Oh, *God*! Doors slamming, noises. She came down and very quietly said I didn't have to eat the food, to go to my room. And he was there behind her in the doorway. I knew he'd kill her. I knew it. I wanted to tell her he was there but I couldn't speak. She told me to go and I ran out, ran away up the stairs, then knelt down in the dark on the landing to watch. So scared he'd kill her. I thought that was what he was doing—killing her. I didn't know. Now . . . I know. It looked as if he was trying to crush her with his body, suffocate her. Pushing up and down so heavily. I could hear his breathing, so loud, falling down on top of her over and over again. And then all at once she went dead and I knew he'd done it. She completely stopped moving, making such sad awful sounds. Then she didn't make any sound at all and she was dead. I ran away to hide in the closet because now that she was dead, he'd come up and kill me too. But not Richie because Richie was only little and asleep and I knew if Richie didn't wake up, but just kept on sleeping, Daddy wouldn't kill him.

"But the next morning, she found me in the closet and she wasn't dead at all. So I told myself it had been something I'd dreamed. A bad bad dream. But I saw it, Jess. I saw what he did to her. All of it. And somehow I knew what it really was. I knew. It threw some sort of switch in my brain, seeing. So that I never wanted anything like that to happen to me. And if you grew up, got married, became a wife and a mother, that's what happened to you. You died at night and came back alive in the morning. That couldn't happen to me. I wouldn't let it happen. So, I held myself in. Kept all of me inside a tight little knot. And began dreaming, telling myself a story over and over again about perfect, antiseptic love finding me. Nothing could ever soil me, mash food in my face, or kill me on the dining room floor. Nothing could touch me.

"But I was wrong. I fell for the first good-looking man to come along and flatter me. Because suddenly I was afraid that the dream wasn't ever going to come true, after all. I was thirty-five and ignorant, so I allowed it to happen. For a lot of reasons. Feelings I had at night, alone, that I didn't know what to do with. How to cope with how my body felt to me. Because it felt like something entirely separate that was making enormous demands, enormous. And I was too scared or too stupid, too something, to figure out how to take care of myself. And besides, I was tired of me. So tired of me.

"Now, I'm trying to make myself believe this is real, this is happening. You're here. You say you want to be here and you're making me see things about myself I've hidden from all my life. I *love* my mother, Jess. I love her so much. And Richard. But my mother. God! She's so courageous, so—*real*."

"You are, too," he said quietly.

"Oh God! I'm not real. I haven't been real in twenty-five years. I'm so unreal I've lost whatever power I might once have possessed for distinguishing between real and imaginary. I'm doing it again. With you. What I did with Ian. Oh, not in the same way. I loathed making love with him. Hated it. And there was nothing, really, with Jimmy. Just affection. And gratitude. But Ian. I was scared to death to let him get by me because no one else would ever come along again wanting me. And I suddenly wanted to be wanted, needed. So I'm doing it all over again. Not wanting you to leave because if you do, tomorrow you might be driving away down the turnpike on your way to somewhere else, never coming back."

"You know that's not going to happen."

"I don't want to think about what's going to happen." She reached for another cigarette. "But it's hard to accept,

Jess. You're almost six years younger. You're handsome and talented. So many things. I have absolutely nothing to offer you. I'm not even good at making love."

"Why do you keep on putting yourself down all the time? It's so stupid! It's so fucking stupid! Don't you think I can make up my own mind about things?"

It's Jimmy again, she thought. The same words.

"I know what I want," he went on, his face formed of serious lines. "I don't need you minimizing whatever it is I happen to like about you. It just makes me mad because it's like saying to me, You don't know shit from Shinola, turkey, if you're so stupid you'd get hung up on me. I love you. I don't care how old you are, how old you *think* you are. It's almost a challenge to me because you've got so goddamned many stupid hangups and I'd like to get your head straightened around.

"And would you mind telling me what you think's so fucking wonderful about being young and good-looking? Would you mind doing that? I don't walk around with a mirror saying, Man, oh, man, are you ever young and good-looking! What kind of shit is that? I just *am*. Whatever. I'm no prize, either, you know. Dad threw me out of the fucking house because he couldn't take it. 'Go scream in the goddamned garage! Go drive somebody else crazy!' Like he thought it was some kind of performance, something I like to do to get my rocks off in the middle of the night.

"And how about all the chicks I thought were so together, so for-real and understanding who freaked totally the second or third time I started screaming and the neighbors called the police because Miss America was getting murdered in 2A. So sorry, Jess, but you understand. I can't have people phoning the police and all. You understand, Jess. You'll really have to go, Jess.

"I can't help it! I can't *help* it! Just like you can't help getting red in the face every time someone says pass the mustard or fuck or something. Don't do that number, Lyle." He softened his voice. "Maybe we're both a couple of rotten losers. I know it was a bad trip seeing something like that happen to your mother. But that was a long, long time ago. It doesn't matter anymore. To me, you're fine. I don't care about how old you are or any of that. I bet you never once thought that I get off on being out with you, having everybody see we're together. You look good. You know that? You look rich! I think it's a gas being out with you, having you look so goddamned rich! How's that for a kink? And I like your crazy old cigarette voice, too. Lots of things, all kinds of things. You're not some lousy lay, either. Jesus! You're better than any of them with their gimmicks and perfumed vaginal sprays and house specialties. How the hell do I know why I love you? I didn't invent it. I just walked in there and you turned me on. Just zap. At first I really thought you hated me and I couldn't figure out why, if you hated me that hard, you didn't ax me. But then, after a while, I got it all figured out and realized it wasn't me you were hating, but you."

The hand had left her mouth and was now covering her eyes.

"What're you crying for?" he asked quietly, his hand palm-down between her breasts, feeling the tremors of her tears through his hand.

"I don't know. I'm just crying. Don't go home."

"It'll drive you crazy," he said.

"No." She withdrew her hand from her eyes. "I know it isn't something you do intentionally."

"I had eleven months with the shrink after I got home. Dad said I was just faking, playing for sympathy. How d'you explain to a guy like that whose only frame of reference is a nice, clean war like World War II? How d'you tell him about bamboo cages and friends you had who turned crazy, or gay, or into dopers because they're somewhere they shouldn't be and don't know why they're there? It's all like *Star Wars* or something to him. But it's real. Jesus, it is real!"

"I know."

"It could be maybe forever. I might scream my fucking life away."

"You won't." She turned on her side, facing him. "One night, it's just not going to be there."

"Don't I wish."

"It won't," she repeated, moving closer to him.

This time, she knew what it was the instant her dreams touched it. And woke up, leaned over to try to wake him up. His eyes were wide open, his lips drawn back. His body slick with sweat, muscles knotted. He screamed. His hands closed around her upper arms. He screamed again, his knees jackknifing, feet flying into her belly. He hurled her through space like a weightless toy. She flew backward across the room into the chest of drawers. Her head colliding with the corner. Something catching her right in the spine. An explosion of pain. A flare of blinding white light and then black.

In the dark, he got up, staggered into the bathroom. Violently sick. Heaving. Trying to throw off the nightmare. A bad one. His head hurt. He turned on the cold water in the tub and put his head under it until the pain ebbed, then turned off the water, toweled dry his hair.

Returning to himself, he tried to piece it together. Had he screamed again or caught himself in time? Couldn't remember and opened the bathroom door, seeing her sprawled on the floor in the spill of light from the bathroom.

"Oh, Jesus!" He threw on the lights. Trembling, scared, dropped down beside her, terrified he'd killed her.

"Don't touch me for a minute," she whispered, eyes closed. "I don't think I can move."

"I'm sorry—I'm sorry. Jesus, I'm sorry!"

She opened her eyes and reached for his hand, held it.

"Okay," she said, slowly straightening her body. "I can get up now."

"What did I do?" he cried. "What?"

"Oh!" She winced, sitting up. "That hurts."

"Where? What did I *do*? Tell me!"

"I leaned over to wake you up and you grabbed my arms, threw me."

"Shit!" He helped her up and back to the bed. "Where are you hurt? Is it bad?"

"My back. Is it bruised?"

Gingerly, he turned her on her side and looked. "I'll get some ice." Frantic, he flew out of the room and downstairs to the kitchen, returning with a dish towel full of ice cubes. He held the ice against her back and she yelped.

"It'll help," he said apologetically, looking her over, seeing the bruises darkening on her upper arms. The look of her back scared him so much he just couldn't tell her. He was so upset, so ashamed. "Didn't I *tell* you?" he said, the shame and upset making him sound angry. "I *told* you, Lyle. It's no good having me around. I'll wind up killing you."

"No," she said stubbornly. "We've got to talk about it. I know you didn't mean to do it. I know you didn't."

"It's the goddamned dark playing tricks on my head. Bad enough the shit that's already in there. But in the dark . . . Does it hurt? Is it bad?"

"The ice is helping. I'll get a night-light, Jess. When you're here, I'll keep a light on for you. So it won't be completely dark."

He couldn't help it. He started to cry. It decimated her. She'd never seen a man cry.

"Oh, *don't!*" she said, sitting up to put her arms around him, the tea towel opening, ice cubes slithering all over the sheets. "Don't, Jess! I'm fine. Really. You shouldn't be alone in the dark. Someone's got to be with you. You can't kill me all that easily." She tried a small laugh that emerged distorted. Her back was filled with pain, from her shoulders to her hips. She ignored it, holding him. "Let's go back to sleep," she said, keeping one arm around him, gathering up the ice cubes with her free hand. "We'll leave the bathroom light on."

"I *hate* myself! How could I hurt you that way? What'd you do with the ice? You've got to keep the ice on it before it really takes hold and starts hurting." He busied himself returning the cubes to the tea towel. "Lie down and let me put this back."

She stayed his hands, kissed his wet eyes, then sat smiling at him.

"We're so funny," she said softly. "Taking turns being wretched messes."

"Come on, lie down. It's a good thing you haven't got eyes in the back of your head. If you could see what I did to you, you'd go bananas."

"Is it bruised?" She craned, trying to see.

"Just lie still and let me get this ice on it. Man, I could kill myself, doing that to you."

"Don't say that! Don't *ever* say things like that!"

Her intensity silenced him.

She stretched out, he returned the ice to her back. She gritted her teeth as the cold ate into the pain. Reliving that moment of flying through the air.

"Jess, lie down with me."

"I've got to keep this ice on you."

"Lie down and do it. I want to see you."

Keeping one hand on the makeshift ice pack, he came down beside her.

"I want to say something," she said, wetting her lips.

"You need more Kissing Potion."

"Not now. There's something I want to say to you."

"What?"

"I'm not sure how . . . Your garage apartment. What's it like?"

"A crap can. No heat. I've got a gas space heater. A john. A closet bedroom. Don't ask me to show it to you," he warned. "I'd rather be immolated by a pack of crazed pygmies."

She laughed. It hurt.

"Do you pay rent?"

"No way! The old man's tight, but he's not that tight. The rent money paid for your Christmas present."

Go ahead! she told herself. He can only say no. But if he says no, I'll die for having asked.

"Come stay here," she said into the pillow.

"What?"

"Come stay here."

"You're nuts! Are you nuts?"

"Yes, I think so."

"D'you know what you're saying?"

"I'm asking you to come live with me."

He looked at her closed eyes, knowing what it had to be costing her.

"I'd wind up killing you one night thinking I was bayoneting V.C."

"I'll risk it."

"Why?"

"Because I want to be with you in the night when you have your nightmares. I just want to be *with* you."

"It's not a good idea."

"You won't?"

"I'm scared to."

She opened her eyes. "So am I. We can be scared together. I want to help you. *Need* to. I refuse to believe you can't get past it."

"I don't want to keep on hurting you."

"Then tell yourself that. Make it penetrate your bad dreams. When you feel them touching you, coming at you, tell yourself, It's Lyle. Not them. It's Lyle. And it's all right."

"Tell myself it's you and not them. It isn't that easy."

"Oh, Jess, nothing's easy. Please?"

"Okay. Yes. Okay."

"Don't you want to? I don't want to force you." He sounded so reluctant.

"Sure I want to," he said quickly. "I want to! It's just that I don't think you know what you're doing."

"Working," she said. "Working at believing."

Fifteen

◆——◆→

It got so that the instant he started, she knew and was wide awake to witness how the dreams took him over, turned his body to dripping steel, sent him screaming. Once or twice, at a safe distance, she sat and smoked a cigarette and watched, trying to interpret what it all meant. His flailing fists, writhing body, grimacing features. The cries. Snatches of words. Shouts. She couldn't imagine the horrors that had to be stalking the arena of his dreams. All she knew was that it was monstrous. And it grieved her, seeing. Made her pray to have it all ended for him so that just once, for just the length of one night, he could sleep peacefully for eight solid hours. It also amazed her that he possessed the reserves of energy he so obviously did. Because he rarely got more than three or four hours' sleep. Neither did she. Yet he seemed to function perfectly, while the lack of sufficient rest was beginning to take its toll on her.

To a great extent, she seemed to be surviving on the elation generated by his presence in her life. As if his reality within touching distance produced enough stimulation for her brain and body to keep her performing on an effective level. Knowing she ought to feel far more tired than she did. Anticipating a point in time when it would surely all catch up with her and send her reeling to her bed where she might stay for weeks, sleeping nonstop in an attempt to compensate for her present wakefulness. But it was so worthwhile to be awake, to be with him.

Between customers at the shop, they were both working on the wildflowers. He was taking photographs of the canvases at every stage. And, when she was unaware, photographing Lyle as well. The after-Christmas business doldrums had set in and the shop was fairly quiet. More and more often, she'd find herself gazing numbly into space, her body craving sleep, long minutes going by when she'd feel herself sinking into herself, exhausted. Telling herself, Just five minutes. Just to close my eyes for five minutes. But then someone would come into the shop or Jess would say something and she'd snap awake and continue on with whatever it was she'd been doing.

It surprised her how readily she adapted to having him in the house. Wanting him there. His presence delighting her. Every time she came into a room, she was astonished anew to find him there. Each time she heard his voice, she was startled by the fact of his substance, the volume of his being. And astonished, most especially, to discover her own insatiable appetite for him.

Yet it was tacitly understood that their connection existed entirely outside the shop. There, they were friendly companions, co-workers. At ease together. But the minute they closed the front door and got into the car, she wanted to leap upon him, wrap him up, disappear into him. A greedy, surging possessiveness she wanted to dislike herself for feeling. Because it didn't seem altogether right to have become so fixated, so dependent upon him. It was a small, ongoing battle between the factions in her brain.

They made love one night in the car, in the dark parking lot. This once, mutually unconcerned about the possibility of being seen. It had to be now, this minute. Caught up in the urgency—was it his, or her own, or both?—she lifted her coat and dress, got her tights down and straddled his lap. The windows of the car going opaque with the steam of their labored breathing. His hands cold on her naked thighs. His mouth hot. She felt—in one lucid moment—wicked, altered, unrecognizable to herself. Then ducked down beneath those feelings, mindful only of his potent presence inside her. They laughed all the way home. She wondered—in another lucid moment—if they were laughing for the same reasons. And berated herself for possessing so little faith, so little ability to believe.

Unexpectedly, one evening mid-January, he began talking about some of his wartime experiences. She wasn't certain how to react—taken aback by his seemingly easy slide into this area—and sat watching him closely, listening. So confused by so many things about him that the confusion threatened to interfere with her comprehension of what she was hearing.

"What bothered me most," he said, a deep worried furrow between his eyes, "I guess was that I kind of liked most of the guys. To begin with. You know? I mean, there were some all-right guys in the squad. Not your lifelong-friend types, but all-right guys. And seeing these people you thought were all right, turn into . . . I don't know what to call what they turned into. It was insane. All of it. The whole goddamned thing." He shook his head. "There were maybe two guys who actually wanted to be there. Hung up on protecting America and that whole bag. Garbage. The rest of us . . . When we talked about being there, why we were there, we none of us knew why, couldn't make any sense out of it. That was way back, right at the first. Before we saw any action. *Action*." He laughed a hard, barking sound. "All that goddamned rotten never-ending rain. So everybody had some kind of something like dysentery or fungal infections or ringworm. Something. Action," he said again. "Fighting shadows. Raiding empty villages. Getting all geared up for the raids, every single time. As if we were actually going to see V.C., fight them. They were never there. Never. Just old women and kids. Daylight raids. Nighttime raids. Rushing in on this big adrenalin high. Everybody positioned right where he was supposed to be—which was a huge laugh altogether. There was this whole set of rules that didn't have a goddamned thing to do with the 'code.' We changed radio men three times because we couldn't find the right *voice*. Can you believe that?" He laughed, less unpleasantly this time.

"Anyway, the guys, they started seeing V.C.—the *enemy*, you know—everywhere. Those little kids, those tiny little old women. Because everybody had heard the stories about little kids or old women who'd smile as they lobbed a live grenade in your lap. They started going nuts. And that afternoon—" He stopped, his eyes watching the film unwind slowly in the replay. "They just went for-real crazy, finally. The only ones . . . me and Fineberg, we just stood there, couldn't even say anything. Because, like, if we'd started putting words to what was happening that would've made it real and we didn't want it to be real. We kept looking at each other, both of us knowing we weren't going to put the words to it. And we couldn't stop them. What really scared me was that I could even understand why they did it. Because it was too much, really too much. All that fucking rain and sickness and shadow-boxing where we never saw them but they always saw us and somehow they managed to kill one of our guys and only one guy in our squad ever got anybody and that was just a V.C. kid. But he got a decoration for getting the kid. Like a prize for killing a shadow. But anyway, it scared me—being halfway able to understand why they were doing it—almost more than the fact that they were . . . I didn't *want* to understand it. But I did."

"What happened?" she asked softly, her heart beating a peculiar rhythm.

He glanced unseeingly over at her, then looked away.

"Another empty village. The last goddamned straw. I think they just got to the part marked 'The End' and couldn't take any more. Not another bunch of little kids and more women in those black pyjamas. So they started on the women, even the one really old one. And Fineberg and me, we were trying to get them to stop because it was so goddamned sick. The women wailing, making these *sounds*. We were shouting, telling the others to get their acts together, look at what in hell they were doing. And then there was a moment, just a couple of seconds, when everything stopped and the rest of the guys turned to look at the two of us. Crazy. Sick, scary crazy. And we knew, right then, if we stepped in, really tried to stop them, they'd kill me and Fineberg, too. Get together and make up some story for later on about how the two of us got blitzed out by snipers or something. So the two of us—it was incredible, as if we'd talked the whole thing over and decided how we'd play it—we just moved on off. Far enough away not to hear. Sat under a tree with the rain dripping down the back of our necks. Fineberg smoking, the two of us talking this nonsense about what we had it in mind to do when we got back home. Nothing-type stuff to make out like it was usual we were hiding while the rest of the squad were just over there, a few hundred yards away . . .

"The thing is, we waited maybe a couple of hours. To give them a good long time to get themselves together, get some of the shit out of their systems. Then, we figured to join up and head on out with them. Except when we got back to the village . . . They were already gone. We couldn't believe it! It was . . ." He shook his head again, grinding his fists into his eyes. "They killed them all. All the kids, the women. The smell. Jesus! So goddamned bad. Blood everywhere and the mutilation . . .

and . . . it was like . . ." He cleared his throat. "Anyway, me and Fineberg, we buried them. Had to. I don't even know why. We just had to. Something else we never talked about. Just got shovels and started digging this big hole in the ground. Not looking at what we were doing, shoveling all the sickness into the hole, covering it over. Then starting toward the rendezvous, when Fineberg said in this very quiet voice, 'We're accessories, Kelsey. We're just as guilty as they are. Now.' It scared me almost more than anything else. Because I'd been thinking about decency, you know. About how it wasn't *decent* to just leave those women, the kids there . . . that way. And he took it, put it into another whole dimension. Well, we didn't talk anymore about it and kept going.

"We expected something or something. It's hard to explain. We got back thinking to see all the guys quiet and subdued or something. Sorry, maybe. Ashamed. But they were all doped-out and wild, kind of. In this old, wrecked temple. It'd probably been really beautiful—before. It was wrecked by then. They looked at us with these eyes, these messages warning us, telling us we didn't see anything and we didn't have anything to say to anybody because we'd get ourselves put in some other hole if we started talking.

"The two of us weren't a part of them anymore after that. Because we hadn't jumped right into the middle of the whole thing with them. So, we moved off to break out some rations, me and Fineberg, trying to dry out our socks and boots over a can of Sterno. And it was like because of what happened and the way the rest of the guys had silenced us into a different corner, I could think Fineberg's thoughts and he could think mine.

"Four women and nine little kids. And one of those women was maybe seventy. I wanted to talk about it. *Badly.* I needed to talk about it more than I'd ever needed anything in my life. And Fineberg kept looking at me and looking at me, the two of us sitting there in the corner with our socks steaming over the stinking Sterno. Looking at me like if I started, he'd pick up and go from there. But neither of us could get the words together. I wanted to. But I couldn't. I should've talked to him. Jesus! I should've." He took a deep, shuddering breath, his clenched fists resting on his knees. "He was such a goddamned *kid*, Fineberg. For all his brains and the rest of it. There was this thing in his face, you know. This kid thing.

And I knew, I goddamned *knew* he wasn't in control of where this whole thing had put him. Put him in such a bad place. Put me there, too. But I was never a kid the way Fineberg was a kid. Sweet. He really was. I loved that guy. I wanted us to come home, be friends, get together every so once in a while for a rap. I could see the whole picture. I *loved* him. Because he was the only one in that whole fucking lunatic outfit with any feelings.

"He hanged himself. He was just there, swinging, a couple of hours later when we all started waking up. And nobody said one goddamned thing. The animal thing was over by then, the guys just guys again. Looking a little guilty, *embarrassed* because Fineberg had to go and do this dumb-ass number.

"I couldn't get myself back inside that squad after that. Because I knew about where they'd gone to inside their heads and how could I ever trust them again, I couldn't because I hadn't ever been one of them, not really, and this just put me farther over on the other side away from them. And the other thing is, it was Fineberg they murdered. Not just the women and those kids. Scrawny, goddamned little kids. And one really old lady. But Fineberg!

"You know what he wanted? He was going to be a pediatrician, loved babies, little kids; wanted to have a practice and take care of all the little kids and babies. He was a baby himself, for God's sake! The company CO wrote this very nice letter to Fineberg's family, all full of lies about how he died. I promised myself when I got home I'd go visit them in New York, tell them the truth. But I knew I couldn't do that, blow his family away with that kind of truth. I shouldn't have started all this," he said abruptly, jumping to his feet. "Jesus! I shouldn't have." He grabbed his jacket saying, "It's okay. I've just got to get out for a while, walk it off. It's okay." And before she had time to protest, he'd left the house.

Her hands were trembling, her stomach knotted. She lit a cigarette and sat gazing at the front door, filled with an image of Fineberg. Someone she'd never seen. A boy who'd sat talking about his future while his friends . . . Jess's love for the boy made her throat hurt, made her feel what he'd felt, brought her face to face with the reality that she could never know all the thoughts, feelings, experiences housed within Jess; she could never, no matter how long she lived and worked at it, know all the surfaces

and corners of Jess or anyone else. It was impossible
to hope to do more than gain some slight understanding of
one's own self. She felt utterly drained.

When he returned just over an hour later, he seemed
himself again; having managed to pull it all back under
control and push the lid down on it.

"I shouldn't have started all that," he said apologetically, reaching for her hand. "I know how things upset
you. Come on to bed. You're wiped."

"Jess . . . ?" She didn't know what to say. Was there
something to say?

"It's okay," he said quietly, leading her up the stairs. "I
know."

Having bathed, feeling horribly uncertain, she climbed
into bed. Trying to understand why it was some people
could find ways to cope with their lives, their realities and
why others—like Fineberg, like me? she wondered—simply couldn't.

He stretched out on his back beside her, sighing tiredly.
Making her think he was perhaps too enervated for love-
making. And she thought that if they didn't, perhaps she'd
sleep, get a bit of extra sleep. Then at once felt guilty for
wanting sleep when it was Jess she wanted, and his body,
if he cared to reach out for her. Wishing she had the capacity to heal his injuries, erase the remembered pain.

He turned on his side toward her. And automatically
she turned to face him. Wishing, more than ever, that she
were more certain of herself, of him, of the ways in which
things were done in the world. There were moments—still
too many of them by far—when she couldn't, simply
could not understand why he was with her. Moments
when she felt pale and old and so completely without appeal that his presence had to be some sort of charitable
act. Moments, like this one, when his hand came through
the air to curve itself over her breast. His eyes closing as
he stroked her slowly, as if reading her through her breast.
A slow hand traveling over and around her breast. Then,
suddenly, gathering her into his arms, pulling her hard
against his body as his mouth opened hungrily over hers.
Leaving her no time, no room for thoughts about her
inadequacies. He seemed unaware they existed. His hand
moving up between her thighs, surprising her into violent
response. Surprising her into the further understanding

that their coming together always varied, wasn't ever the same. Each time was different. She opened herself, closed around him as if her flesh might, in its motion, wear away his pain. A little bit at a time.

By the end of January, she felt as if she were staggering around inside a lead overcoat that was slowly dragging her to the ground. Constantly yawning, her eyes watering. Tired.

He couldn't help seeing, couldn't help feeling guilty.

"I'm wrecking you," he said. "You've got to get some sleep."

"I'm all right," she insisted, trying to suppress a yawn.

"Okay." He backed down.

"I'm getting used to sleeping with you. I probably wouldn't be able to sleep without you now."

"Okay," he said, unconvinced. Bothered by the circles forming under her eyes, her obvious weight loss. Hounded by guilt because his presence in her house, in her bed, was responsible for all of it.

There was an ice storm the first weekend in February and they went to bed without benefit of electricity. The absense of the night-light worried her. But she was too worn out to give it any thought.

They made love, moved apart to sleep. Happily sated, she was asleep in seconds. And woke up to a beating. Fists slamming into her body, into her face, her head. She screamed and a pair of hands fastened around her throat, squeezing, cutting off the scream. Panic. She was strangling. Thrashing. Unable to get him off. He was sitting on her rib cage, his knees digging into her, choking her.

You were right, she thought, losing consciousness. You did wind up killing me.

She came to some hours later, blinded by the light. Tasting blood. Jess wasn't there. She opened her mouth to call him but found she hadn't any voice. And it hurt to swallow. She made her way into the bathroom and gasped at the sight of herself in the mirror. Her mouth and nose bleeding, a bruise on her cheek. Bruises around her throat. She hurt all over. Particularly when she took a deep breath. She cautiously cleaned her face, then took another look at herself. It doesn't look quite so bad now, she decided. But where was Jess?

She pulled on her robe, feeling her ribs protesting, and went downstairs. The house was empty. Every single light on. But no Jess. She went to the front door and looked out. His car was still there. So was hers. She looked beyond, at the beach. Someone was there. She pulled her boots on over her bare feet, wrapped a scarf around her neck and put on her fur coat. Everything frozen, glistening as the sun started its rise. The road a sheet of ice. The trees, down to the smallest twig, ice encrusted.

She picked her way over the road and down to the beach. She could see him a hundred or so yards away. Sitting on the sand. She went toward him, finding it difficult to move, her side paining with each breath.

He was sitting on the frozen sand, crying.

"Jess?"

He wouldn't look at her, covered his head with his arms.

"Don't do that, Jess."

Tucking the coat under, she sat down beside him on the sand. The air made her face sting. She touched her fingertips to her face, inspecting the sore areas; watching the horizon. A magnificent sunrise.

"You're missing it, Jess, and it's beautiful."

"*What's the matter with you?*" he shouted, uncovering his head. Furious with her for being out in the freezing cold with bare legs and nothing on but a thin silk robe and a fur coat. "You'll *freeze!* You'll get *pneumonia* and *that* will be my fault *too!*"

"This is a very warm coat," she said, her voice not much more than a wheeze. "And since we're both here, we might as well watch."

"You're making me *hate* myself!" he cried. "I can't stand it, having to look at you, see what I did!"

"If I can stand it, so can you."

"No, Lyle! You're playing it like some kind of martyr. It's not right!"

"I wish I had a cigarette," she said, tucking her hands up inside her sleeves. "I could use one."

He sat glaring at her, already defeated by her refusal to rise.

"Your eye's turning black," he said hoarsely. "You can't go anywhere looking like that."

"I'll stay home for a day or two. You can take care of the shop."

He clenched his fists, threw his head back and howled. A sound of rage and frustration and pain.

"I'm sorry," she said, longing to touch him, "but I just can't blame you for something I know isn't your fault. I'm not happy about it, by any means. But I know you can't help yourself. It's the same as my blushing. I can't help that. And you can't help this. I won't give up on you that easily. No one's ever meant to me what you do. And I found out quite some time ago about paying for things."

He was looking at her in disbelief.

"I mean it," she continued, confronting his disbelief. "If it was intentional, if you derived some sort of sick satisfaction from hurting me, I'd be able to write you off, see you on your way. But that's not what it is and I know it. So, there's really nothing very much more to say."

"How're you going to explain the way you look?"

"I don't *have* to explain myself to *anyone!*" she said fiercely. "That's one of my prerogatives."

He started crying again, banging his forehead against his knees.

"Are you angry with me," she asked, "or with yourself?"

"Both of us!"

"That's intelligent. That's wonderfully intelligent."

"You don't even sound like you," he said accusingly, wiping his nose with the back of his hand.

"I'm tired, Jess. When you're tired, all the defenses seem not to exist. All the pretences and games kind of have a way of disappearing. I don't have the energy to patronize you. Caring about you takes all the energy I have."

"I'm no fucking charity case!" he snapped.

"I always thought *I* was," she said, finding the irony in the situation. "I thought it was why you were so diligently working to knock down my defenses. Because you were sorry for me. Or out to prove something. And now, here we are, and you think I'm sorry for you."

"Well, what the fuck are you, then?"

"God knows! Right now, I'm cold. And I need some coffee and a cigarette. I think I've got a broken rib, but I'm not sure. I really ought to drive down and have an X ray."

"Looking that way? What're you going to say?"

"What do you want me to say, Jess? The man I live with, sleep with, did it. He couldn't help himself. I understand it. Nobody else has to. Jess, I don't *care*! Could we go back to the house now? It's really too cold to be sitting out here feeling sorry for ourselves."

"Ah, shit!" he said dejectedly. "It's what I'm into, isn't it? Self-pity. Jesus, I hate that!"

"Then stop doing it. It's my understanding that the conscious mind and the subconscious dreaming mind are closely related. Of course, I don't have a degree in dream therapy or anything like that. But it would seem to me that if you wanted to, you could force yourself to get past it. When I have nightmares, I make myself wake up before they become unbearable. Couldn't you try?"

"I *do* try!"

"It was the blackout," she said, reaching out to touch him. "You haven't ever been as bad as this. There wasn't a night-light."

He held her hand against his eyes, then wrapped his own around it.

"Why?" he asked, choked. "You're getting the dirty end of the stick. Why bother?"

"Why are you willing to allow me to watch you suffer?" she countered.

"I don't think of it that way."

"Neither do I, really. But you're here. Why do you come back every night?"

"Because I love you. I want to be with you. But I don't want to put you away for good while I'm out of my mind in some spaced-out nightmare."

"I told you, Jess. Try to stop them before they go too far."

"Come on," he said, pulling her to her feet. "Let's get you back inside."

"Don't run away," she said. "Not from yourself and not from me. I love you, Jess. If I die as a result, it's worth it. But I don't believe for a minute you'll let yourself go that far. You're the one in control of your dreams. Not some gang of Asian soldiers. *You*."

"You really think your rib's broken?"

"Feels like it."

He put his arm around her.

"You've never said it before," he said as they were crossing the road.

"I know."

"Why now?"

"Because you needed to hear it. I know I needed to say it."

He stood open-mouthed listening to her coolly tell the doctor in the emergency room that she'd fallen down the stairs.

"Because of the blackout," she said. "Did your power go off, too?"

She went off with the doctor and Jess looked around for somewhere to sit. There didn't seem to be any place. So he walked halfway up the corridor, turned around, walked back, turned around. His head filled with racing thoughts.

At one point, having waited close to an hour, he decided he simply had to get some air, get outside; and went out to stand in the parking lot, looking at the now-melting ice on the trees. Asking himself, What am I doing to her? All of that and now she's in there lying for me. What's taking so long? He felt like running, wished he could take off down Lake Avenue and run for maybe five miles, sweat out his thoughts. Run right down Lake to Lyle's mother's house. Talk to somebody about what he was doing to her. He could almost feel his legs lifting, heart pumping; the good, clean feeling he got running. Instead, he pushed back in through the doors and leaned against the wall to wait some more.

Another thirty-odd minutes and the doctor came out, saying, "Step in here, would you?"

He followed the doctor into a room where Lyle was sitting on the side of a bed. Looking embarrassed.

"I want to admit her," the doctor said, looking at Lyle with an expression of sorely tried patience. "She wants to go home. Maybe you can talk some sense into her. She's got two broken ribs and a perforated lung."

"I'll be all right," she said.

"Hey, Lyle?"

"I'll leave the two of you to talk it over." The doctor closed the door and went out.

"I'm fine," she said, suddenly wanting to cry. Hurting, tired. And at a loss as to why she was doing the things she was doing.

"You've got to stay," he said, sitting down on the bed beside her. "You can't walk out of here with broken ribs and all the rest of it."

"I feel fine," she insisted.

"Lyle, I want you to stay. If you don't, everything we talked about this morning doesn't mean shit. I mean it! You walk out of here all banged up and go home and I'll go crazy. Because it's martyr material. It's bad enough having to hear you lie for me. But there's no way you're not staying."

"But I want to be with you."

"You'll be with me when you've done your stint here. I'm not going to split on you or anything like that. Is that what you think? You think I'm going to take off on you?"

"I don't know."

"Listen." He put his hands on her face, turning her head to face him. "I'm responsible. I know it and you know it. And you can't *do* this! Not to me and not to you. Okay, I can handle it that I go insane with the nightmares and do a lot of things I never meant to do. That's one thing. It's absolute fucking hell to have to wake up in the morning, turn over and see you lying there, bleeding. For one sick, goddamned minute I thought I'd really done it, really killed you. It's so *hard*! *Please*! Do what the medic wants you to do. Get checked in here and let them patch you up. I'll take care of the shop. I'll take care of everything. But do it! You've got to trust me. Saying you won't stay, you've got to come home. That's not trusting me. It makes me feel like I'm some kind of genuine, certifiable crazy you've got to watch night and day. You understand?"

She nodded.

"Your goddamned lips are all split and everything."

She closed her eyes. I won't cry I won't there's no need.

"I'll go back to the house, get some stuff together for you and come back."

"Okay," she whispered.

He kissed her on the forehead, got up and went out into the hall to tell the doctor, "She'll be staying. I'm going now to get her stuff."

"I'll have the nurse get the admit forms."

Jess went back into the room. She hadn't moved.

"D'you really understand?" he asked.

She nodded.

"Okay," he said, holding both her hands. "Don't think about it, don't worry. I'm okay on my own. Nobody gets hurt that way."

She tried to withdraw her hands, frightened by what he seemed to be telling her. He wouldn't let go.

"I'm telling you I'll keep the goddamned night-light on. And I'll work at putting you right into the action when it starts getting heavy."

"I love you."

"I love *you*. I'll be back with your things."

He hurried out. The door swung to. She sat staring at the closed door.

Frances said, "He beat you!"

"He didn't beat me. It's very complicated."

"I've got all the time in the world. Try the complications out on me."

"Are you being sarcastic?"

"Not remotely. But an explanation would go a long way."

As briefly as possible, she tried to explain. Frances listened closely, intently. And at the end, said, "He's right, you know. He could kill you. Poor Jess."

"Poor Jess isn't going to kill me. He's going to get past it!"

"Don't try to play God, Lyle. That's reckless, foolhardy."

"If no one took risks, we'd all be savages."

"That," Frances said, "is dangerous generalizing."

"So is life. Dangerous."

"You're risking your life, Lyle. Have you any idea what you look like? It's dreadful! And your breathing. It hurts me just listening to you. This is *dangerous*!"

"Just as dangerous as defending an eight-year-old who wouldn't eat her dinner."

Frances's eyes widened. "You remember that?"

"All of it. I saw."

"You saw?"

"Why is it different?" Lyle asked, touching her mother's face. All over. Delicately, like someone newly blinded. "You love someone, you try for that someone. I love Jess. I'm not some poor deluded afternoon drinker in love with 'my Bill,' Mother. He's someone good. You said so yourself. He can't help it. And he's trying. I've got to help him in every way I can. You said one time that you loved me and you loved Richard, that it was the only kind of love you understood. That's no longer the case, is it?"

"No, it isn't."

"Okay. It's better than walking into the river because someone who didn't even really care for me did some pretty sadistic things to me in the name of love. At least I know this is real. God! I'm almost thirty-six years old. Isn't it about time I had some sort of life?"

"It's time, certainly. I'm just very worried that thirty-five is all you'll ever get to be."

"We'll work it out."

"You've made up your mind," Frances said helplessly.

"Mother, I don't want to be a female version of Richard. Showing up every few weeks with another new beauty, afraid to feel, afraid to care."

There was a lengthy pause. Frances tried to think, to untangle her thoughts and fears.

"I've never," she said finally, "wanted to face what I saw happening to the two of you. All the cruelty. He was such a cruel man. I don't know where it will end for Richard."

"He might find his way out."

"You *saw*?"

Her hand returned to her mother's face.

Part Three

Sixteen

——◆——

He was being so tender, so unhurried and gentle that she simply couldn't respond. It didn't feel right. She'd never before failed to respond to him. But this time she simply couldn't make herself unaware of what was being transmitted through his hands, his entire body. And found herself in the uncomfortable position of objective viewer instead of active participant, waiting it out; helping him to finish. Wanting it finished. It was all too labored, too programmed, too obviously directed toward her pleasure for her to derive any.

He ended with none of his usual explosive excitement and she lay motionless, holding him; waiting. Wondering what was bothering him.

"Lyle." He leaned on his elbows, looking into her eyes. "We've got to talk."

"All right."

"I've been thinking it through," he said, looking pained. "Trying to come up with an answer." He could feel her tensing, her eyes focused on his mouth.

"Go on."

"It's no good," he said, "the way things are. Hating myself, getting angry with you because of hating myself. I've thought about it until it's all I *do* think about. And there seems to be just one answer. I've got to get away, go off on my own for a while, work this thing out."

"Get off me, Jess," she said evenly.

"No, listen."

"Get off me, Jess!"

"Please! We've got to talk about it."

"*GET OFF ME, JESS*!" She screamed so hard, so loud, it felt as if her head might burst open. He jumped away and she leaped off the bed. Shaking. Making strange sounds. Moving this way, that way, everything jarred into motion; her head going back and forth, back and forth.

She grabbed up her robe and pulled it on, oblivious to the fact that he was sitting, stunned, watching her dash this way, that way, mumbling to herself.

"Listen." He tried again. "It's not for good, not forever. But I can't see any other way. This is something I've got to get straight for myself. I want to do it so I can come back and we can be together without any of this grief."

"Just go!" she said wildly. "Just get all your things and go! Go away! Go on! If you have to go, you have to go right now, right away."

"You're not listening to me! I'm trying to tell you and you're running around the room like a crazy, not listening."

She stopped at the foot of the bed, quivering, palsied.

"Correct me if I'm wrong," she said. "You're going? Is that correct?"

"Yes, but . . ."

"If you're going, then *go!*"

"Be reasonable," he begged. "At least hear me out."

"I'll be reasonable next week, next month. Not now. I can't be reasonable just now. I want you to go right away, get your things, go now."

"I'm not going away from *you*, Lyle. I'm going to try to get myself together so we can make the two of us work."

Not again, she thought, unable to stand still. Not another. Once, not twice. I can't, can't! A variation on a theme. That's all it is. Boiling down to the same thing, the same, the same. God! Oh God!

"You're being impossible!"

"Yes. I know. Impossible. God! I know."

He began pulling on his clothes, somehow infected by her urgency, so upset his thoughts were becoming jumbled. Why wouldn't she listen? He got his sweater on and tried once again to talk to her.

"Quit that!" he shouted, taking hold of her arm. "Just stand still for a minute and listen to what I'm trying to tell you. I'm trying to tell you I'll be back. Why are you acting this way? I don't understand. It's not like it's forever. It's for as long as it takes me to get my head in gear. I'm doing it *for us*, not to hurt you. I'm doing it 'cause I'm fed up with hurting you. It never got this far before with anyone. Now, I care and I've got to get some control going. For *you*, for *us!*"

"I wanted it to be me," she said, strangling.

"It can't *be* you! You'd be dead. I don't want to be responsible for killing the only person who really cares. I can't handle it anymore, Lyle. I don't *want* to go," he wailed. "I'd like to just hike on downstairs, light the fire and put my feet up. It's stupid! Neither of us can pretend this isn't real, isn't serious! I'm going to get away somewhere by myself and face this whole fucking thing, get the better of it. And it's something I can't do here, with you. Not when I have to wake up every morning and see that I've done yet another lousy number on you. Please don't go off all crazy this way! *I'll be back!*"

"When?"

"I don't *know* when. As soon as everything's straight."

"Go on," she whispered. "Part of my head knows why. The rest of me's going crazy, telling me none of what you're saying's true. It's just another story, another someone doing his best to get out. I'll work at putting the pieces in perspective some other time. Right now I want you to go so I can fall apart without an audience. Okay?"

"D'you believe me?"

"If I'm still here when you get back, you'll know I believed you. Take everything, Jess. Everything. I'll see you . . . whenever."

She brushed past him, went into the bathroom and locked the door. Quickly turning on the shower, climbing in. The water drowning out any extraneous noise. Thinking, He's right and I'm acting like a lunatic. But the feeling, it hurts, oh my God I don't want to go back to being alone and he'll never come back no matter what he says he won't be back. Hurts more than anything else, more than being thrown through the air, or beaten. Hurts. Breaking me.

She leaned against the wall and cried, stayed there crying until the water ran cold and she had to get out. And, of course, when she emerged from the bathroom, he was gone. Except for the note he left.

I'll be back. I love you. Jess.

Monday, Tuesday, Wednesday. She couldn't face leaving the house, going down to the shop. Couldn't be separated from the pain, the tears or the fire she kept going night and day. Didn't eat or do much of anything except make fresh cups of coffee and open new packs of cigarettes. Traveling back and forth between hurt and anger.

Ignoring the telephone when it rang. She'd have ignored the doorbell, too, except that it wouldn't quit. So she had to get up and go open the door.

"I've been worried half out of my mind!" Frances declared. "*What* is going *on*?"

"Would you like some coffee?"

"No. I want to know why the shop's closed and why you haven't been answering the telephone. Where's Jess?"

"Gone. Off into the world to straighten out his head. Sure you won't have coffee? I'm going to have another cup."

"He's *gone*? Where?"

"I have no idea. Coffee?"

"All right, yes."

Frances followed her out to the kitchen. "Why?"

"It made him feel too guilty to look at what he was 'doing' to me. So, he's gone, he says, to get everything together."

"That sounds reasonable. Why are you behaving this way?"

"I don't know. I'm just doing what I feel like doing."

"But the shop. What about the shop?"

"I'm never setting foot in that shop again as long as I live," she said heatedly. "I'm selling it. I listed it today."

"But why? What will you do?"

"Why? Because he made the place into a work of art. It doesn't belong to me. When it was mine, it was . . . I don't know what I'll do. Something. Or maybe I'll just do nothing."

"Lyle, it seems to me that what he's doing is very sensible. What doesn't make one bit of sense is the way you're acting."

"He won't be back," she said, plugging in the coffeepot. The feeling between her breasts now was an empty, hollow one. What had begun to take root there was gone, ripped away.

"You don't know that."

"If I think it, I won't be disappointed."

"Lyle, that's crazy!"

"*Mother!*" She stopped abruptly at the demented sound of her own voice. And dragged it back into control. "I feel crazy," she said quietly. "What am I supposed to do? I can't just go on as before. It feels too . . . I also can't just sit here day after day waiting, wondering if today's going to be the day Jess comes back. It's . . . What is it? I don't know. Something. What guarantee do I have that he won't get himself all nicely glued back together and decide the last thing on earth he needs is someone six years older who was capitalizing on his problems. He won't need me. God! I've really outdone myself this time, playing the fool."

"If he says he'll come back, he will. Jess is honorable."

" 'So are we all honorable men,' " she quoted dryly, getting two cups from the shelf. "God save me from honor and men. I think I've had enough of both to last a sizable lifetime."

"I don't believe this is you." Frances sat down heavily. "I don't believe it."

"I know." Lyle gave her a bizarre smile. "I just went all the way up the scale and now I'm coming down the other side. Fast."

"I think you're wrong. He's doing the sensible thing. And you were wonderfully understanding. It had nothing to do with capitalizing. You're frightening me with all this."

The shaking again. Like the victim of some horrendous disease. Shaking so much she had to hold on to the counter for support. "I was so self-righteous and smug," she said in an uncertain voice. "Spouting home-grown homilies, being magnificently philosophical. Like a goddamned Joan Crawford movie! Convinced of my own omnipotence, positive I could cure him of everything from warts to nightmares. Condescending in my thoughts of Richard, feeling so superior. It isn't Jess, Mother," her voice sinking low, lower. "It's me. Making a fool of myself. I threw him out when he said he wanted to go." She was off, the tears running. "I don't know why I did that but I couldn't help myself, couldn't help feeling I'd counted on too much, jumped in too quickly, too deeply."

"Come sit down. Let's talk about this rationally. It's awful seeing you so upset."

"It's just that I wasn't expecting it, you see. Of all the things I'd considered, his leaving wasn't one of them. I wasn't ready. How could I *do* that to him?" she cried, despairing. "Screaming at him, not giving him any sort of chance to explain. I don't understand what's happening to me."

"Would you like to come stay at the house for a while?" Frances offered. "I've got quite a lot of vacation time accrued. I'll take a week."

"No. I'm not fit for human consumption right now. But thank you."

Frances got up to pour the coffee.

"A trip south?" she suggested. "Somewhere warm?"

"I don't want to go anywhere. I've got to stay here and do my *own* piecing together. I've probably driven him away for good. You should have seen me." She laughed miserably. "It was quite a spectacle. Screaming, muttering, running around. A spectacle," she repeated, the laughter turning to sobs. She put her head down on the table.

"What can I do for you?" Frances asked. "You're making me feel so . . . useless."

Lyle's hand crept across the tabletop. Frances took hold. What was there to say after all?

She accepted the first offer on the shop, drove down, cleared out her personal belongings, threw everything into the trunk of the car and returned home to pace back and forth in the living room, in the grip of desperation. Wishing she'd behaved more intelligently with Jess, bemoaning her irrational tantrum. Asking herself again and again, Why did I do that, say those things? Why? Unable to provide any sort of viable reason for the way she'd reacted. She couldn't stop thinking about it. Was determined to try to stop.

Finally gathering herself together sufficiently to take stock of both herself and the house, deciding both needed cleaning, she dumped the bed linens and her dirty clothes into the washer on top of a number of items already in there. Got the machine going and went through the house on a manic cleaning spree. It was when she was removing the clothes from the dryer that she discovered the jeans he'd left in the washer.

She sat down at the kitchen table with the jeans and cried all over them, holding them to her face, soaking them with her tears. Then, her crying ended, she held up the jeans, looking at them, turning them this way, that way and finally removed her slacks and tried them on. They fit. It gave her the strangest feeling standing there in Jess's jeans. She smiled, feeling fractionally better. And wore the jeans constantly from that point on.

After several weeks of being housebound, she decided to venture out. For groceries. For air. And was somewhat revived by the bracing air and the mindless act of wheeling a cart up and down the aisles of the supermarket. Returning to the house, though, was like burrowing into a dark tunnel in the ground. She wanted air, light, something to do with her hands; something to ease the awful agitation.

She couldn't read, couldn't sit still long enough to watch television, couldn't even think about working at her needlepoint. She wanted to sketch, to paint; to make vast color-laden canvases. She wanted to bleed on canvas. To paint with tears and blood and anger. She went back out to the car and drove into town to get some supplies. Brushes and an easel, some prestretched canvases, some turps and a small set of oils. A palette, palette knife, some charcoal sticks. Not daring to stop in the midst of her frenzied purchasing to question her actions. Wrote a check and carried everything out to the car in two trips, then drove home. To be confronted, upon arriving, with the reality of having nothing she cared to paint. But not to be deterred, telephoned the Artists' Guild, asked about classes and arranged to enroll in an oils class that had already started. Her first session would be the next evening.

She ran upstairs to look in each room, trying to decide which offered the best light, which would lend itself to her efforts. The attic? What about the attic? She switched on the light and went up to have a look. A lot of dust and cobwebs. But so much room. And four windows, one for each exposure. If she got a carpenter to come in and finish the walls, put in a skylight, she'd have the perfect place to work.

In a froth now, she tore downstairs to look through her address book, trying to remember the name of the carpenter she'd had do some minor work on the house a few years earlier. She found it, called his home, left a message with his wife and asked to have him call her back. She was trembling, soaked with perspiration, feverish. Wanting everything done right away, that minute.

Hungry, she put away the groceries then set about preparing an enormous meal. Steak and a baked potato, salad, bread, some corn. Food. Threw the potato into the toaster oven, set the thermostat to five hundred and started the salad. Put the undressed salad in the refrigerator while she stripped the corn, threw it into a pot of water,

slammed on the lid. Put the steak on the broiling pan, left
it on the counter, then set the timer to go off in twenty
minutes. By then the potato would be pretty well done and
she'd cook the steak.

Grabbing up the vaccuum cleaner, pausing only long
enough to pin up her hair, she lugged the machine up to
the attic and began attacking the years' accumulation of
dust. That done, she carried the vaccuum down again and
prowled through the house looking for bits and pieces she
could move upstairs. Thinking she might just move bodily
into the attic and that way never have to come down for
anything except meals and classes and more supplies.

The timer went off and she ran to turn it off, shoved the
meat under the broiler, reset the timer and went into the
downstairs bathroom to wash her hands. Caught by the
sight of her face in the mirror. You look insane, she told
her reflection. Crazy! Hair hanging half up, half down.
Dirt smeared over her face. She washed her face. If I am,
then I'll be. Crazy.

And the next morning, slid into the jeans without underpants. Pulled on a sweater without a bra. Shoes without
socks. A rubber band to take care of her hair. She cleaned
the attic windows, the sills, dragged an old rug up from
the cellar. Then stopped. Realizing she'd have to wait. The
carpenter would make a mess. She'd have to wait. Turned
off the light, went down the stairs, closed the door to the
attic. Stood in her bedroom feeling her nakedness under
her clothes. Jess's jeans. She closed her eyes and she was
wearing Jess. He was under the jeans, inside. As if over-
taken by a fit, she unzipped the fly, inserted her hand
through the opening. Jolted by the touch of her own hand
on her bare flesh. Put her other hand up under the sweater
over her bare breast. *Jess!* God come back Jess I'll die if
you don't.

Seventeen

———◆◆◆———

She couldn't stand to be in the house while the carpenter was working. So she sat on the beach in the cold, clad in boots, jeans, sweater, and fur coat, sketching the houses rimming the beach. And the cafés. Quick sketches of people strolling the sand. Rudely discouraging interested passers-by from standing watching her work. Wishing the damned carpenter would hurry up and finish so she could get into the house and really get to work. Her urgency and frustration reflected in the sketches. Thick, bold, slashing lines. A minimum of detail. Shading here, a line or two there. Strange, somehow haunted drawings of houses and people. She destroyed most of the sketches, feeling hamstrung; not doing what she wanted to do.

The instructor of her class stopped frequently to observe her at work. Finally leaning down one evening to say in an undertone, "You don't need to be here. If I could paint as well as you I wouldn't be teaching. You ought to be somewhere painting full time."

She looked at him in surprise, charcoal held in midair. Was he serious?

After the class, he waved her over, saying, "You're no beginner. Where did you study?"

"Pratt."

"I can't teach you anything. You're wasting your money."

"I need the models."

"Have you shown?"

"I haven't got anything to show."

He looked astonished. "Are you putting me on?"

"I haven't held a piece of charcoal or a brush in fifteen years."

"Christ!" He laughed. "It should happen to me. Got time for a coffee?"

"Sorry, no. I really haven't."

"Maybe another time."

"Yes," she said, and dashed away.

What did he mean? "I can't teach you anything." Never mind. She wasn't there to be taught. She needed the discipline of the classes two nights a week, the models. Have you shown? What does it matter to show? This isn't for showing. It's for me, for my life. I've lost my life. Perhaps he knows things—about life, about painting—I need to know.

She hurried back, coming to a dead stop in the classroom door. He was talking to the last of the students, looked over at her and brought a hurried end to the conversation. She wanted to change her mind again, leave. Especially now when they were left alone in the deserted room and he was collecting up some books, pens. His attitude, his entire posture one of certainty. Certain of me, she thought. That I'll stand here dutifully and wait.

"Changed your mind," he observed, not looking at her until he arrived at the doorway and reached past her to switch off the lights. His arm grazing her breasts. "Good," he said. She was too shocked to speak. What did it mean, his reaching across her that way? It couldn't have been intentional. After all, he was the instructor. And she was simply one of the students.

He took her arm, a gesture that further jarred her. Mixing up her feelings so that she didn't know what she wanted or why she'd come back.

"What did you mean?" she asked, walking with him out of the building.

"About what?"

"About not being able to teach me anything. I have my own car."

"That's all right," he said easily, as if this was something he'd done many many times before. "Follow me."

He went off to get into an old Chevy station wagon with fake wood paneling, and she had no choice but to go to her car, get in and wait to go where he went. Thinking, all the way, that she should just fall back, let him get well ahead, take some right turns and go home. But curiosity and a grinding, permanent-feeling anxiety kept her twenty or so feet behind his taillights. Stopping finally, when he did, at a restaurant/bar on the Southport line. The sort of clubby-looking place she'd never been in, had always been curious about.

At once disliking the smell of the place, the thick over-hot air, the look of the people. Nothing felt right. Especially being here with this man she didn't know at all. This man with a wide wedding ring and a way of repeatedly looking first at her mouth and then at her breasts that caused something inside her to cringe.

"What'll you have?" he asked. And, irrationally, she thought, Jess. Or my life the way I once knew it. Something. Both. Anything.

"Coffee, please."

He ordered a Bloody Mary and a coffee, then sat back looking at her. At her mouth again, and then at her breasts. Penetratingly, as if she were sitting there bare-breasted and he couldn't quite make up his mind whether or not he approved of the way she was put together.

"What did you mean?" she asked a second time. "About not being able to teach me anything."

"You don't need lessons," he said flatly. "Practice. A lot of practice. But not lessons."

She felt suddenly tired. "I enrolled for the classes . . . to get practice," she explained. Hadn't she told him that earlier?

"Getting divorced?" he asked, his face shrouded with knowingness as he watched her light a cigarette.

"Divorced? No."

"Thinking about it, then, eh?" he persisted.

"No."

"I think about it all the time," he said leadingly, sliding the ashtray over the table closer to her. Waiting for her to respond to his opening. His clue to the state of his availability.

"Do you?" Why aren't we talking about painting about my not needing lessons about who needs lessons and who doesn't and why should I show am I good enough to show?

"About once an hour, at least." He gave her what looked like a well-used smile, containing elements both of bitterness and expectation. "Don't you really?" he coaxed.

He thought she was married and for some reason she felt safer having him think it. But why did he think that? Did he just assume that all women of a certain age were married or about not to be? She said nothing to clarify matters. Instead, answering, "No."

"Oh, come on!" His smile broadened. "Sure you do. It's okay to admit it."

"No," she repeated. "You actually think I might show my work, that it has . . . merit?"

"Oh, sure," he said offhandedly. Making it plain it wasn't art or her attempts at it he was interested in discussing. "There's a lot of strength there, a lot of power. A nice feel for space and line. Seriously"—his tone altered—"you do, don't you?"

"Do what?"

"Think about getting divorced, or maybe just breaking out."

The coffee and his drink arrived. She busied herself adding cream, sugar, trying to think how she could escape this. It had been a mistake coming out with him, hoping he might have something to say, something that might enlighten and enlarge her perspectives. Feeling deeply betrayed by Jess right now, because she was too defenseless. Alone again, having to cope; hating it. She could feel all the prior gains evaporating, leaving her almost worse than before. Inarticulate, unable to play this ludicrous game, ignorant totally of the rules.

"Okay," he said. "We'll change the subject."

Optimistically, she looked across at him. To discover he was engaged in taking his eyes on another tour of those parts of her body within view. Like an eager gourmand appraising the game fowl in some exotic butcher's shop. She wanted to strike him.

"Do you teach full time?" she asked, her mouth dry. The coffee too strong, bitter. The bottom of the pot.

He laughed. "I'd starve to death, for chrissake! I work in an agency, in the city."

"An agency?"

"Advertising."

"Oh! What do you do there?"

"Usual thing, you know. Art department." He was patently bored in this area, eager to shift elsewhere.

"I see." She tried another taste of the coffee. Too bitter. She wouldn't drink any more of it, but finish her cigarette and then leave.

"Why don't you relax?" he suggested.

"Relax? I'm relaxed." She loathed being told to relax. Only stupid people talked about relaxing.

He took a long swallow of his drink, then set the glass

down, smiling at her. "You're about as subtle as a car crash," he said, sounding now as if he were being tremendously indulgent of her many failings.

"I beg your pardon?" She wouldn't bother to finish the cigarette. She'd just pick up her bag and leave.

"Why did you change your mind about the coffee, come back?" he asked teasingly. As if pointing out to her the fact that she'd started this. Not him, despite his invitation to come out for coffee.

"To . . . I wanted to know what you meant . . . what you said."

"Hey!" He chuckled. A grating, nasty sound. Making her think, I despise you, people like you, telling me to relax, trying to make it seem I came back for reasons other than the ones I had. "It's okay. You can drop all that now."

"I think I'd better be going."

"Nervous. That's cute. It's really cute. You've been thinking about it, deciding to give it a try. Got a little brave back there, but now you're getting scared. That's cool. I can relate to that."

An idiot. He was looking, sounding and behaving like an idiot. And what am I? she wondered. Sitting here with you.

"I have no idea what you're talking about. Thank you very much for the coffee. I really do have to go now."

"Take it easy," he said, unruffled, glass in hand. "I'll walk you out to your car, at least."

She didn't want him to do anything. But manners—was it that or something else?—kept her there waiting while he finished his drink, waiting for him to see her out to her car. Because, bad as he was, someone worse might accost her between here and the car. It was a possibility. One she wasn't prepared to face.

It took forever when all she wanted was to be out of there, on her way home. He first had to finish the drink, then get the waitress's attention, give her the money, wait for his change, deliberate over how much of a tip to leave. While Lyle sat with a second cigarette, trying to look unbothered, feeling a fool for having instigated this ridiculous meeting in the hope of a scholarly conversation, something with meaning.

At last they were leaving the bar, going out to the parking lot. And she took deep breaths, glad to be out of the thick, fetid air and away from the crush of damp bodies inside the bar. She moved toward her car with him right beside her. Waiting while she fumbled with her keys.

"Nice car," he observed. Sounding as if he was praising her for, if nothing else, marrying someone with the money to provide her with these luxuries. A Mercedes, a leather handbag. Other things. Freedom to pursue undesirable men after class. Leaning too close to her, an arm either side of her, hands braced on the roof of the car. He had her trapped. If she moved, some part or another of her would have to touch him.

"Take it easy," he said maddeningly, shifting so that the lower half of his body was now resting against her. And panic, like an injection directly to the heart, raced through her bloodstream.

"Please." She tried to raise her hands but her handbag collided with his arm. "I have to go now."

"Just a minute." He smiled horribly. She glanced past him, wanting someone to come into the parking lot. Someone to rescue her. He wasn't even especially good-looking, she thought irrelevantly. Although his attitude led her to believe he thought he was. A man of forty-five or so. With a too-narrow pair of shoulders, hard eyes. Hair meticulously, expensively cut. Looking hair-sprayed into place. Faded jeans, a sweaty-smelling T-shirt.

She could tell from the tilt of his head what he was going to do and felt like screaming. Felt even more like it when his wet, open mouth clamped down over hers and something too close to insane claustrophobia came awake inside her, causing her to bring her fists together between them in an attempt to push him away. Succeeding only in bringing an end to the kiss. His hands like slithery fish moving here, there.

"Please!" she said, not wanting to touch him but forced to in order to stop his hands' progress over her breasts. "*Please!*" She tried to turn, open the door. He was a large boulder impeding her progress. And suddenly, it had all gone too far. Everything. All of it. She shoved him. Hard. Her chest heaving, voice gone crazy with rage. Demanding to know, "What do you think you're *doing? Stop it! Get out of my way!*"

"Goddamned cockteasers you're all alike!" he accused, red-faced.

"You don't have the *right* . . . Get away!"

If he didn't move, she'd kill him. She knew it. It was that simple, really.

He moved.

She wanted to strike him, battled down the impulse and leaped into the car instead. Jammed the key into the ignition, floored the accelerator—something she knew it was absolutely wrong to do to the car—got the engine going nevertheless and backed up. Then, tires screaming, she drove without looking straight out of the lot into the road. Looking up, briefly, into the rearview mirror to see him sill standing there, a diminishing figure. The murderous impulse causing her hands to shake so badly she could scarcely keep the car going in a straight line. Racing down Route 1 on her way home. Knowing she wouldn't go back to the classes. She'd never have to see him again. She didn't need classes.

Jess!

She was running away, the voice in her head told her. Calling her those names. Insults, insinuations. That feeling of wanting to destroy him. Didn't even remember his name, doubted he knew hers, so why did he think he had the right to do those things, force himself on someone else that way? Too reminiscent of Ian, that night . . . Her stomach heaving, trying to overturn. And needing badly to go to the toilet. Not in the car. I won't. Appalled by the images both of soiling herself and the car. All the muscles in her body knotted against the several needs as well as the continuing rage. Her body trying to go crazy now, too, in the aftermath of what she tried to tell herself was a meaningless confrontation. Something that was inevitable in the lives of women. But was it that, or simply additional proof of her inadequacies?

She made it home and ran upstairs to the bathroom.

Later, sitting in the kitchen, nursing a fresh, decent-tasting cup of coffee, smoking one cigarette after another, she tried to understand what the encounter meant. There had to be women who enjoyed that sort of thing, went out looking for it. Unimaginable. Wanting to be treated in that deplorable fashion. I'd prefer to do without, she told herself; again feeling that swelling rage. Thinking of Jess and all at once unable to conceive of doing without.

I won't be Richard, making a pretence of feelings but always leaving, changing partners before the feelings have a chance to take hold. I won't be one of those women, either; expecting to be taken without even benefit of an introduction. But what then?

Thinking, for no reason, of Fineberg. Jess's Fineberg. With his "kid" face and Jess, near-crying, exclaiming, "I *loved* him!"

Will I have to die to have you love me?

It took weeks to get the attic done. Storm windows and paneling and reinforcing the floor in several areas where there'd once upon a time been dry rot. Or something. And then conferring on the skylight; the carpenter advised two instead of one.

"Them bubbles," he said. "For what one of them costs, you could get yourself two big safety-glass skylights maybe eighteen square feet each."

"Go ahead, do it."

More work, more weeks. She was frantic to have him pick up his saws and his drills and his level and be gone. And went up every evening after he left to inspect the place, driven half mad by his slow-moving efforts. Knotting her hands into her hair as she stood looking at this that was only half-finished and that over there waiting to be done. Pulling the hair almost out of her head, wanting to scream. Jess would have had it done in three days. God! You might come back to find I died.

At last, after seven weeks, it was finished. And the carpenter sat down with her at the kitchen table with a little coiled notebook, the stub end of a pencil, and a pocket calculator. To tally up the costs, the hours.

"Three thousand, six hundred and twelve dollars and thirty-six cents. Let's call it an even thirty-six hundred."

She wrote a check, thanked him. He went away. She tore upstairs to look. It was done. Except that there was an even bigger mess than she'd anticipated. Bits of wire, odd ends of lumber, wood chips, nails. She once again dragged the vacuum cleaner up the stairs and started cleaning.

And when she was done, stood in the middle of the room, turning slowly, breathing in the fresh wood, new paint smell. Perfect. She laid down the rug, brought up all her accumulated art supplies. And the percolator, the toaster oven. A chair, a table, the old radio from the kitchen. She tore down to Norwalk to get some tension rods so she could throw some curtains up over the windows.

Then she went to work. With no idea what she was doing. Only knowing she was rejecting everything she'd ever learned, ever been taught. Wanting to go at it raw, start from scratch. As if she'd never been told about perspectives, depth, shadow, any of it. Just put a big canvas on the easel, mixed some colors that had the right feeling, struck the proper note inside her, and went directly to work on the canvas without even bothering to rough in first in charcoal. She needed to get right into the colors. Laying them on thick. Levels of feeling, a frenzy of overlapping tones and shadings. Attacking the canvas, dealing with it as she couldn't deal with her life. In control here. Scraping, changing, adding more, scraping again; shaping, building with thick layers of paint. Building out from the canvas, erecting a multidimensional monument to something critically injured. Not caring about anything, just waking every morning to fly upstairs, get the coffee going, prowl about the easel, narrowing her eyes, her perspectives. Whipping up a brush, her palette, going at the canvas as if it might fight her back, given any kind of chance. Working until the light died. Then sitting on the floor studying what she'd done, chainsmoking, drinking yet another cup of coffee. The days and nights merging. Hating having to break out of the spell even to see her mother or Richard. But emerging weekly, clad in her old, now peculiar-feeling clothes to drive down to Greenwich for dinner with her mother and Will. On those occasions when Richard was present, she studied the most recent girlfriend, knowing Richard cared little or nothing for these women, wishing she could invite the girl of the moment back to the studio and ask her to remove her clothes, pose. But of course she couldn't do that. Although certainly Richard wouldn't have cared. So, instead, she made hurried mental sketches, then raced home to throw off the awful-feeling clothes and, not wanting to waste any time for fear the details would leave her, set the latest canvas to one side and made sketch after sketch on huge newsprint pads she bought six at a time now. Naked. The charcoal often splintering from the pressure of her attack. She lunged at the paper, her arm and hand flashing, slashing. Like a murderer repeatedly stabbing her victim.

Richard said, "What's happened to you? Every time I see you, I get the feeling you can hardly bear sitting still for however long Frances manages to detain you. What are you doing?"

"Nothing, nothing."

He studied her face, finding her altered beyond measure. Driven. Visibly longing to be somewhere else. He wished he knew where Jess had gone. He hated so much what was happening that had he known where to find Jess, he'd have gone after him to try to bring him back. Knowing his thinking was off beam but wanting someone to return her to the way she'd been before. At Christmas. That morning. Like someone who'd been in a coma for years and years and had, that morning, finally come out of it and found the world beautiful.

When he asked about her paint-stained hands, she looked down, laughed a forced-sounding laugh and said, "I'm doing over the attic."

And when Frances asked, "What are you really doing?" Lyle lied to her, too, saying, "Investigating properties. I've been thinking about opening another shop."

"And they've all just been newly painted." Frances took hold of Lyle's right hand and held it in the air between them. The evidence.

"I don't want to talk about it." Lyle yanked her hand away, her eyes burning into her mother's.

Chilled, Frances said, "All right. We won't talk about it."

After Lyle left that evening, Frances sat down with Will in the living room.

"I think she's having a breakdown. I'm terribly worried about her."

"I think she's breaking out," he said, looking askance at his pipe. "Damned thing's gone out again."

"Breaking out of what?"

"Out of Lyle. Leave her be, Frances. Lyle's not the sort to break down. She just wishes she were."

"I hate to question these profound insights, but may I ask how you managed to arrive at that conclusion?"

He laughed. "I love the way you become very English and very precise when you've got a temper on."

"My mother was English. Answer me."

"I don't recall your ever mentioning that," he said as he scraped out the tobacco and began repacking the pipe. "She's redirecting her emotions," he said. "Trying to work them all out of her system. She won't break down. She'd die first."

"*What?*"

"I think what she's doing is healthy."

"She doesn't look at all healthy," she argued.

"That's just because you're used to her looking like Sybil in—what was that movie?—*Separate Tables*. I swear, for years, every time I looked at Lyle I thought of what's-her-name who played it."

"Deborah Kerr."

"No, no. On Broadway. Margaret Leighton. She was so repressed it was just beautiful to see. Fine actress. Died awfully young. A pity."

"You're changing the subject."

"Not at all. The interesting thing to me about the production of that play"—he struck a match on the side of the fireplace—"was that Leighton played both parts. The spinster and the other woman." He got the pipe lit and tossed the match into the fireplace. "The messed-up sexpot and the repressed neurotic. Schizophrenic, seeing the one woman playing both roles."

"Are you trying to tell me that that's Lyle?"

"Oh, no!" He looked surprised. "I was talking about Margaret Leighton."

"I'm going to hit you!"

He laughed. "Calm down, Frances. I think the truth is you're just bothered because she isn't choosing to confide in you."

"Of course I'm bothered. Wouldn't you be?"

"No, I wouldn't be. You always seem to forget that I've got children, too. By the time kids get to be thirty-five or six, I figure they're on their own. I don't expect them to come to me every time they have to make a decision."

"You're saying I'm treating her like a child."

"Not quite. She doesn't need your protection now. So leave her alone. He's been gone several months. The time for her to have broken down was when he first left. It'd be too late now to be legitimate. She's working it out as best she can. Stop fussing at her. I mean it, Frances. Every time she comes here, you try every way you can to dig at her, get her to tell you what she's doing and thinking and why. It's her right to silence."

"I hate being on the outside," she admitted. "Not knowing."

"Madame"—he smiled to take some of the sting out—"that *is* your place. Outside."

The letter from Jimmy arrived on her birthday. She'd forgotten altogether writing to him, so was surprised and pleased to get his answer. And smiled, reading the letter; so much of him returning to her via his simple, direct statements. He was, he said, coming to America. Stopping in San Francisco to visit the old friend he'd told her about. Then continuing on to New York where he'd be for a day and a night before flying on to Ireland, to look at horses. Would she be able to have dinner with him in New York? He gave the various dates and she sat down immediately to answer yes. Then, once the letter was mailed, forgot.

The heat and frenzy were abating somewhat. She was working more slowly, steadily going from one piece to the next; accumulating pieces she stacked against the attic walls. Drawings she tacked up on the paneling. Moving into watercolor to see if she had any facility with the medium. Deciding she couldn't cope with the delicacy of the technique, although she liked the speed with which she was compelled to work. It seemed to suit the racing of her blood through her veins. She put aside the set of Winsor and Newton discs and returned to the oils. Branching experimentally into acrylics. But they dried too quickly. She couldn't make the changes she often wanted to make upon viewing her work a day or two later. So the oils, the charcoal won out.

As the weather warmed, she ventured outside. Driving along the Saugatuck to stop, park the car, roll down the window and do sketches of the people fishing along the shore. She went to Sherwood Island to capture the beach there at the end of winter. And, one afternoon, to New London. On a whim. To draw the Fishers Island Ferry and then the Block Island Ferry. Frozen half to death by the winds whipping in across the Sound, the sketches completed, she walked stiffly back to the car and headed home. Setting off most days in search of things, faces, scenes. Sketchbooks piling up in a corner of the attic.

It was as if the world were suddenly revealing itself to her. As a series of shapes. And she had a tremendous compulsion to put all of it, every last bit of it, down on paper or canvas. Transposing line and color, mood and feeling.

Her work was most often nonrepresentational. Simply how what she saw felt. How what she felt looked. And sometimes, too, photographic; every last detail worked to microscopic perfection. Spending an entire week on a crocus in the front garden. Going deeper and deeper into the flower until the final painting was of its core.

She worked and worked and when she wasn't working, dreamed of forty-foot canvases she raced back and forth covering with painted shapes. Images of immense scope, intense feeling. She dreamed one night of an enormous elaborate painting of Jess and forced herself to wake up.

Her hair grew long. She pinned it up out of the way. Her fingernails broke. She got out the scissors and cut them off. Her body grew thin and hard, her breasts shrank. She didn't care. It didn't matter.

She was burying Jess under piles of paper, under coats of oil paint. Burying him. Pushing him farther and farther away, deeper and deeper down. Trying to reject every thought of him that attempted to penetrate her consciousness. I won't think about him won't can't! Work! Keep working, keep moving!

She washed and wore Jess's jeans until they were faded and soft and familiar and no longer his but entirely hers. And abandoned altogether the drawerful of underwear, not even bothering to put any on when visiting her mother. Underwear meant something. She wasn't at all sure what. Just something she no longer wanted anything to do with. Hating having to drag out something traditional, something sensible to wear for her Sunday visits. And, finally, one Sunday didn't bother. Just put on a clean shirt, an old Shetland and the jeans. Some reasonable shoes, with socks. Brushed out her hair and presented herself at her mother's front door looking, Frances claimed, "About twenty years old! Is this you?"

"Do you mind?"

"No, I don't mind. Not at all. I'm just a little surprised. I've never thought of you as the jeans type."

"What type did you think I was?"

"The type you were."

"She died."

"My God, Lyle!"

"I mean it."

"Are you going to talk to me?" Frances asked hopefully.

"What about?"

"What you've been doing for the last four months."

"Painting."

"I thought so. Would you let me see your work?"

"No. I'm sorry. I can't."

"I see."

Lyle put her hand under her mother's chin, raising her face, gazing into her eyes. "You really are beautiful," Lyle said softly. "Beautiful."

"So are you," Frances said huskily.

"No," she said, her eyes never leaving her mother's. "I was for a while. I could feel it. But you just are. Someday, I'll let you see. Someday."

She'd forgotten all about Jimmy. So when he telephoned, she was very surprised. And pleased.

"I'll get changed and drive in right away," she said. "I can't wait to see you."

"I've been looking forward to seeing you, as well," he said. Sounding strange. Because they'd never spoken to each other over the telephone.

She dug out a dress, one that didn't bother her too terribly, then tried to do something with her hair. At last brushing it all up on top of her head, she twisted it into a knot, jabbed in half a dozen pins and let it go at that. It made her face look very angular but she was too anxious to see and talk to Jimmy to waste any more time on her hair. She found a pair of shoes, snatched up her bag and keys and ran out to the car.

The air was lovely, warm. She found herself smiling as she raced down the turnpike, doing a good fifteen miles over the speed limit. Feeling bold.

She parked in the lot under the Americana, found her way to the entrance and rode the elevator up to his room. She knocked. The door opened. And they gaped at each other, speechless for a moment.

"You've lost so much weight!" She laughed, hugging him. "My God! You look wonderful!" He was at least thirty pounds lighter. And looked years younger.

"I'd've known the dress." He smiled. "You wore it every day, remember?"

"God! I'd forgotten all about that."

"I hadn't," he said, closing the door. "But I doubt I'd have known you." He tilted his head to one side, studying her. "You don't look the same woman."

"No," she said, looking around the room, hating it. "I've made a reservation for us. At Le Chanteclair. Do you like French food?"

"Beautiful!"

"Good. Why don't we talk there over a drink?"

"Fine with me," he agreed, noticing her look of distaste for the room. "Shocking place, isn't it? Not much of a view, either."

In the taxi, she took hold of his hand, smiling at him. "I never thought you'd actually do it. But you're here!"

"Didn't truthfully think I'd get to it myself. A lot's happened the last months. Mag and me finally came to the end of it. We're getting a divorce."

"That's too bad."

"It isn't, really. Just a long time coming. And what of you?" She wasn't at all the same. Looked younger, thinner, somehow more alive.

"I'm painting," she confessed.

"No! You're not!"

"I am. And I don't care if it's good or bad. I'm just painting."

"Isn't that fine!" he said admiringly. "You've come quite a circle."

"Several."

Over dinner, he told her about his plan to meet up with his sister in Ireland, and how they'd be returning together to Australia. She told him about selling the shop. And a little about Jess.

"I can't think about him," she said. "And I really can't talk about him, either."

"Good or bad, you know, Lyle, he's done well for you."

"How? What do you mean?"

"You're more forward now. More homely."

"Homely?"

"Attractive, relaxed."

"My God!" She laughed. "Here, that's a very insulting thing to say to a woman."

"No! What does it mean, then, here?"

"The exact opposite."

"Well, it's not at all what I intended."

"I'm glad to hear it." She smiled.

"You're not so shy as you were," he said. "Not by any means."

"I suppose not. Having someone saying 'fuck' every other word all day every day for months, you get used to it after a while."

He laughed and squeezed her hand.

"It's so good to see you," she said, over coffee, "talk to you."

He looked suddenly thoughtful, holding his cup with both hands.

"There's always a place for you," he said, at length, "if you fancied the long flight."

"Oh, Jimmy." She placed her hand on his arm. "You're so kind. My God! The kindest man in the world. I'll keep that in mind. But right now, I feel as if I've been watching one of the world's longest movies. Or reading a six-thousand-page novel. And I've got to see it through, find out how it ends."

"I know that feeling well enough." He smiled a little wistfully. "It's a pity I've so little time."

"When does your flight go?"

"Midday tomorrow."

"So soon. It's not very much time, is it?"

"Too little."

"You look so well," she said. "Really! So well."

"And you." He'd lost her. Not that he'd ever had her. But he'd gone along on a slim hope. And it was too late.

"God, I wish you lived nearer!" she said. "I'd love to be able to call you up, talk to you."

She insisted on paying for the dinner. And he, in his gracious fashion, accepted with a smile. When they left the restaurant, it was raining. Hard.

"We'll never get a cab in this," she said. "We're going to have to either wait it out or walk back."

"Shank's mare. Never hurt a person."

He put his arm through hers and they set off back toward the Americana. They were both thoroughly soaked by the time they got there and pushed in through the entrance, laughing.

In the foyer, their hair plastered to their heads, they stood smiling at each other, holding hands.

"I've loved seeing you," she said.

He nodded his agreement. "What will you do?" he asked, looking past her at the rain outside.

"My car's parked right here. I'll drive uptown and spend the night with Richard."

"And if he's not in?"

"I have a key. It'll be all right."

"It doesn't seem enough, does it?" he said sadly.

"Somehow, nothing ever does." She kissed him and disengaged her hand. "Send me a postcard from Ireland. And write to me." She kissed him again, turned and walked across the lobby to the garage entrance.

Richard was out. She left a note on his bed, then made herself comfortable in the guest room. After a shower, she lay in the narrow bed with a cigarette, listening to the city night noises; the sirens and sudden shouts of people in the street below. Feeling odd, unfamiliar to herself. As if, for almost five months she'd been smashing her way through a concrete wall with nothing more substantial to aid her than a child's plastic shovel. But she'd managed somehow to make a hole in the wall. And she hadn't thought about Jess in over a week.

They were collecting garbage. Or maybe just knocking over cans for the hell of it. Whatever it was, it might have been happening in the next room. She woke up and turned on the light to see it was just after five. The sky a dull grey.

Just after five and wide awake, she lit a cigarette and sat on the side of the bed, thinking. Remembering Jimmy telling her he got up every morning at four-thirty in order to drive out and tend to his girls. She jumped up and crushed out the cigarette.

Her dress was ruined. But there was bound to be something in Richard's closet she'd be able to wear. She tiptoed out of the guest room and over to the door of his bedroom, about to tap quietly. The door swung gently inward under the slight pressure of her hand. He hadn't come home. There was her note still on his bed. She turned on the light and went through his closet, found a pair of Levi's and a shirt, pulled both on, wrote a new note, borrowed his toothbrush, remade the guest room bed and took off.

She called from the lobby, feeling horribly premeditated.

"You told me you get up at home at four-thirty to feed

the girls. Was that just a story, or are you a person of habit?"

He laughed. "No story. I've been up for quite some time."

"Great! I'll come up and have breakfast with you."

He opened the door to her, saying, "I thought you were ringing from your brother's flat."

"No. Downstairs." She'd never be able to go through with it. Couldn't. It smacked too much of revenge. And on whom?

"You're just in time," he said. "I've a trayful of food here. Only one cup, though. We'll have to share."

"Fine. I'm starving."

They sat down on the side of the bed with the tray between them and in hungry silence devoured every last bit of food. Then shared the remainder of the coffee.

"This is the noisiest city on earth," she said, removing the tray to the desk, then lighting a cigarette and returning to sit beside him. "I swear people were vandalizing trashcans this morning. Anyway, I wanted to see you again. Why didn't you plan to stay longer?"

"I don't know why," he admitted. "Part of it was my not wanting to bank too hard on the invitation."

"Jimmy, I *meant* it. This isn't nearly enough time. It takes me two days just to think of all the things I want to talk about with you. Can you stay over?"

"Can't I'm afraid. The thing's booked through. If you change anything, there's a whopping surcharge."

"You won't even get to see Connecticut."

"Haven't seen all that much of New York."

"And you're flying home from Ireland?"

"England."

"No changing that either, I guess."

"That's right." He put his arm around her shoulder. She leaned against him, smoking out her cigarette. Knowing it was hopeless. "Next time," she said, knowing they'd never see each other again; knowing he knew it, too, "we'll have to work it out to meet somewhere halfway. What's halfway between here and Perth?"

"Don't know. Pago Pago?"

"Raratonga?"

They laughed. She sat slightly away from him. "Tell me something," she said, looking at his mouth, then at his eyes. "Do you still feel overweight, even though you know you're not anymore?"

"When I think about it."

"It's the same," she said. "I still feel shy. We'll meet halfway?"

"Can't see why not."

"I'll send you a ticket to somewhere."

"Knowing your fondness for flying," he said, "I'd say that'd be about as good as a trip across the Nullarbor."

She gave him a brilliant smile and a one-armed hug. "I'd do it for you, Jimmy."

She reached past him to put out the cigarette, then with both arms around him sat for several seconds absorbing him, breathing him in, memorizing him. "I've got to move my car, get out of the city before the rush starts. You'll send me a postcard?"

"First thing I'll do."

"Goddamn it!" she said softly. "I've got to go."

He kissed her on the mouth and she wished she could have accomplished what she'd come for. But she couldn't make love to him. She got up, bent to kiss him again, picked up her bag and headed for the door saying, "Don't forget that postcard!"

"Cook Islands," he said. "Next year."

"God! I love you, Jimmy," she said, then closed the door.

He got up off the bed, hurried to the door, threw it open, stepped out into the corridor and called to her just as the elevator doors were opening.

"It's mutual," he called. "Mutual."

Eighteen

The idea of a self-portrait occurred to her one afternoon in early September at the beach. She put aside her sketchpad to lie propped on her elbows watching two small children playing at the water's edge, thinking about it. Wanting to do it. For any number of reasons. But primarily because recently she'd been feeling invisible. As if nothing of her existed but her eyes and hands, the paper or canvas upon which she worked. She too often had the feeling people weren't seeing her. Which, of course, wasn't the case at all. She knew that. But felt it all the same. And wanted suddenly to know what she looked like. And, also, to stop and take stock. A little bothered by how completely she'd allowed all her prior practices of self-care to lapse.

Her legs needed shaving. And her underarms. Her hair badly in need of professional attention. Bleached by the sun, ragged-looking, dried-out. These were things she could readily see. But what about the other things, the ones she mightn't have noticed? She threw her things into her canvas carryall and hurried back to the house. To stand in front of the bedroom mirror, critically surveying the landscape of her image. Seeing herself thin, and tanned, and somehow wild-looking. Starting to appear a little too much like those women she'd seen for years and years. The ones who wore out-of-fashion artsy clothes, shawls. Aging, but with long, free-flying hair; usually already grey. The ones who spoke in earthy, low tones ringing with ambitious sincerity and a hint of possible madness. Maybe it wasn't madness. But they took what they thought of as their freedom so seriously, so defiantly, with such a strong element of manic determination. And it wasn't the way Lyle wanted to appear, not the impression she wanted to create—even accidentally.

She wasn't overly concerned with other people's opinions of her, but rather with her thoughts of herself. They didn't quite fit. And she wanted, more than anything else, to make herself fit her concept of herself. So she made an appointment at the hairdresser's. Then unearthed her shaver and did her legs, underarms. Aware of a peculiar sensation after. As if she'd shaved off an entire layer of skin.

Her trip to have her hair done was an unsettling experience. Something she'd previously done for years without a second thought was now a demoralizing venture. Bothered by the supercilious smile of the receptionist, the smell of the place, the overheated air. The row of women all staring at themselves in the mirrors while this and that was being done to their hair. The woman who washed Lyle's hair was new, though. And gentle. As if she, too, had had the base of her skull cracked more than once against the basin and wasn't about to do it to someone else. She hummed quietly as she soaped, rinsed, soaped, rinsed Lyle's hair, then, with a smile, indicated Lyle could leave the chair.

To stand waiting for Charles to finish the woman he was doing. Blowing dry a headful of bone-colored bleached hair. With a look of intense concentration on his face. A ceremonious feeling to all of this. Ritual. A lot of women silently insisting, Make me beautiful, and the hairdressers silently responding, This is the best I can do for you.

He gathered Lyle's hair into his hands, making eye contact with her in the mirror. That invisible feeling was at once upon her. But now, instead of eyes and hands, she was eyes and hair.

"What d'you want done?" Charles asked.

"It needs trimming."

He looked at his hands filled with her hair. "You'd look good with it cut short," he said. No smiles. Serious business.

"How short?"

"Short. Soft." His eyes gone somewhere, seeing her already shorn, altered. "You want to trust me?" he asked, somehow implying if she refused she'd be defying him. "Or d'you just want the trim?"

Short hair. That year, that night in the dining room, she'd had short hair. Why think of that now? It wasn't relevant.

"All right," she said, boldly confronting an entire vista of old ghosts. "Cut it."

He said, "Good!" and smiled. He approved of her decision.

Reaching for a small pair of scissors, he sectioned her hair and began cutting. Making comments now and then. Saying, "Got some nice natural curl here." And, "This'll be good for your face. Small face like yours looks good with a short cut."

Small face? She wouldn't listen. Studied instead the faces of the other women. So nervous. What did it matter? Just hair. But it wasn't the hair, it was this place. And the irrational feeling being in this place gave her. Of belonging to no one. The feeling compounded by the wedding rings she saw on every left hand within view. Women working to be beautiful for someone else's benefit. This is for me, she told herself. For me. But what for?

Why was it so much like suffering, having to sit there in the overheated, hair-laden atmosphere of the salon, while Charles cut and cut and cut and hair was in her ears and down the back of her neck, on her arms, everywhere? The smock sat too loosely on her naked upper body. She glanced up to see if he was looking down the front of her smock. He wasn't. He didn't even know she existed except as a head covered with hair. She wanted to get out of the smock, avail herself of the talc kept in the small bathroom; have him finish so she could leave, go home, get back to work, get past this experience. Hating the feelings being aroused in her. Hating feeling like something unattached merely floating senselessly through space. An old maid with an overly large capacity for making a complete fool of herself. The first time in a very long while she'd felt this way—old and stupid.

Speculating on what her status might have been had Jess not gone away. Horrified to realize that her status depended on no one but herself and that she had, for too long, given lip service to any number of beliefs while in reality disbelieving all of it. Looking for someone to come along and supply her with an identity she couldn't supply for herself.

It was all over now. Whatever her life was, whoever she was, it was entirely up to her to give her life, her self, credibility. Because no one else could do that for her. If there was a point to her life—evident or not—it was solely up to her to find and work toward it. And Jess's presence in her life couldn't affect that one way or another.

It's up to me, she thought, a panicky thumping in her chest. Just me. Nobody else. This present, this me, is all I have to work with. And I've got to make it mean something.

What alarmed her immeasurably about this was the fact that she wasn't at all sure she had the strength or the determination or the motivation, or even the interest, to make her own self the entire focus of her existence. It hardly seemed worthwhile.

Finally, Charles finished. She said, "It's fine," refused his offer of a hand mirror so she might inspect the back, and quickly left the chair to go into the bathroom. Getting the smock off, shaking talc into the palms of her hands, feeling it easing the itch and irritation of all those loose hairs on her back and shoulders, as well as the irritation of her thoughts and the knowledge that she was someone who was completely out of place here. She buttoned her shirt, hurried to pay the receptionist. Went back to give the shampoo lady a dollar because the shampoo lady seemed the only real person in the place.

Then out. Into the fresh September air, breathing with relief. Climbing into the car. To touch the back of her neck. Startled. No hair. An exposed nape. She ran her hand over her hair, afraid to look at herself and see she'd done something dreadfully wrong in consenting to this drastic move. She drove home.

She made coffee, carried a cup upstairs, then down; walked through the house with her too-light head, her coffee, and cigarette. Imagining Jess coming to the door. Not recognizing her. No! She returned upstairs to the attic, set down the coffee, put out the cigarette, then lugged the large mirror up from the guest bedroom to prop it against the wall at an angle that allowed her a full-length view.

Stripped, charcoal in hand, she studied the mirror image and began roughing in. The exterior lines simple enough. Form. Simply form. Like working with a nude model who happened to move rather often. But once the lines were down, it began to change. Her focus of necessity narrowed in on precise details. She saw the width of her shoulders, the rounding of bones just there, the line leading from shoulder into neck into head. The lines leading from

shoulders down into arms, into chest. Her breasts. She
stopped. Looking at her breasts, eyes moving back and
forth between the reflection, the reality. This is me, how I
look, how I feel. This is the shape of me, the size, the con-
tour. Look! Here is your model: me. How do you like
what you see? Do I like seeing me? Eyes on the mirror.
This is my reality. As much as I can attain. Holding this
part of me in my hand; to know its weight, its texture, its
color. A flush of pleasure realizing she liked what she was
seeing. There's nothing ugly here, nothing deformed or of-
fensive. This is me.

She continued roughing in. An infusion of satisfaction,
steadily growing; discovering a fondness within her for the
parts of herself. The artist approving of the model. She began to work with more abandon, less of a critical eye. No
need finally to narrow the eyes because she knew this
model, after all, and approved her absolutely. Approving
the model, flying headlong into the job of putting the
essence of her vision and approval down on the paper.

Dressed again, she tacked the best of the sketches to her
drawing board and began copying the essential lines onto
the canvas. Making certain modifications. Omitting background altogether. Omitting a line here, one just there,
eliminating certain details; searching for the core. Anxious
to be at the point where she could put flesh to the bones,
color to the flesh; make it all real.

With the canvas at last ready to receive paint, she
stopped. The light was going. And she was hungry. And a
little too frightened to proceed any further.

Frances called just as Lyle was about to sit down at the
kitchen table with a bowl of soup. Her appetite in the past
month having disappeared almost entirely. She'd taken to
opening cans of soup. She'd often open the refrigerator
door, look inside at the contents, feel herself gagging and
close the door.

"I had my hair cut," Lyle told her.

"Cut short?"

"Very. I keep touching it and wanting to laugh. Or cry.
How are you? How's Will?"

"We're both fine. Will you be coming Sunday?"

"Don't I always come Sunday?"

"You do," she said. "But you're no longer predictable
and I like to be sure."

"I'm no longer predictable?"

"You're not, dear, are you?"

"Is that a crime against motherhood and country?" Frances laughed. "Naturally not. How are you?"

"Fine. Busy. Working."

"Are you going to start another shop, Lyle?"

"No."

"You'll get hit heavily for capital gains."

"That's all right. I've got the money to pay."

"You're just going to keep painting?"

"When I die," she said, looking down at her cooling soup, "it'll probably be a little like the Collier brothers. They'll have to dig their way past my collected works to get to my corpse." She laughed. "I have no intention of doing anything else, ever again. I don't *need* anything else."

"What about Jess?" Frances asked quietly.

"What about him? He went away quite some time ago. Don't you think it'd be just the faintest bit idiotic of me to be mooning around here, waiting for him to come back? He's probably found himself a nice young girl who suits him down to the ground."

"I don't think so," Frances said.

"Oh, for *God's sake*, Mother!"

"Why are you so angry, Lyle?"

"I'm not angry. I'm just trying to make you understand that I'm not sitting here wasting my time, my life, waiting for Jess to come back. I'm doing what pleases me, what's important to me, what I need to do. I'm not interested in talking about Jess."

"All right." Frances sounded hurt. "You needn't shout my head off."

"Sorry. I'm sorry. Just, please, don't talk to me about Jess. I can't take any more of it. I'll see you Sunday. My soup's getting cold."

They said goodbye. Lyle hung up and sat staring at the soup. Shoved her chair back from the table, marched upstairs, stripped off Jess's jeans, yanked the night-light out of the wall, marched back downstairs and outside to deposit the jeans and night-light in the trash. Returned inside, locked the back door, sat back down at the table in her shirt and underpants, suddenly trembling, battling down an overwhelming desire to hurry back out and retrieve the things from the trash. Forcing herself to remain at the table, spooning the cold soup into her mouth, mechanically swallowing. Tears running down her nose, dropping into the soup.

Going back over the conversation with her mother, trying to find the fault. Because there was something that had been wrong with it. Something that didn't fit. She dialed her mother's number.

"Why did you really call?" she asked.

"What do you mean why did I *really* call?"

"I mean *why* did you *call*? What was all that business about Jess?"

Frances sighed. "Will ran into him in town, Lyle."

"Oh God!" The trembling, fear and panic, started up at once. "Where? When?"

"This morning. Will was on his way up Greenwich Avenue to his office and ran into Jess in front of your shop. He'd been there looking for you. Will explained to him about your selling the place."

"Looking for me. *God!*" She turned toward the front door, all at once desperate to get out of the house, get away. "I've got to go now."

"Lyle! Don't run away!"

"Was he there when you called me before?"

Frances didn't answer.

"How could you do that to me? *Mother!* How could you *do* that? It's not *fair!*"

A car in the driveway. The engine being turned off.

"I'll never *forgive* you for this!" she cried into the telephone. "*Never!*"

She threw down the receiver, bolted through the house and up the stairs to her bedroom. Pulling on a pair of slacks as the knocking started at the front door. She wouldn't answer. Just go upstairs, wait in the attic. He'd go away. But all the lights were on. It was obvious she was home. Calling me to make sure I was here so he could come, certain of finding me. Conspirators. I don't want to see you, don't want you here, you'll just start it all up again, go away.

Nowhere to hide. No closet big enough. Nothing to do but go woodenly down the stairs and open the door. To see this big bearded stranger grinning at her.

Her chest was filled with rattling tin cans and other debris.

He said, "Hi!"

She stepped away from the door saying, "Do you want

a cup of tea? I've stopped buying coffee. A one-woman boycott because the prices are too high. An entire South American country blackmailing us. Just like with the oil. And we're allowing it to happen. Except that I'm not. I'm not buying any more after my supply runs out. So there's tea. I'll put on the kettle."

He came inside, closed the door and followed her out to the kitchen. Stopping in the doorway to watch as she snatched the kettle up off the burner, held it under the faucet, turned on the water. Returned the kettle to the stove, switched on the burner. Keeping her back to him, refusing to look at him, not wanting him here, wishing him away.

"How come you sold the shop?" he asked from the doorway. "I really like your hair. You look terrific!"

She grabbed her cigarettes from the table, managed to get one lit, looked anxiously over at the kettle. Moistening her lips, groping for words, for something to say.

"You're still pissed off at me. I told you I'd be back."

"You can't *come* back!" she shouted, her voice totally out of control. Shouting, wondering why she was saying, doing the things she was, but unable to stop. "You can't just come and go when it suits you, thinking you can just walk back in and I'll take you, want you. I don't *want* you back!"

"What I did," he said calmly, leaning against the doorframe, "I took my stuff and camped out. In the wildest, most desolate goddamned places you ever saw. Got right down into the scariest part of the whole nightmare and said, Okay dreams, come on and fight me! Screamed my fucking head off night after night until it just didn't make any sense for me to be out there with nothing much around but a few animals, some snakes; scared of V.C. who were going to start coming out of the trees to get me. I just stayed there day and night, sticking you smack into the middle of every goddamned nightmare until one night I dreamed about you. Right the way through. Didn't wake up at all. A week or so later, I did it again. Then I did it two nights in a row and had a little celebration. Drove into town to get some more supplies, and a bottle of wine. Anticipating this whole long lifetime from now until forever, all quiet nights. Drank too much and screamed my nut off for two solid weeks. So I had to start all over again. Waking up in the middle of the goddamned night, black as fucking pitch in the middle of this goddamned forest. Fighting the air, fighting my stinking sleeping bag. Stepped into the fire and would've burned my foot off but I had on my heavy socks you gave me so I just got this enormous blister on the bottom of my foot. Gee," he said in a heavily sarcastic voice, "I just had the neatest time. Perfectly swell. Howling like some fucking animal. Rushing around beating up trees. It was just *neat*."

"I'm not interested," she lied, unable to look at him. His voice was eating into her ears, like acid on her skin.

"You wouldn't listen then and you won't listen now. You've got no goddamned *faith*, Lyle. You know that? D'you *know* that?"

All she could think of was that she should have thrown the jeans and night-light away sooner. As if that might have kept him away, prevented him from returning.

"Faith," she said, the word awkward and heavy on her tongue. Like a lump of cement she was expected to chew up and swallow, like a good little girl. "*Faith*." She dared meet his eyes, looked at his mouth.

"Yeah, faith," he repeated, folding his arms across his chest. "You don't believe anything, not one damned thing. You don't have to be some kind of religious fanatic, but you've got to have some kind of faith."

"Oh, go *away*!" she said, turning off the stove, then crushing out her cigarette. "Go away, Jess! I'm not in the mood for a sermon."

"You don't mean it," he said evenly. "You hardly ever say what you really mean. You're still mad at me for doing something both of us knew had to get done. But you said if you were still here when I got back, it'd mean you believed me."

"That's no longer the case. Things have changed."

"You've changed," he said. "You got your hair cut. And given up bras." His eyes penetrated her shirt, wounding her in the breasts. She wanted to hit him. Had to clench her fists, hold herself rigid in order not to fly across the room and start hitting him.

"Like a goddamned little kid," he said. "Getting mad because you fell down and hurt yourself and want to yell at somebody because you're mad that you hurt yourself. I love you," he said simply. "You look like if I hand you a knife you'll stab me with it."

"I will," she said coldly.

"Why? I didn't do anything to you that I didn't do to myself. It was no sweet picnic alone in the stinking boonies for months on end. Getting eaten alive by gnats and mosquitoes. I hate snakes. And all those weird beetles and owls."

"I don't want you back."

"You're lying!"

"I *don't* want you *back*!"

"I want to be with you. I even lined up a job, talked my old man into letting me do a junior executive gig so I'd have the bread to be able to take you places, do things."

"Oh, yes," she said stiffly. "I forgot. I have a check here for you."

She brushed past him and went into the living room to her desk, opened the drawer to pull out an envelope. "Your last salary check." She held it out to him.

"Don't do this," he said quietly. "This isn't you."

"*You don't know what's me and what's not me!*" she shouted.

"And you're not going to give me any kind of chance to find out, either. Okay! Okay!" He pushed away from the door frame, did up his jacket, then walked straight past her, opened the door and went out.

The door closed. She stared at the closed door. Then started screaming.

He stood in the driveway, listening to her screaming, racked by indecision. Covering his ears with his hands, doubling over, hearing her screams. What was he supposed to do? Shit, shit! What? He couldn't stand it. The key was still on his ring and if nothing else he'd shut her up because he couldn't just get in the car and drive back to the garage with her screaming in his head.

He opened the door and stood there, looking at her. Like a crazy, on her knees in the middle of the living room, pounding the floor with her fists, still holding his check. Her screams going ragged, her voice giving way. Screaming, sobbing.

"You're stupid," he said. "You're so fucking stupid!"

He closed the door. When he tried to touch her, she pulled herself away, hands flying out, trying to hit him. Her eyes gone crazy, too. It made him mad. He grabbed her wrists and shook her, saying, "Stop all this shit, Lyle! It's so fucking *dumb*!"

She couldn't talk, just sobbed noisily, clamping shut her eyes. She wouldn't look at him. But his arms went around her hard, squeezing the air out of her and she opened her eyes to see he was going to kiss her. And she held still until his mouth covered hers, sending her into a frenzy of wanting him. They attacked each other's clothes. He got her slacks down, dragged her pants down with them, and fell on her. She opened her legs. He stabbed into her. She cried out, hurting. Then wound herself around him, hurtling past that moment of pain directly into the heart of the most intense pleasure. And a few minutes later, lay quiescent beneath him, slowly extending her legs. Her slacks and pants caught around her left ankle.

His hand stroked her cheek, her hair, then slid up under her shirt to cover her breast. His voice soft.

"I love you," he said. "And I *know* you love me. That's my faith, my believing. I came back to *be* with you. I'm funny sometimes, I know. But I'm no goddamned comedian."

"I don't know anymore," she whispered, her throat raw from screaming. Her fingers investigating the depths of his beard. "I just know it can't be the way it was. Because *I'm* not the way I was."

"Can we go upstairs?" he asked, lightly teasing her nipple. "I want to make love to you. Not like this."

"All right." She sighed and sat up. "I'm going to take a shower." She got to her feet and without looking at him freed her foot, picked up her clothes and went up the stairs. He watched her go, then went into the downstairs bathroom.

Under the shower, she asked herself, What am I doing? What do I want? Needing answers, terrified of supplying them for herself. Searching for something. He called it faith. She might call it dependence. But was that so terrible? Don't know, I don't know, don't know.

He was in her bed. She switched off the bathroom light and stood looking at him. Waiting there in her bed.

"What happened to the night-light?" he asked.

"I threw it away."

"I don't need it anymore, anyway."

She slid in beside him, at once betrayed by the luxurious satisfaction of coming up against him skin to skin. So warm, so familiar, so strong.

"You really didn't believe me, did you?" he asked.

She longed to close her eyes, keep them closed forever; dispense with thinking, words, the need to create and supply them.

"I don't know," she whispered. "I don't." Let's just do this, I want so much to do this, need the feeling.

"You look so pretty," he said, tracing the line of her jaw. "Like a little girl with your hair this way."

"I'm not a little girl," she whispered.

"You're not old, though."

"No. I'm not."

"That's another change," he said, kissing her throat, robbing her of her breath. "And you're way too skinny now." He lifted his head to smile at her. "More changes. Like the way you always say the opposite of what you really mean. Drove me bananas until I doped that out." A smile. Then his head dropped, his mouth on her breast, hand on her upper thigh. She shifted, opening, rendered heavy by the weight of renewed lust. Her thighs weighing thousands of pounds each, arms made of lead. His beard grazing her breast, her belly, as his tongue went from hip to hip, then following the line of the scar down. His mouth descending on her. She was dragging air into her lungs in small, painful gasps; her hands wound into his hair, whispering, "Oh God! Please! I . . . please . . ." Sounding like No, meaning Yes.

I do love you I do always lying eternally lying to myself to you to anyone who'd listen, claiming not to need not to want when I need want. You did come back you said you would and you did, I should believe you and why is it wrong to want to hope you'll stay? Make me believe because you're right there's no faith how am I to know it won't become a matter of me dying every night, being alive again every morning? Is that faith? To trust in you, to learn to believe.

His mouth delivering her into well-remembered madness, she twisted around to remind herself of the taste and feel of him, the hardness of his thighs, the soft place at the back of the knee.

Love God it hurts so much I don't want to but I do love you.

She sat over him on his lap, her face hidden in the curve of his neck as his hands rippled up and down the length of her back. Hiding from him so he wouldn't have to see her eyes.

"I do love you, Jess."

"I know. I know that."

"But it can't be the way it was."

"It's not going to be."

"I mean it. I have my painting and no one's to see. I don't want to share that. It's for me."

"That's cool! Don't! I wouldn't make that kind of demand on you."

"I don't know if I can sleep with you."

"One step at a time. Sleep comes later."

She lifted her head, searching his eyes.

"Why do I feel as if it's wrong to admit I want you?"

"You think I'm going to split again."

"Yes."

"No! There's no reason for it."

"But it's how I feel, Jess. I can't help how I feel."

"I'm all straight. Now we'll get you all straight."

"Two lousy losers?"

"So what? Who cares! Unfold your legs." He patted her knee.

She did and he lowered her down. His hands covering her breasts. His palms very warm.

"Jesus, you're so hot!"

"I'm very close."

"I know." One hand left her breast, moved down, touching. She shuddered. "I love you so much," he said. "And you better *believe* that. I know you don't want to because you've all along had this thing in your head that I was not to be trusted, I was out to take something away from you, or make you do some stuff you didn't want to do. But even so, feeling that way, you had to be fair, had to give me things; and put up with the night sweats and the screaming. And you would've kept on putting up with it all. But I couldn't do that. You're the only one who's ever really been fair and straight with me. The only one. Jesus! I went around shaking my head all the time trying to believe I could get that lucky. It's what you gave me. If I hadn't made the move when I did, if I hadn't gone, we'd've wound up some kind of accident. I had to do what was right. And getting away was the right thing to do. Now it's done. It's all over, all of that. I don't have to do any more going away. And you've got to start believing that this is where we start."

"I want to!" she whispered. "Oh! *God!*"

Her hand gripped his forearm, her body lifting from the bed, straining toward him. She closed her eyes. He stirred in her. She moved against him. His hands insistently caressing. She tightened her grip on his arm, welding his hand to her breast. The pressure building, sweet delirium. Flashing images whizzing across the whitelight of her eyelids, body gone wild gone mad, a sob of pleasure breaking the silence.

She returned to herself slowly, elated to bear his weight as he sank down upon her. As if he might impress his reality upon her by the very fact of his substance. Automatically caressing him, holding him close. Deciding, there are no simple answers, no easy ones.

"Stay," she whispered. "Tonight. Sleep with me."

He held her closer still.

"Isn't it . . . supposed to be wrong of me? All those lies . . . You won't want someone else?" she asked.

"I want you. *You*."

"And that's enough?"

"Is it enough for you?"

"Before you left, I thought it was . . . would be. Enough. But while you were gone, I had to have something more. I need that, too."

"Hey, lady!" He smiled and covered her mouth with his hand. "I need my gig, too, you know. And anyway, your mom told me about how you did up the attic and haven't come out since. I think it's a gas. It's where you should be. There's probably six zillion dynamite paintings up there. And, knowing you, one day in about twenty-seven years you'll maybe trust me enough to show me."

"Maybe." A smile forming.

"Okay." He grinned. "So thirty years."

"Maybe."

"Thirty-five years?"

"We'll see."

"Okay. Now we shut up and go to sleep."

She smiled, turned her face into his neck and closed her eyes. Faith. I'll get some. Eventually.

NEL BESTSELLERS

T51277	'THE NUMBER OF THE BEAST'	*Robert Heinlein*	£2.25
T50777	STRANGER IN A STRANGE LAND	*Robert Heinlein*	£1.75
T51382	FAIR WARNING	*Simpson & Burger*	£1.75
T52478	CAPTAIN BLOOD	*Michael Blodgett*	£1.75
T50246	THE TOP OF THE HILL	*Irwin Shaw*	£1.95
T49620	RICH MAN, POOR MAN	*Irwin Shaw*	£1.60
T51609	MAYDAY	*Thomas H. Block*	£1.75
T54071	MATCHING PAIR	*George G. Gilman*	£1.50
T45773	CLAIRE RAYNER'S LIFEGUIDE		£2.50
T53709	PUBLIC MURDERS	*Bill Granger*	£1.75
T53679	THE PREGNANT WOMAN'S		
	BEAUTY BOOK	*Gloria Natale*	£1.25
T49817	MEMORIES OF ANOTHER DAY	*Harold Robbins*	£1.95
T50807	79 PARK AVENUE	*Harold Robbins*	£1.75
T50149	THE INHERITORS	*Harold Robbins*	£1.75
T53231	THE DARK	*James Herbert*	£1.50
T43245	THE FOG	*James Herbert*	£1.50
T53296	THE RATS	*James Herbert*	£1.50
T45528	THE STAND	*Stephen King*	£1.75
T50874	CARRIE	*Stephen King*	£1.50
T51722	DUNE	*Frank Herbert*	£1.75
T51552	DEVIL'S GUARD	*Robert Elford*	£1.50
T52575	THE MIXED BLESSING	*Helen Van Slyke*	£1.75
T38602	THE APOCALYPSE	*Jeffrey Konvitz*	95p

NEL P.O. BOX 11, FALMOUTH TR10 9EN, CORNWALL

Postage Charge:

U.K. Customers 45p for the first book plus 20p. for the second book and 14p for each additional book ordered to a maximum charge of £1.63.

B.F.P.O. & EIRE Customers 45p for the first book plus 20p for the second book and 14p for the next 7 books; thereafter 8p per book.

Overseas Customers 75p for the first book and 21p per copy for each additional book.

Please send cheque or postal order (no currency).

Name ....

Address ....

....

Title ....

While every effort is made to keep prices steady, it is sometimes necessary to increase prices at short notice. New English Library reserve the right to show on covers and charge new retail prices which may differ from those advertised in the text or elsewhere.(7)